VICTIMS

After winning the Crime Writers' Association John Creasey best first book award with *The Latimer Mercy*, Robert Richardson wrote five more Augustus Maltravers mysteries before turning to psychological novels. *The Hand of Strange Children* was immediately shortlisted for the CWA's Gold Dagger, followed by the highly praised *Significant Others*. A former chairman of the CWA, he is also a journalist who has worked for, among others, the *Observer*, *The Times*, the *Independent* and the *Daily Mail*. Married with two sons, he live in Old Hatfield.

VICTIMS

ROBERT RICHARDSON

CASSELL PLC

VISTA

First published in Great Britain 1997
by Victor Gollancz

This Vista edition published 1998
Vista is an imprint of the Cassell Group
Wellington House, 125 Strand, London WC2R 0BB

A catalogue record for this book is
available from the British Library.

ISBN 0 575 60134 5

Printed and bound in Great Britain by
Caledonian International Book Manufacturing Ltd, Glasgow

98 99   10 9 8 7 6 5 4 3 2 1

For James

Author's note

Books require a location, and for no especial motive I decided to set this one in Suffolk. While writing it, I visited the county and came across a village that filled the role of my imaginary Finch; about a quarter of a mile away was a farm that could have been the reality of the fictional Tannerslade. In these circumstances – and the fact that Cambridge University and Suffolk Constabulary obviously exist – I should emphasize that this story and the people in it are complete inventions.

Death

Although he was the first to be shot, Benjamin Godwin died last because the heavy leather saddle he was holding partly protected him. But as the storm of shotgun pellets hurled him backwards, stray ones striking glittering orange sparks off cavities and goitres of black and dulled silver flints in the barn wall, the gunman was convinced that so old a man could not survive. He left Benjamin bleeding on scattered straw, his mind vandalized with pain and helpless fear.

Mandy, Benjamin's ten-year-old grand-daughter, ran to her death, shouting in alarm as she raced across the poplar-shadowed farmyard where hollow echoes still seemed to roll among startled, squawking chickens. She shrieked as the man came out of the barn, then the second shot turned her primrose T-shirt scarlet and she was dead before her body had completed its jerked puppet somersault through the air.

The first thing Annie Godwin saw as she appeared in the doorway of the kitchen was Mandy, lifeless by the tractor; the last was the figure less than fifteen feet away, practised fingers thrusting fresh cartridges into smoking barrels. Too stunned to react, even to scream, she stood totally still for the final seconds of her life, shaking her head in bewilderment and pleading. Then it was as though she almost welcomed what happened because reality could not be borne.

With the angry, rash courage of thirteen years, Thomas died in the kitchen, kicking, fists lashing out at the destroyer of those he loved, a hopeless valour from a raging heart that would have been irresistible if matched to a man's strength. After the first

7

explosion he had rushed to the bedroom window, from where he had seen his sister shot, and had heard the death of his grandmother as he dashed downstairs. There had been no thought of running away; the Godwin metal in him had been steeled as long ago as Ypres and El Alamein, even in the desperation of Corunna, and, like his father's, his hair flamed with the Hood temper. Thomas fell defiant, like ancestral warriors before him.

Ears clamped in foam headphones filling her half-asleep mind with Abba, Cheryl, the children's mother, did not hear the first three shots from outside, but twitched and cried out as the fourth blasted through the house. For a few seconds she lay dazed and petrified with shock on the tapestry sofa, then was scrambling to her feet in panic as the gunman ran into the sitting room. She flinched in terror as he raised the gun.

'No,' she begged. 'No . . . please. Where are my children?'

She screamed and backed away as he moved towards her, half stumbling against a pie-crust table, regaining her balance only for him to hit her across the face with the gunstock. He took a fifth cartridge from the pocket of his denim jacket as she moaned at his feet; she had seen him more clearly than any of them. Delicate glass in the teardrop chandelier tinkled violently with the last bellow of death.

The anonymous white van left twenty minutes later, loaded with silverware, an early landscape given by the young John Constable to his friend Matthew Godwin, a pair of eighth-century terracotta Chinese figures, a basket-hilt Toledo rapier and a German headsman's sword, a gold goblet used at the coronation of George IV and thirty pieces of rare porcelain, including a vase said to have been designed by Josiah Wedgwood. In the wide, vacant tranquillity of a barley-tanned Suffolk after-noon, it appeared to be the only moving thing, rocking frantically as it tore along the straight, stone-pitted access road that ran from the farm, pale dust swirling behind it; it reached the gate and tyres squealed as it swung violently left, then there was a grinding clash of gears and a raging growl of acceleration before it sped away.

As silence settled on the farmyard, chickens began to peck

scattered seed, nervously stepping away if they approached Mandy's body, and a pair of crows settled on the gable end of the farmhouse roof. In the barn a distressed horse whinnied at the scent of blood and pounded the wooden walls of its stall, seeking escape from Benjamin's dying presence. In the kitchen the stench of burning fruit, put on to cook for cold summer pudding that evening, rose from the copper pan on the Aga. A game of computerized slaughter flickered on the television monitor in Thomas's bedroom to a background of repetitive synthetic music, and downstairs the phone rang, chirruping for a minute before it stopped. More than two hours later Benjamin Godwin died beneath the oak cattle manger that his great-grandfather had built.

All this happened between 1.42 and 4.30 on the afternoon of Wednesday 11 July, 1990.

Early the following morning Sam Pulfer, one of Benjamin Godwin's farmhands, arrived to be given his day's orders and saw the bodies of Mandy and Annie. As he stared, he was conscious of a sense of human absence amid the chatter and bustle of poultry. He cautiously approached the child, the sight too grotesque to accept until he was close enough to see her blood, flecked with greedy iridescent blowflies; he felt a compulsion to wave them away, their swarming presence an additional obscenity. Before he reached Annie he recognized that she was lying in a position impossible for a living person to maintain; her eyes were still open. Now unnatural hush carried the menace of evil, and he had to thrust down a shudder of fear as he entered the kitchen. The Aga had gone out, heat transformed into the acrid smell held in the cold, blackened crust roasted into its iron surface. Inquisitive and nervous, a powder-blue budgerigar repeatedly hopped from bar to swing and back again in its cage suspended from the ceiling by the window; it was the only life in the house. For some reason it was the sight of Thomas, face twisted with dying fury, that was impossible to tolerate; retching with revulsion, Pulfer spun away and ran back to the open air.

When he recovered, he felt convinced that whoever was responsible was no longer at the farm. Forcing himself not to look at the boy's body by the kitchen table he went back inside, terrified of discovering Benjamin Godwin – he owed the farmer ten pounds and felt irrationally guilty. The telephone was in the hall, so he did not see Cheryl.

'Police.' The act of starting to tell someone brought up an immense wave of shock and pity. His voice cracked into a desperate croak and he began to cry like a terrified child. 'Hurry ... Tannerslade Farm ... near Finch ... please ... they've all been ... Jesus, Mary and Joseph! Help me!'

When the first patrol car arrived, they found him halfway down the path, from where he could see the building but not any of its horrors. He was sobbing uncontrollably. He had three young children of his own. For more than a year afterwards he was unable to sleep without the aid of drugs and all his dreams were hideous.

The final paragraphs of a report in the *Observer*, Sunday 2 September, 1990.

Five pine coffins, two of them heart-breakingly small, were borne from the church amid a great gathering of hushed mourners. With slow, solemn dignity they were carried to the sunlit patch of grass beneath looming yew trees where the opened earth waited to receive them, deep, grim pits softened by bright garlands of flowers.

Sombre men lowered the coffins on canvas straps – Benjamin Godwin and his wife together, their daughter buried with her children – as the vicar, voice firm with a strength governing awful grief, pronounced the church's promises for all those who die in the Lord. Bewildered by the mantle of sad ceremony, a little girl gripped her mother's hand for reassurance, and a farmworker, uncomfortable in an ill-fitting borrowed black suit, lowered his head as he shook with sorrow. During the final moments of private prayer the hum of television cameras ceased and all that was audible was birdsong and the soft crying of a baby.

Then it was over and people turned to each other to offer comfort of word or caress. The vicar stood immobile by the graves for a few moments, then went to speak to those closest to the victims before quiet black limousines bore them away. Finch, which had seemed totally stilled since daybreak, returned sadly to its placid rural life, harrowed by death and an insufferable Suffolk afternoon.

For reasons of space, the reporter's final paragraphs were cut:

Senior officers leading the murder inquiry had joined the mourners, and opposite the lychgate of the church three men and two women watched everyone discreetly but intently. It was an agonizing reminder that whoever violated Tannerslade Farm is still out there somewhere. Nearly six weeks after the killings a massive police hunt has brought no arrests or the emergence of a real suspect since Cheryl Hood's estranged husband was cleared of any involvement.

Whoever murdered Benjamin Godwin and his family also destroyed an innocent community's sense of security, a belief that brutality only occurs in dangerous, distant cities or in the excesses of fiction, where violent death does not bring such real and terrible anguish.

Killers

Coal-black and moonlight silvered the river slid silkenly beneath
Clare bridge, the hollow wooden knock of moored punts
curtseying softly against each other on undulating water the only
sound until bell answered bell as clocks marked three o'clock
in the summer morning. Apart from the two figures on the
sloping bank the Cambridge Backs were deserted, chapels and
colleges like abandoned civilizations awaiting dawn and discov-
ery. Lying with his hands locked behind his head, Giles Lambert
raked through the remains of a childhood passion for astronomy
as he gazed up at remote constellations: Lyra with bright blue
Vega, Cygnus and Draco, ancient Greeks in limitless space.
Randall Jowett sat beside him, elbows on raised knees, thumbnail stripping bark from a twig, concentrating as he tried to
invest the pointless with importance, in an attempt to hold
horror at bay. Only his 21-year-old pride prevented him from
crying.

'Why did you kill them?' Unshed tears stained the words, his
voice dared no louder than a painful whisper in the silence.

'Does it matter?' Lambert sounded bored, as though he had
already explained something several times and Jowett was being
perverse in not understanding. He felt irritated as another name
remained just beyond the rim of memory, glimpsed but indefin-
able as the most distant stars. 'Anyway, I had no choice. When
the bloody elastic on that mask snapped he saw my face.'

'But you killed all of them! Including the kids! For fuck's
sake, did you get a kick out of it?'

Lambert looked reflective, as though the suggestion was novel but intriguing. 'Perhaps I did. I certainly couldn't stop once I'd started.'

'You said that sodding gun wasn't loaded.'

'Well it was.' Lambert nodded to himself as the name came back: Cepheus, father of Andromeda, containing eight stars above the fourth magnitude. It was a brilliant night, residue of the day's clinging warmth held beneath a pinpoint-clear dome of black; a night to spend with a consenting girl, not the panicking man beside him. 'The important thing is that nothing went wrong.'

Jowett laughed bitterly. 'Except that five people are dead.'

'We can't do anything about that now. But everything else went perfectly. We weren't seen and our alibi's rock solid. Nobody's going to connect us with it.'

'Jesus.' Jowett's head sank between his knees, as if cutting out the sight of Lambert, the dim-lit walls of the colleges, the river, trees and grass, even the sky and the night itself, would somehow allow him to return to how things had been before it all began. Before he had hired the van; before they had found the farm; before Giles had written the initial outline; before that night in the Gog and Magog when they had lingered over halves of bitter, all they could afford, resenting the fact that they were permanently, embarrassingly broke, joking of ways to raise money – an official university brothel, kidnapping the vice-chancellor (abandoned because no one in their right mind would pay for his return), fixing the Boat Race – until Giles had suggested a robbery . . .

'OK, we'll start with the moral arguments in favour. "All property is theft".'

Randall laughed. 'Piss off. Marxist-Leninism isn't cool any more.'

'Thank you, Karl. We'll call you if we're interested.' Giles used humour a lot in those early stages, making what they were contemplating more acceptable, somehow lighter. 'Very well, unreconstructed capitalist running dog, answer this. How much does a man need to be classified as obscenely rich? A million pounds, ten million or a hundred million? Candidates must select only one option.'

'A million.' What Randall's father had speculated he could be worth within five years until a series of high-risk investments had imploded and real debts had become as massive as fantasy fortunes.

'Ergo, if a man has two million pounds, you can justify taking half of it off him. He remains very rich and everything's insured anyway, so he gets back what he's lost and is no worse off. But the thief's lifestyle has been greatly improved. Finally, there's no victim.'

'What about the insurance company?'

'Bollocks. They're investing billions all over the world. They can make fifty times what they'll pay out in a couple of seconds.'

'But somebody pays,' Randall argued. 'There's no such thing as a free lunch, yeah?'

'Sure someone pays.' Giles was dismissive. 'A bunch of peasants get ripped off or have to work in a Far East sweatshop. Are you bothered about them? If you are, go out and change the bloody world. I'm talking about us, about the fact that we're so broke we can't afford a Big Mac without worrying about paying the rent. We're not used to that.'

'Supposing we get caught?' Jowett found himself analysing his motives for the question the moment he asked it. Was fear of capture terrifying him more than guilt? If they got away with it, would he start to rationalize? What sort of person did that make him?

'That was always a risk. It didn't bother you before.'

'But we'd just have been done for robbery. Not . . . not this.'

'We're not going to get caught. Why should we be?' Lambert sat up. 'Just hang loose, OK? Take it a day at a time . . . You're not really thinking we should admit it, are you? What's the point? They'll lock us up and throw away the key so that society

14

can feel better. But they'll still be dead. Our lives will be ruined and nobody will be any better off. Get real.'

His calmness, acceptance, skill at argument was a balm for Jowett's fright and shrieking nerves, a hiding place from conscience. He could have stopped it at any time, and regretting now that he hadn't was as futile as wishing the sun could be moved back or the endless flow of the river reversed.

Once the decision had been made – and Randall recognized he had finally been willing, not coerced – the first stage proved temptingly simple. They were looking for an isolated house at least fifty miles from where either of them lived; East Anglia had almost suggested itself. They drove around the countryside south of Bury St Edmunds spotting possibilities, but not knowing if they contained valuables worth stealing and, if so, what security protected them. Then, when they stopped at a village shop because Giles wanted cigarettes, he returned with a county magazine, bought on impulse because it might be useful; inside was the article about Tannerslade Farm. Owned by the same family for generations, obviously with money. One photograph showed the woman with a Georgian tea service, a Constable hanging on the wall behind her; another, the man holding a fifteenth-century Spanish sword, glimpses of silver and gleaming porcelain in the background, plus a comment in the text – 'a farmhouse filled with secret treasures'. How had they let them publish an open invitation to be robbed? Perhaps they were simply trusting, this defenceless elderly man and woman living alone.

They located the farm on an Ordnance Survey map and drove past just once, but slowly enough to take photographs through the car window. It stood about a hundred yards off the road, sentinel Lombardy poplars behind it, at the end of a straight stone-rough track with ragged grass growing down its centre, lined on one side by a hawthorn hedge. Adjacent fields lay fallow or were growing what looked like barley. In the few minutes they observed it, no vehicle passed them in either direction and the only other building they could see was the roof of a cottage glimpsed in a dip of land half a mile away.

Giles developed the photographs himself – 'People have been caught because they were dumb and sent things like this to the local chemist's.' Slightly blurred images emphasized the farm's solitude. They examined them with a magnifying glass, plotters trying to assess peril or opportunity, but all they identified was a window which appeared to be the one from an interior shot in the magazine. The fact that they now knew which was the main living room brought a sense of achievement.

'I'm going to be sick.' Jowett swayed as he stood up, then lurched down the bank, grasping an overhanging sycamore branch as he doubled over with the excruciating effort of trying to vomit when there is nothing in the stomach to expel. Lambert looked away in distaste at the sound of tortured gasps and gurgles.

'Keep quiet, you prat. Sounds travel at night.'

Jowett swung on his arm as he went dizzy, and for a moment it seemed that he would fall into the Cam. Lambert leapt to his feet and reached him in two long strides, tearing his shirt collar as he pulled him backwards violently. 'Come on! There's no point in sitting here. I've got some stuff at my place that'll sort you out.'

'I'm not taking anything!'

'Don't worry, it's good shit. Peterson sold it me. He's OK. You need a few hours of unreality.'

Panting on the grass, Jowett shook his head. 'No way. Not unless it's enough to kill me.'

Suddenly Lambert lost his temper, kneeling beside Jowett, his fingers digging deep into bony shoulders as he shook him furiously.

'I'll fucking kill you if you don't loosen up! They're *dead*! Got that? We did it – you're as fucking guilty as I am. But nobody is going to suspect us unless we do something stupid. So we don't. I'm not about to sacrifice my bloody life for this.'

He thrust Jowett back on to the grass as though throwing something away and stood up, staring across the river at the shadowed soaring walls of King's College Chapel. Now Jowett was looking at the sky; stars he could not name, moon of creamy wax, winking lights of an airliner, unheard and far, far above him. Two hundred or so people, probably asleep, unknowingly passing through a few moments of his awareness. Innocent people who were able to fly away.

Randall could not understand why he remembered something as meaningless as the weathervane on the gable end so vividly; the silhouette of an angler cut out of metal, dark against a sky of pale, solid blue. He recalled thinking that someone must have taken a lot of trouble over the details: tufted hat, outline of thigh-deep waders, rod thinning until it blended into the wire used for the curve of the fishing line. It was too high up to be certain, but there might even have been a tiny pipe in the mouth. The afternoon was very still, the miniature man facing south-west, motionless since his last rotation. Why was it so memorable? Perhaps because it was the first thing he had consciously seen as they reached the farmhouse, a touch of the domestic, a symbol of normality. He saw it through the eye-slits of the plastic Margaret Thatcher joke mask – Giles had bought two of them in a crowded W. H. Smith's on a Saturday morning when no one would remember him; he constantly drew Randall's attention to his care over the smallest details.

'Never speak,' Giles warned again. That he had felt the need to repeat such a basic precaution gave the impression he was nervous, but Randall, rigid with excitement, did not think about it. Giles reached behind and took the shotgun from the metal floor of the van. Just to frighten them, he said; in case they resisted.

At first they thought the house was deserted. The farmyard was empty and there was no sound as Randall turned off the engine. Three cars were parked next to a tractor: a Vauxhall, L-registration Volvo and a Golf hatchback.

'Windows are open,' Giles muttered. 'They're here somewhere.'

They got out, uncertain despite all their planning as to what exactly they should do. Randall had imagined knocking on the door, pointing the gun at whichever one opened it as a mute order, entering the house to find the other conveniently inside, tying them to chairs, loading up the van—

'In the barn!'

Randall heard it as well – what sounded like a creak and the rustle of feet on dry straw, loud in the simmering afternoon. The wall facing them was blank, and they ran to stand with their backs to it before edging towards one end, a parody of small boys imitating television heroes in a game of cops and robbers. Randall felt a sudden impulse to run, a last-minute surge of panic . . . but Giles had already reached the end of the wall and was turning the corner, shotgun raised.

'Who the devil are you?' The question was aggressive, half shouted, not afraid.

Randall's scream dissolved into the first explosion and his crotch felt warm as he wet himself. He could hear Giles cursing, then there was a cry of alarm from the house. The next few moments were no more controllable than events seen in a film. As Giles reappeared, a little girl ran into the yard; she seemed to have no fear as he drew nearer. Surely he wouldn't . . . As Giles shot her, Randall banged the back of his head against the flint wall, hurting himself, needing to suffer, and clasped his arms across his stomach. Then the old woman appeared, and it made no sense that she just stood in the doorway as Giles fumbled in his pockets and reloaded. For God's sake run away . . . She couldn't now.

Randall's legs lost their muscles and he slithered down the side of the barn until he was sitting in the dampness of his urine, sobbing with terror. He heard the fourth and fifth shots faintly from inside the house. Then he was aware of nothing until he felt a violent kick against his leg.

'Move it!'

'Sure . . . yeah . . . shit . . . what . . . ?' He didn't know how he was managing to struggle to his feet, but at least the van was only . . .

'Where the fuck are you going? We've got to get the stuff.'

'The stuff? Oh, yeah. The stuff. Right.' He had no more control over his speech than his actions. He followed Giles into the house, where the sight of two more bodies had no capacity to deepen fear already inflamed to its limits. His hands felt sticky inside the rubber gloves, but he followed Giles' orders as they collected the most obvious valuables and piled them on the living-room table.

'Get that picture down while I get the bags,' Giles snapped.

The Constable hung above the sofa in front of which the woman lay. Randall forced himself not to look down as he stepped over her and muttered 'Sorry', as though he were being ill-mannered. He briefly felt the warmth of her body through thin socks as his ankles touched her, then stepped on to the sofa and fumbled with the frame, pulling the hook out of porous plaster as he wrenched it from the wall. Fragments sprinkled down, bouncing off the sofa back, one larger lump landing in the woman's shattered eye socket, instantly starting to soak up blood. He wanted to brush it away. From out of the headphones lying on the carpet beside her seeped the faint, tinny sounds of disco pop.

'Here.' Giles returned with the black bin bags, holding one up then pulling it swiftly downwards so that the thin plastic crackled and billowed open. He dropped silverware in carelessly, but took more time over porcelain and glassware. They rapidly filled five sacks, then carried them all to the van in one journey.

'Where's your mask?' As they put the last bags in the back, Randall had suddenly registered that he could see Giles' face.

'Fuck, it must be in the barn. Turn the van round.'

He ran across the yard and disappeared for what seemed a long time, then emerged carrying the mask, white loop of elastic flapping loose from one ear. As he opened the passenger door and scrambled in, Randall was fumbling with the unfamiliar seat belt.

'Leave it, you stupid cunt!' Giles reached across and Randall's mask split as he snatched it off. 'Just fucking get going!'

'Do you think they'll have found them yet?'

'There was nothing on TV about it. That's good. They can't start an investigation until the morning.' Lambert wondered if Jowett would feel better if he went over all the precautions they had taken. 'Think about it, Randy. We tested the bloody plan to destruction. Everybody thinks we were in London – we showed them what we bought. OK? Nobody knows we got off at Luton and picked up the van.'

'But I gave them my real name when we hired it!'

'We discussed that. If they'd checked back and found anything dodgy, they'd have been suspicious. But you were just another customer who wanted to hire a van for the day. And why should anyone connect it with something that happened nearly a hundred miles away?'

'Somebody could have seen us leaving the farm.'

'Think, dickhead. We didn't see another vehicle until we'd gone through the village. And what would anyone have seen anyway? A van with two men in it. Do you think they stopped and wrote down the colour, make and number? Just in case there'd been a murder and the police would be asking for witnesses? People do that all the time.

'We were bloody careful to make sure there wasn't a mark in the van. We used clean plastic bags and wiped the steering wheel before we returned the keys. Anyway, how the hell can the police find it? There are bloody millions of hire vans on the road. And we certainly didn't leave any prints at the farm.'

'What about . . . tyre tracks or something?'

'If there are any, they're no use unless they can find what made them. So the police have a run-of-the-mill tyre track, but experts can tell them the make. Big deal – unless they've got someone with a crystal ball who says, "Hey, why don't we look at vans hired from that place in Luton? Then we'll catch them." They're not Sherlock Holmes, Randy, they're thick country coppers. The clothes and shoes we wore are in that mechanical skip at – Christ, I can't even remember where it was. But that bag's crushed between God knows what else by now. Come on, we covered every bloody thing.'

Giles had argued that only stupid crooks were caught, and second-year Cambridge undergraduates were not, by definition, stupid. They had approached the idea at first as a piece of research, reading about police investigations and watching television reconstructions of crimes, noting where criminals had made fatal mistakes. It was interesting that insane coincidences occurred much more in reality than in fiction. One man had been caught because he was seen passing a house at the precise moment a goal had been scored in the Cup Final, which wrecked his alibi; in another case, the police traced a girl's killer because a cab driver at Waterloo station happened to notice her shoes, a man had been recording car numbers following a completely unconnected robbery in the area where the body was dumped and a dentist's assistant had found a cast of the murderer's teeth which was thought to have been thrown away. Giles had dismissed such incidents as chaos theory, impossible to allow for. And how many crimes remained unsolved because they had not been exposed by such freak chances?

There would be no reason for them to be suspected, but they ought to have an alibi. Two weeks before the robbery Giles had gone to London, where he had paid cash in the Virgin record store and for the clothes at Mr Byright on Oxford Street, throwing away the receipts, but keeping the carrier bags. He knew Randall's sizes, and had shopped while both shops were crowded. He had returned when his parents were in bed, so they had not seen what he had bought. Everything was in his rucksack when he arrived to spend a few days with Randall, and they had hidden it all in the boot of Randall's car, still in carrier bags. Giles had also brought his shotgun; both he and his father were licensed owners and he'd been shooting since he was fourteen. His father was away and his mother would not notice that one of the guns was missing. He had promised Randall it would not be loaded, but why should anyone hand over their possessions to unarmed men? Randall had felt uneasy, but by now the plan had achieved a momentum that was sweeping him along with it. He did not know that the bag Giles used to carry the gun and the clothes he would change into for the robbery also contained ten cartridges.

They left Randall's house early and parked near Bedford station, then bought return tickets to London. The train was full, and they were among several passengers who got off at Luton. Giles had added the farcical touch of a false moustache; it looked ridiculous, but he said it was a misleading detail that people would remember in the highly unlikely event that someone noticed them and gave a description to the police. They collected the van, booked by phone the previous day. As the receptionist checked his licence, Randall casually mentioned they were helping a friend to move and what was the latest time it could be returned? By ten o'clock the following morning, but they could drop the keys through the door before that as long as they made sure the petrol tank was full again.

Giles insisted they put on rubber gloves the moment they got in the van as a precaution against leaving any traces of their presence. As they drove towards Suffolk, staying with other traffic on main roads as much as possible, he discussed the precautions they had taken as though admiring a well-written thesis. Stopping for lunch was out of the question – someone might remember them – but neither was hungry. Carefully observing speed limits, they were near Tannerslade Farm by half-past one, the timing Giles had worked out in advance; people rarely made visits at lunchtime, so the couple would be alone. They pulled in to the side of the road and climbed into the back of the van in turn, putting on jeans and denim jackets, old shirts and worn trainers, nondescript clothes that would be thrown away later. Tension that had started to build up imperceptibly with the planning, more vividly with the establishing of the alibi, relentlessly since they had set off that morning, was acting like a stimulant. As the gate to the farm appeared, Giles' breath came faster and Randall's mouth felt dry.

Giles murmured reassurance as the distance diminished; no cars in sight, no one in the fields. Turn. Stop. Masks on. Let's do it.

Randall was gibbering within minutes of them rejoining the main road, and Giles yelled at him as the van swerved crazily.

'You stupid bastard! Slow down!'

'They're dead! They're all dead!'

For a nerve-racking moment Giles thought the van was going to crash into the ditch, but he grasped the wheel and hauled it away.

'Look! Just ahead . . . pull in there.' Randall obeyed and Giles leapt out and ran to the driver's side. 'Move over. I'll drive.'

'But you've not got a full licence. You need L-plates.'

'L-plates!' Giles screamed. 'Jesus fucking Christ! Just move!'

Randall scrambled into the passenger seat as Giles climbed in, then wrestled with the gearstick before the van moved forward jerkily. Randall was staring out of the side window, twitching with muffled, hysterical sobs; inside the rubber gloves his fists were fiercely clenched.

'We'll stop in a minute,' Giles assured him, as they passed a sign that welcomed careful drivers to Finch. 'Once we're through this place. Open the window. You need some air.'

Randall wound the glass down, then moved his head so that the wind struck his face. Giles glanced at him occasionally as they drove through the village and out again, back on to deserted roads. In the two years they had known each other, Randall had always been susceptible to persuasion, even allowing Giles to mock him into taking the drugs they had become unable to afford. Giles began to look for somewhere to stop; nowhere too visible or the van might be seen and remembered, but it had to be soon. Trees appeared on the left and he saw a narrow dirt path leading into them. The van rocked over dried mud, then he stopped, anxious lest he hit something and marked the bodywork.

'OK,' he said. 'Just a couple of minutes. There could be someone around. You want to throw up?'

Randall shook his head. 'They'll hang us.'

'For Christ's sake, they stopped hanging people fucking years ago! Anyway, they're not going to catch us.'

Randall turned to face him, disbelieving. 'You mean . . . we just . . . just carry on with it?'

'What else is there?' Randall winced as Giles, the captor of his mind, leant towards him. 'You know the next stage. We worked it all out. Let's just do that, OK? Afterwards we can talk it over. There's a lot to take on board here, but we can't piss about now.'

'We just go ahead? Hide it like we planned? Then go home?'

'That's what I'm saying.' When Randall remained silent, Giles leant across him and opened the passenger door. 'Or you can get out now. Go back to that village and find the local copper – but just give me time to get out of here. You want to do that?'

'No.'

'Good. Then close the door.'

As Giles started the van again and struggled to find reverse, Randall slammed the door, conscious that he should have refused, but the impact of metal on metal was helpless commitment.

Back in Bedfordshire they stopped in an isolated lay-by, and while Giles plunged into the bushes to hide the bags Randall climbed into the back and changed again, stuffing the mask and the clothes he had worn at the farm into another plastic sack. Giles returned and did the same. The risk of someone finding the bags in the next few hours was minimal. Just outside Luton they pulled into the council rubbish tip, where Giles casually walked past waiting cars to drop the sack of clothes into a skip, mechanical steel jaws crushing it up with garden refuse, building rubble, household waste, a pair of decrepit deckchairs. They returned the van by six o'clock and caught the next train to Bedford. Back at Randall's they displayed what they said they had bought in town; Giles' present for Mrs Jowett to thank her for having him as a guest – a headscarf printed with London landmarks – had been a neat touch.

Randall appeared just about under control, but Giles was

24

apprehensive that he might suddenly go to pieces. But Isobel Jowett, obsessed only with the disaster of finding herself in an alien world where the cost of a hair appointment was now a problem, had not noticed anything. All that mattered to her was that her husband's financial crisis denied her the right to entertain whenever she wanted; that she would fail to become the ladies' golf captain because the membership fees could not be met. She had paid scant attention when Giles mentioned meeting a friend on the train who had invited them out that evening and that they might stay over. They left the house again before nine o'clock.

Randall said he could not eat, but Giles bought himself a Chinese takeaway and ate it in the car before they went for a drink; it was still summer light and they could not return to the lay-by until darkness fell. They chose a busy pub, where they would not be remembered; Giles remarked that they – he – had thought out even the tiniest details. He was unable to decide if Randall was becoming calmer or had fallen into some sort of inertia; he would not talk and two young men sitting drinking in silence might be noticed. So Lambert was loquacious, telling jokes, inventing college gossip, asking questions that forced Randall to respond. Both of them stared at the television over the bar when *News at Ten* came on. They could not hear it, but headline footage of George Bush, African famine, a rock star kissing a supermodel and a shot of a cricketer meant that a multiple murder at a farm in Suffolk was not the main story; after a few moments someone changed channels.

The pub was still crowded when they left and drove back through the darkness to the lay-by. While Giles recovered the sacks, Randall stood by the road, watching for approaching headlights. Twice he called out a warning and hid behind a tree, but each time the cars swept past. It was after midnight when they returned to Cambridge and no one saw them unload the sacks in the walled yard behind Giles' flat and carry them up the fire escape. Randall immediately turned on the television for the latest news on Ceefax, but the only reference to a murder was a stabbing in Tyneside.

'I'm going out,' he said suddenly.

'Where to?'

'Anywhere. For a walk.'

'I'll come with you.'

'It's all right. I'd rather be—'

'I'm coming.'

Left alone, he might have walked straight into the nearest police station . . .

So they ended up on the deserted riverbank, silhouettes amid charcoal trees, talking softly of guilt and justification, of fear and contempt of fear. And Jowett was aware of finding himself in a moral desert, where guilt was so gigantic as to be beyond any redemption. What values of right and wrong he had been taught or had absorbed were now meaningless. He had not confessed – not gone back to that village when Lambert had offered him the opportunity – because he had been incapable of any action. A memory of his heightened nine-year-old imagination conjuring the Devil in the darkened corner of his bedroom, horned and marking him for hell, relentlessly returned, childish superstition more powerful than reason, turning it to insane prophecy. He could no longer think.

And Lambert, unexpectedly, found himself remembering his grandmother, privileged by wealthy parents and a richer husband, contemptuous of any who dared question the superiority of money and position. A stern, distant, imperious woman, who had paid him no attention until he was old enough to understand what she said and follow her example. Who had brought out leather albums with a proud melancholy and shown him sepia photographs of long-dead Kemp-Howards at Biarritz; standing by Bentley convertibles at Ascot; holding slaughtered grouse on Scottish estates; attended by white-coated stewards on exclusive decks of transatlantic liners. Who had once remarked that laws were passed by people of her class to control the lower orders. She regarded the century in which she had grown old distasteful, and deplored the fact that Harrow had rejected her grandson and he would have no private income.

'Whatever happens, Giles,' she told him during her final illness, as she confidently prepared to enter the Heaven set aside by a Conservative God for his chosen people, 'remember that you are a gentleman and that a gentleman's actions are always correct.'

His fourteen-year-old instinct to mock such antique attitudes had been silenced by his awe of her, by the fact that he had been conditioned to love a woman who was unlovable . . . by the fact that she represented money. Now he found his perverted justification in what she had taught him.

Aftermath

Committed in the dog days of summer when news was slow, the murders remained screamingly prominent as journalists constantly forged new angles to keep the story going. It appeared to Jowett that people talked about nothing else and he felt a permanent, irrational conviction that he bore a visible brand of guilt. He could not confess, but there were times when it would have been almost a relief to be exposed. The situation became surreal when his father asked him to sign a petition drawn up by the Bedford Conservative Association calling for capital punishment to be brought back. As he wrote his name – how could he refuse? – it seemed insane that so immense a lie would not be recognized.

He escaped in early August to take a vacation job at an international campsite near St Raphael, but even there other students asked him about *les tueurs de Tannerslade . . . Une affaire atroce . . . et Cambridge, c'est loin du Suffolk?* He drank cheap wine until he was sick, and one night a girl fought him off when what she sought as playful love-making with the handsome Englishman became a fury of violent sex. Afterwards, she and the other girls avoided him and told the men to do the same. But their distance meant no more questions and Jowett secretly felt too much an outcast for it to matter. He needed to see Lambert – the only other one who knew the truth – but he was working in a bar somewhere in Spain and had not given an address. Jowett rang him just before the new term began, but he would not talk on the phone and refused a meeting before they returned to Cambridge. When they did meet, Lambert was impatient.

'Loosen up!' he snapped. 'It's nearly three months now. There's no way they'll get on to us – unless you screw it up. You've seen what the papers have been saying.'

'I don't read them any more. I can't . . . I daren't.'

'Prat . . . the latest thing was that they reckon it was a gang from Essex. They let the husband go.'

'What husband?'

'Christ, don't you know anything? The father of the kids. He was separated from her and they suspected him. Obviously they would. Those reports we read showed that murder's a family crime. Anyway, he had an alibi, so now they're concentrating on professionals. They say it didn't look like an amateur job.' Lambert sounded satisfied, as if that were a tribute to his abilities.

'Don't you worry about it, though?'

'Bollocks.'

Now every day was bad, recollection constantly waiting to ambush Jowett with accusation. Exhaustion would finally bring fretful, thin sleep, then consciousness returned early; not gradually, but with the searing impact of an arc light switched on in the brain . . .

You were there, you saw the murders but did nothing to prevent them, you robbed the dead, you haven't confessed . . . The police are hunting you . . . She was such a pretty little girl in that photograph under the headline 'BUTCHERED IN COLD BLOOD' . . . When it comes out, everyone will condemn you . . . Your mother be despised for breeding you . . . The police will beat you up and claim you were resisting arrest . . . and afterwards the prison scum will turn on you – even the worst of them hate child killers – and one night you'll be alone in your cell and they'll come in . . . It won't be quick; you'll see the loathing in their faces as you scream . . .

But Jowett was long past screaming; waking, he would lie paralysed, with his eyes closed for several minutes, accepting images of renewed torment, then his eyelids would squeeze tighter, as if struggling to block them out. The emotional exertion required to move had become like some disease that froze his muscles in the night, and he had to ease them back agonizingly into endurance of another day.

He had developed a strict routine from the moment he got up. His radio was tuned to a pop-music channel and concentration on each song, however trite, occupied his mind as he washed and shaved. Preparing the simplest breakfast of cornflakes and tea had become a ceremony requiring meticulous attention to detail. Only eight teabags left, write a reminder to replace; this would taste better with banana, buy some tomorrow; how many added minerals and trace elements can I remember without reading the back of the cereal box again? Time check on the radio. Eight fifty-six. First lecture in an hour, but read those two chapters beforehand. No, don't think about that . . . just find the book. Read it aloud, that helps.

Other students asked if he was all right, even the men, who never noticed such things. He made excuses: been sick a couple of times, should see the college quack; been drinking too much; might be a touch of flu. I'm all right, OK? Butt out. He broke down twice in the first weeks, leaping from his seat and running out of the lecture room when normality became too unbearable. He apologized to each tutor, telling them his mother was seriously ill and he was worried. They were understanding, too much so, insisting that he must go home to be with her, and in his confusion the lie had become more complex. She was in an isolation ward and visitors were not allowed; his father was keeping him informed. Later he said she was recovering in case someone started making inquiries. By that time he was more in control in public; horror waited for him in the night.

Convinced Jowett was too scared to talk, Lambert found it interesting to reflect that he was capable of killing. His ability at self-assessment had always been prejudiced to his own advantage, achievement admired and failure rationalized. Moral questions were irrelevant – remorse would not raise the dead – so what he had done he interpreted positively. He was not ruthless, but determined; not evil, but efficient; when the going got tough, the tough got going. The world was a hard place and rewarded those with no weaknesses.

His only problem was what the police superintendent leading the murder hunt had said on television immediately after the murders. At first Lambert had listened cynically to assurances that the killers would be caught; more than seventy officers were working on the case, information was pouring in, the standard spiel.

'The murderers will make a mistake eventually, or someone who knows them will start to have suspicions. I realize that whoever you suspect may be a relative, your husband, son or brother, or a close friend. It won't be easy to come forward, but remember that five innocent people, including two young children, have been brutally killed. I was with Mr Godwin's son when he identified the bodies. If you had seen that man's face, you would not be able to stop yourself talking to us.'

Crap, copper, Lambert thought. Emotional blackmail. You've not got a sodding thing to go on, and—

'—I am also appealing to anyone who deals in jewellery or antiques who may be offered some of the stolen property. Under the terms of his insurance policy, Mr Godwin had all his valuables photographed so we have excellent descriptions . . .' The screen blinked and a landscape appeared. 'For example, this is an early painting by John Constable and these Chinese figures are—'

Lambert's contempt was replaced by startled alarm. He realized that much of what they had stolen was rare, some of it unique, but now the police were saying they knew exactly what it looked like. So if they tried selling even the smallest item . . . ? Bloody Godwin and his insurance company. Perhaps if he acted quickly, before the police had time to circulate photographs . . . too risky. Think. Would they really be unable to shift anything from those plastic bags? What about abroad? Vaguely he thought he'd heard that Amsterdam was a good place. But they'd have to get it all through customs . . . 'the murderers will make a mistake eventually'. Not this one, PC Plod, even if it means waiting for years. Shit.

At the beginning of December Lambert was in the college refectory reading Haigh's *The English Reformation Revised* over his coffee. He had grown a beard since the murders, so that thick waves of pale hair washed over his ears before mingling with tight, wiry curls coating cheeks and jaw; his wide lips were like slices of peach in a crust of spun blond. A Danish sailor, father of a son born to a nineteenth-century housemaid in Scarborough, had injected Viking blood into his family, and the beard and grim-humoured blue eyes echoed violent invaders. The refectory was almost empty; Christmas vac started in less than a week and many students had already left. Lambert was scribbling notes on his pad when he realized someone had walked over to the table. He looked up and saw Jowett, wrapped in the Army surplus trench coat that had always been too big for him.

'I want to talk,' he said urgently.

'For fuck's sake.' Lambert sounded weary. 'What about now? And keep your voice down.'

Jowett pulled the tubular steel and cane chair away from the table and sat down. 'You've still got it? The stuff.'

'Of course I have. I told you how long we'll have to wait before it's safe to sell it. Bastard. Anyway, I've moved it to—'

'I don't want to know,' Jowett interrupted. 'I don't want to know anything about it. Ever. Got it? I want out.'

'What do you mean, out?'

Jowett leant forward. 'Don't argue with me about this, Giles. I don't want anything more to do with this. You keep the stuff, but keep me out of it. You can have everything.'

Lambert looked at him guardedly. Jowett had . . . not aged, but changed since Tannerslade Farm. He was thinner, ochre skin concave beneath sharp cheekbones, twin hollows emphasized by the nose that formed an almost exact right-angled triangle, like a child's drawing of a profile. Long, swept-back black hair fell to his collar. Seen walking through Cambridge, he would have been classed as a serious student, committed to some esoteric discipline, an embryo professor devoted to pure knowledge, a male virgin, not a fun person. Yet before the summer he had been loud in the raucous Friday night union bar, a beer and pizzas party animal.

'Everything?' Lambert repeated. 'You mean all of it?'

'Yes.' Jowett nodded. 'The lot . . . and that's the end of it. I don't want to hear from you again. I'm not coming back next term. Don't try to find me. OK?'

Lambert closed his textbook. 'Let's get this straight . . . You're pulling out. Finito?'

'Totally. You won't hear from me again. I'll just . . . forget it. I've thought it through. I don't want to know.'

'And how can I trust you to keep your mouth shut?'

'Come on, I don't want to go to gaol. I'm never going to talk. I don't even want to think about it.'

'Yeah?' Lambert sounded cynical. 'Until you give the police an anonymous tip-off and I'm in the shit.'

'No!' Jowett's deep cinnamon eyes lit with a pleading passion. 'If I did that you'd tell them about me as well, wouldn't you?'

'They might not believe me. Come on, Randy. I'm not falling for this crap. You could tell them just before vanishing to Australia.'

'For Christ's sake! I'm not going to talk . . . ever!'

'And this is going to make you feel better? You expunge your guilt by not taking the money?'

'I don't know . . . perhaps in a way. I'm so fucking screwed up, I'm nearly suicidal. Just believe me . . . If you don't, I probably will crack and blurt it out.' He suddenly became insistent. 'You've got a choice, Giles. Let me handle this my way or I probably *will* go to the police.'

Lambert stared at him. 'You mean that, don't you?'

'Believe me. I don't care how you live with this thing, but I've got to get right away from it. I don't want anything more to do with . . . with that bloody farm and those . . . Please, Giles! I'm giving you the lot. Live and be happy, you know?'

Lambert paused while he rolled and lit a cheap cigarette, all he could afford, then blew out the smoke. 'Giving me your word, are you?'

'If I could find a way to prove it, I would. Look, you've got nothing to lose. If I stay like this, I'm a danger to you. I dream

33

about it, I've ballsed up my course because of it, I *live* it! It's being here, seeing you, remembering. If I go away, I might be OK.'

'What are you going to tell your parents? About quitting university?'

'Anything . . . It won't matter. They're so bloody hung up about being broke, they won't be interested.'

'Where will you go?'

'I'm not sure yet. I've been checking out jobs. There's a company in Bristol looking for insurance salesmen.'

Lambert grinned sourly. 'Don't mention insurance companies. I'd like to piss on the lot of them.'

'It's just something to get away to . . . It's OK, then?'

'I'll think about it.'

Jowett shook his head. 'No. This is it. We agree now or I'll—'

'Don't crowd me, Randy,' Lambert warned.

'I'm not . . . All right, I am. But that's it. We just let it go and I'll . . . I don't know. Try to find a way to handle this.'

'I don't know where you're coming from here. What we've got is worth . . . a hundred and fifty grand? More? You want to just walk away from that? There's no problem – apart from the timing thing. But we'll be able to sell it eventually. Maybe five years, perhaps less. It's a fucking fortune.'

'That won't help me.' Jowett looked down as he began to rotate the tin ashtray on the plastic table top. 'I don't know if it's guilt or being shit scared or . . . You can't relate this to anything else. I can't imagine what I'll be like in a few years' time. There must be people who've done murders and got away with it. Perhaps they find a way of living with it. Perhaps I will – but not if I take any of the money. Somehow I know that . . . Come on, you can't force me.'

Lambert crushed out his cigarette stub as he thought. His greatest concern had been that Jowett's conscience would one day make him talk – but now he was suggesting that by running away he might be able to keep it under control. Lambert found it incomprehensible, but who needed understanding? Jowett could piss off and enter a monastery for all he cared. Or he could top himself. Or perhaps, one day, Lambert could simply make sure he never talked to anyone. When the going got tough . . .

'OK,' he said finally. 'You're fucking spineless – you always were – but it's your choice. But you say one word and I drop you right in it as well. Got it? They'll keep records at that place we hired the van from, for a start. I'll tell them it was your idea in the first place; I'll say you fired the gun. Are you hearing me?'

'You don't need to say it.' Jowett stood up. 'OK . . . thanks . . . I'll . . . All the best, you know? I hope you . . . you . . . shit, I don't know what to . . . live with it.'

Jowett turned and walked away. Hands thrust deep into his pockets, from the back he resembled a hunched and hungry refugee stalking a bleak, hostile world. Lambert watched him push open the plate-glass door of the refectory and cross the frosted paving stones of the quadrangle, before vanishing through the Victorian Gothic arch opposite.

'You're a loser, Randy,' he murmured.

Chapter One

Straightening up from smoothing the duvet, Joyce Hetherington paused and became judgemental as she caught the movement of her reflection in the long wardrobe mirror. At eighteen she had spent hours on body, face, hair, eyes and hands, emerging sleek and glistening as a racehorse; in her twenties she had been less obsessive, but still meticulous, applying soft oils, shining lipstick – for a brief, mannered period in the seventies, mauve – subtle traces of exclusive scent. In the early years of her marriage she had been the glossy trophy wife until, seeded first by Annabel's birth, then Rupert's, a blight had begun. Time, once plentiful, had become a luxury, snatched minutes to skim *Homes and Gardens* or *Vanity Fair* while attending to the ruins of her nails, legs crossed as she rotated each ankle in turn to tone the muscles. But, relentlessly, the house, the children, Ralph's expectations of domestic perfection and something akin to surrender had increasingly cramped her. Moving to the country had been an important factor. London imposed demands of style and appearance; rural Suffolk granted girls a brief blossom spring before dark leaves of mature summer and fading autumn. What West Kensington would approve, even envy, as ripened glamour, would be dismissed as gaudy in Finch Post Office.

Then had come the first stirrings of private rebellion. She'd given up her career, been the breeding mare, accepted more than her share of the demands of infants, and wanted something back. Ralph had passed from repeated, demanding – and admittedly for a long time mutually enjoyable – sex to siring his brood to obvious boredom with her body, and once The Affair had gone beyond evasion and denial to become blatant and admitted, Joyce had begun to resent what she had allowed to happen, angry at her own retreat. Work would have meant commuting into Ipswich at least, which presented difficulties, but when they had bought Windhover Ralph had been quite happy for her to take over the problems of holiday letting, even though he insisted the income had to be put through his books because of some complicated tax avoidance involving him claiming her as his secretary (she had caustically remarked that unlike several men she knew he didn't sleep with his secretary). The next stage had been paying more attention to her appearance again, so . . . She checked the latter-day achievement of forty-four years.

Waist and hips intact, if fractionally tense against her Levis; breasts fuller – going without a bra would be both unwise and more uncomfortable than it had been twenty years ago; ankles and legs still good; corn-gold and burnt-honey highlighted hair, curled and expensively casual; face . . . She stepped closer. Nothing could harm the bone structure; aquamarine eyes remained clear and the skin had been nourished rather than coarsened by open air; she had always tanned evenly, unexpected in a natural blonde. But what had the salvage operation been for, except personal satisfaction? The nearest she had ever come to making use of it had been at one of David and Paula's dinner parties. It had been early in the fightback and the reaction had been gratifying; the men positioning themselves to admire, the women – except Fay, who had thoroughly approved – slightly affronted at competition from an unexpected quarter, as though a sparrow had challenged kingfishers. Desmond – predictably; his ego fed on asset stripping and sexual conquests in equal measures – had wondered if she ever got up to town . . .

'Sod it,' she said aloud, with amused recollection. It had been a wry daydream imagining catching a London train from Ipswich, taking a taxi from Liverpool Street, ignoring the receptionist's discreet intrigued glances as she waited in the enamelled marble foyer of his offices, the civilized, flirtatious lunch . . . No need for him to return to work . . . Nothing so sordid as a hotel, but his high, compact flat in Legoland Island Gardens . . . Gazing down at the sickle sweep of the Thames as he stood behind her at the window, kissing the side of her neck, hands sliding up the front of her dress from waist to . . . but she hadn't been ready, so she'd never accepted. Sometimes she regretted it, even though an affair with Desmond would have been the sexual equivalent of accepting a free sample in the supermarket. And now his company had moved him to Singapore. Hey-ho.

Carrying the used bed linen, she mentally ran through her standard checklist as she went downstairs. Kitchen cleaned and everything returned to its place (why could people never remember where they had found things?). Carpets hoovered, meter emptied, flowers in the sitting room a touch of welcome from her own garden, windows polished, space beneath beds examined in case another soft porn magazine had been left behind – it had only happened once, but she would have felt dreadful if an outraged mother had faced her with it – ad hoc paperback collection tidied, noting that the Joanna Trollope had disappeared. The couple who had moved out that morning had seemed so respectable; perhaps it was an oversight and they would post it back. The next visitor had said he would arrive around six o'clock, so . . . She stopped as his name refused to come. When he had first telephoned it had struck her as unusual, and the fact that she could not recall it irritated her; as Sir Malcolm's PA, Joyce Carstairs had been able to remember two dozen things at once. It was a make of car. Morris? Ford? Austin? Something more exotic. Jensen . . . no, Jowett. She'd had an uncle who'd owned one. It was also unusual that he was apparently coming on his own and had booked for five weeks. The cottage could sleep six with the bunk beds, but few holidaymakers wanted to spend longer than a fortnight in so isolated a place as Finch, even at the height of summer. Perhaps he fished or watched birds; they were always solitary types, usually with patient wives who . . . God, was that the time? Ralph would be back in less than an hour expecting lunch to be ready, and she'd promised to run Annabel over to Suzanne's.

Then Marion was coming to discuss the pageant, which would leave very little time to rearrange the chaos of the flower rota . . .

New graffiti had been added to the bench by the lychgate of St Matthew's; mindless vulgarity that riled her. It would be the brats from the council estate again, probably the same ones who had pushed over the medieval Plague Stone, another act of boorishness and spite that caused offence and distress. The parish council had leafleted all eighty homes, but the only result had been complaints from several parents that their children – all, allegedly, little lower than angels – had been singled out for blame and none of the 'posh houses' had received warnings. It had exacerbated the situation, climaxing in one teenage girl shouting obscenities at Joyce outside the baker's, then standing defiant when Joyce had turned to reprimand her.

'What yer going to do then? Tell me mum and dad? God, I'm shitting meself. And if you bloody dare hit me, I'll have you for assault, right?' She had sneered at Joyce's dismay. 'Fat cow.'

Better to ignore them, wait for them to grow up and leave Finch, get pregnant, in some cases surely end up in a juvenile offenders' home or worse. But such jeering insolence was contrary to all her values, her expectations that parents should set examples and exercise control . . . All the attitudes she had mocked in her own parents before being caught by them herself. And there was the trap of class stereotyping; Mrs Barron, plump, loquacious and shrewd, who cleaned Joyce's house twice a week and had once returned a 10p piece she had found under a sofa, lived in one of the council houses.

Mother had come downstairs, and was peering round Joyce's kitchen like a puzzled, inquisitive magpie, lifting random objects to look beneath them, muttering in impatience and frustration.

'What have you lost this time?' Noticing that she'd left her hearing aid off again, Joyce raised her voice.

'My library book. It was a Catherine Cookson.'

'Well, you're hardly going to find it underneath the flower vase.'

'No, but I've run out of logical places. I've prayed to St Anthony, but he's not helping.'

'I'm positive you've not brought it down here. Let's look in your apartment.'

'It can't be there.' The tone said it mustn't be, because that would mean she had failed to find it in any of the logical places.

'Perhaps it fell down the back of the bed.'

She had become noticeably slower on the stairs, but still managed them, refusing Ralph's regular suggestions of installing a chair lift. For some inexplicable reason the book was in her bathroom, half hidden behind the curtain.

'Oh, dear.' She pulled a face of chagrin. 'I really am losing it, aren't I?'

'Don't be silly.' Joyce kissed her cheek. 'Have you got your lunch sorted out?'

'Yes thank you, dear. Cold tongue and tomato with some of Mrs Barron's home-made chutney . . . Oh, and I think I heard your phone ring twice, but it stopped each time. The machine must be on. Where's Ralph?'

'Golf club. It's Saturday.'

Grace Carstairs smiled, remembering a fragment of contented years as a passive, dutiful wife. 'Your father enjoyed his golf so much. I couldn't play for toffee, but why don't you take it up?'

'We've been through that.'

'So we have.' She had obviously forgotten. 'Anyway, I'm going to watch that Bette Davis film this afternoon. I'll probably cry as much as I did when I saw it at the old Picturedrome in Salisbury. Ralph's put the video in for me and written down which buttons I have to press.'

She'd been right about the answerphone – her hearing could be curiously selective. One message was from Marion cancelling and the other was from Ralph announcing he'd been held up, slightly whining, put out that she was not at home to take his call.

'. . . anyway, make lunch for about two o'clock. That's all.'

So we're not taking it in liquid form at the club today, O Master? But we will doubtless fall asleep in the chair watching whatever European football match you've been obsessed with for weeks. Just don't wake up again full of petulant comments about the times you could talk me into afternoon nookie – can you hear yourself saying that, for God's sake? What sort of mind is it that can switch off everything that's happened between us? Do you really despise me so much that you think I'm going to be grateful for whatever you have left over from servicing Gabriella? We found that flat together, our *pied-à-terre*, when we moved here, so convenient for when we went to the theatre in town, as well as your Monday to Friday base. I haven't been in it for more than five years and I expect she keeps some of her clothes there now – when she's wearing any. Meanwhile, you've found the perfect gaoler in my mother. I'll cry my heart out when she dies, but at least I'll have the satisfaction of soaking you for so much of your precious money you won't believe it.

Absently humming the duet from *The Pearl Fishers*, she began preparing cold lamb and salad, another offering without love.

Reading the *Guardian* while they ate was casual sniper fire in the cold war; given the chance, Ralph would have knelt in the mud to kiss the hem of Margaret Thatcher's gown and constantly dreamt of a Second Coming. The eighties had been his Promised Land, the advertising business floating on a tidal wave of multi-million-pound campaigns; champagne fountains of money to turn round fast, buy and sell shares, take in and out of property – ideal in East Anglia, where prices had remained low for longer, before the glittering, fragile bubble burst. He'd sold like fury in the black October of 1987, screaming down the phone at his broker as the roof fell in, taking every reduction in inflated profits like a personal insult, despite the fact that in many cases he still came out ahead. Before that, at least on paper, he'd briefly been a millionaire, and it was as though he'd been robbed.

'Did I tell you we didn't get that pet food account?'

'I didn't even know you'd pitched for it.' She went on reading, emphasizing her lack of interest.

'Of course we did.' He rubbed his fist against his breastbone, as if he had a spasm of indigestion. 'But Maurice landed it. Bastard.'

She turned a page without looking up. 'I can remember when he was your hero.'

'Well, he's a bloody greedy animal now.'

'Unlike you, of course.'

Such exchanges would once have drawn blood, but there was little left to spill and neither of them had reason to break the brittle ceasefire. As Ralph pushed his plate away and left the table, Joyce frowned at another story about the Dunblane school massacre; evil and senseless, the horror felt all over the world had plucked at terrible memories in Finch, part of a bitter register – Hungerford, Warrington, the cenotaph at Enniskillen. Photographed or faceless, Hamilton, Ryan, hooded IRA bombers and Tannerslade's unknown murderers were devils who cursed the places they had stalked, their acolytes plagues of rabid journalists and sick tourists who came to stare. It would have been Cheryl's birthday next week ... Joyce shook her head sharply to dismiss the anger and grief that could still torment after six years, and moved her attention to something else. From the living room came the frustrated roar of a crowd and Ralph announcing aloud that some England player was a useless wanker.

She went outside to what was her unstated territory, tacitly off-limits to Ralph whenever she was in it. As the children had begun to grow up and away, and the bleak prospect of a withered marriage had emerged, the house remained shared, but the garden was Joyce's equivalent of his golf club or the enemy-occupied Camden flat. He had never dared to question how much she had spent on wrought-iron arches, stone seats, chimney pots and immense glazed amphorae filled with flowers, the gazebo and Elizabethan knot garden beyond the rose trellis, all researched and planted at delicious expense. It was her private country, not another battlefield. She rarely hired help from the village, jealously keeping the work for herself to prove she could create something that had value.

Punching numbers into her mobile phone, she juggled the

church flower rota. If Jackie filled the gap left by Isobel and Mrs Woodhouse would do two Sundays in succession, then surely she could talk Amy into dealing with the wedding at the end of next month. The Barnards were due back from Vancouver on the eighteenth, so . . .

Twenty years earlier, the possibility that her life might diminish to the point where such trivia became important would have been laughable. Now it wasn't funny – but had to be endured.

Chapter Two

For six years Finch had existed only as the place where guilt lived; Jowett could remember nothing from passing through in 1990, shaking with terror, mind seeing only broken bodies and death. He still carried the image of a television report with a church in the background, the horror professionally condensed into a closing soundbite after a voice-over for shots of the farm, cars and policemen, red and white striped tape across the gate they had driven through, stunned villagers, fields and a photograph of Benjamin and Annie Godwin, smiling and alive. '. . . their daughter, Cheryl Hood, and grandchildren, Thomas and Amanda, also died in a crime that has shattered this peaceful village. Martin White, BBC News, Finch, Suffolk.' For days afterwards glaring headlines glimpsed on newsagents' shelves had shouted accusation at him until he had run away – only to discover there was no escape.

What he had achieved since had been a constant, growing rebuke that evil could lead to such rewards. But it was the inevitable result of an obsession with work. After a brief period selling insurance, family influence had gained him a position with the Midland's Hong Kong and Shanghai Banking Corporation, his lack of degree compensated for by his total commitment. At twenty-seven he was a currency dealer at the Thames Exchange in Queen Street Place, bonuses and commission pulling in more than seventy thousand a year, with only himself to spend it on. And other deaths – torturing his conscience further, the remnants of abandoned faith which had taught him that the dead saw and knew all about the living – had brought him more that he did not desire. A heart attack had killed his father in 1993, his mother had died a year later after an overdose which a sympathetic coroner had decided was accidental, and Jowett and his sister had shared the estate, enlarged by life policies he had sold to his parents. He was envied, independent: a flat in the Barbican's Lauderdale Tower, an MGF. He tacitly encouraged envious office rumours of a flamboyant secret life to explain his need for privacy. The reality was nights spent alone, occupying his fearful mind with mental discipline – teaching himself French, memorizing poetry – or indulging in lonely self-abuse, crude fantasies fuelled by magazines that he shamefully hid even though there was no one who might find them, his release bringing with it a sense of humiliation, self-inflicted and squalid.

At the beginning he had grasped at sex, constantly paraded as a panacea for all problems. He had stalked the wine bars and the clubs, stitching on a smile of pleasure, temporarily forgetting as amplified disco drums throbbed in the alcohol-flooded chambers of his mind, groping on packed, strobe-blinked dance floors. There had been Sara, dreaming of hairdressing, in her Gloucester Road bedsit, enthusiastic and giggly; Helen, the law student he had met at a Proms concert, intellectual and intense; Sindy, drunkenly selected one night from the grubby cards displayed in a telephone box near King's Cross, efficient, bored and cynical; a handful of others who now had no names. But he had always been back in the wilderness when it was over. After that he had explored other standard escape routes. Travel to India and Burma, where philosophical monks had failed him; a brief period of voluntary work that felt as hypocritical as his donations to homeless, starving children or research into ugly diseases, when there was no cure for his own.

Finally he had lain in a warm, embracing bath, a sliver of blue blade held across the artery of his rigid wrist. Shaking with fear he had scratched at the promise of ultimate relief before shuddering and hurling the razor aside, weeping at his coward-ice, until the water had grown cold and the cleansing blood sacrifice had turned into a grotesque pantomime of self-delusion.

It was the chance encounter with Giles that had driven him back to Finch. They had met on Moorgate when he was returning from lunch with a client, another anonymous face passing unseen, suddenly recognized, the voice calling his name unnervingly normal, surprised and amused with recognition. *Christ, it's been years. What are you doing these days? How about that? I went into finance as well. Fund manager with Mercury Asset Management.* They had moved aside to let others pass. *Where are you living? Hey, swish. We're in Highgate . . . Yes, I married – a father for God's sake. Rebecca, nearly three. You? Stay like that; it plays havoc with your social life. Just kidding. It's great. Anyway, I've got to get back. Here, have one of these. Call me sometime and we'll have a jar. Great to see you. Cheers.* He had gripped Jowett's hand, smiled and walked away, another assured, well-cut professional suit heading towards London Wall. Holding the business card, Jowett had stared after him, keeping him in sight to confirm that the moment so often played in his mind had actually occurred, conscious that he had failed to say any of the things he had planned, that neither of them had even hinted at . . . that it had been so insanely like dozens of other chance conversations on the crowded City pavements; the casual news and questions, the oblique boasting, the printed oblong of pasteboard from the wallet, the departing invitation rarely followed up.

Back at the office he had locked himself in a lavatory cubicle, his sweating forehead pressed against cool white porcelain. Giles' normality had been a new form of torment, an unspoken, smiling contempt at Jowett's weakness and inability to dismiss guilt as irrelevant. *Get a life, Randy. It was forever ago. They'll never catch us now.* The trembling that had suddenly squirmed through his body had taken on the qualities of a trip, simultaneously uncontrollable and opening doors on vivid perception: the only place left to run was to go back. To the farm, to the village that had known them and the people he had hurt. Rational motives were impossible – laying ghosts a cliché, psychological hairshirts an indulgence – but then nothing had been rational since the blood-spattered frenzy of that summer afternoon.

But Finch was the last place to run to and the only road out of it led nowhere except the perpetual insanity of a life he could neither tolerate nor find the courage to end. He asked for unpaid leave to be added to his holidays – claimed as a need to chill out, to rethink his career schedule. It gave him five weeks from the eighth of June, which would include the anniversary. And all contacts would be closed, no address, mobile phone disconnected. He would step outside his walls and face the creature they guarded him from; the Randall Jowett born screaming and helpless amid gunfire and innocent blood.

Spring was late in coming, sunlight canopied its remains in haze and heat. May had been the wettest in Britain anyone could remember and the glare of yellow on fields of oil seed rape, candled chestnuts, hawthorn blossom like unmelted patches of snow, dull purple of lilac bushes still lingered. The delayed ripening was rich and lush, landscape moulded into endless hollows and shallow domes, a motionless heaving sea of green. As soon as he had left the main road out of Ipswich the countryside had become deserted; the occasional car, a lone cyclist, hamlets he entered and left without seeing any life, wide fields of silent growing. At one point he took a wrong turning and stopped by an isolated signpost to consult his road atlas, parched air scented with dust and the odour of barley seeping through the car's open windows; Stoke by Walsham . . . Ash Sounder . . . Cheslebrook . . . A bead of perspiration trickled from his forehead and dripped a stain on to the map . . . Where was he in this labyrinth of twisting, empty lanes? There . . . he should have taken the left fork. As he straightened up the desire to find the trunk road again and drive back to London returned, but he forced it away by going over the directions he had been sent. 'Watch out for the Shoulder of Mutton on your left, straight on at the crossroads, then we're the house with the iron railings at the bottom of the dip. I'll leave a pint of milk in the fridge at the cottage and you can buy food at the village shop, but I'm afraid it's rather expensive. Most people use the supermarket at Bury St Edmunds or go into Ipswich. Thank you for your deposit. I hope you have a good journey and enjoy your stay.' It had been written on a word processor, then signed, the 'J' and 'H' flamboyant.

The road sign appeared abruptly as he turned out of a stretch of high trees and hedges: Finch. Twinned with Bad Wildegun. Thousands of Allied aircraft had risen out of the East Anglian plain north of Suffolk to attack the German enemy; now peace meant civic delegations and school exchanges. Was that a form of forgiveness for murder? He caught a glimpse of council houses, bleak grey concrete with crude ears of satellite dishes, three youths standing by mountain bikes, a family sitting outside. But the estate was hidden down a side road, a parasite its host did not wish to absorb. Then he was on The Street, long, straight and house-lined, empty except for a young woman with a pushchair and a boy on a skateboard. The frontages were clapperboard or plain plaster, painted lemon, pink, washed orange, pale lime, the roofline of russet pantiles broken by one patch of blackened thatch ... And rising up ahead the square tower of the church where the Godwins had been buried, surrounded by love and grief. What would it be like for him if the truth became known? Within the walls of the prison he would be sent to for the rest of his life, a warder to witness the chaplain granting him token ceremony. Buried in quicklime that would eat his body. Did they still do that? Would someone secretly take a photograph and sell it to the tabloids so that they could write a hate-filled epitaph? 'JOWETT IS BURIED LIKE A DOG TO ROT.'

He concentrated on the directions again; the pub, almost the only touch of brick, its outside tables shaded by canvas umbrellas; the crossroads – the church stood on them and he forced his eyes ahead – then the Finch of social status. Individual detached homes behind hedges, double garages, a private tennis court, gardens that glowed with attention, a row of almshouses originally built for the poor and elderly, now redeveloped for young executives who gave to charity after balancing the monthly accounts. This was where the real money was, solid in property and gleaming BMWs, Mercedes and Range Rovers. It reminded him of the area in which he had grown up on the select edge of Bedford: children at boarding school; mannered dinner parties and coffee mornings; flower arrangement classes; voting Conservative; discreet afternoon indiscretions in Strachan Studio bedrooms; the gîte in Brittany; the wine cellar. Of where, after impatient rebellion, he should be himself, a carbon copy of his father, with a wife like his mother, first child asleep in the Lloyd Loom crib beneath Peter Rabbit murals in the pastel nursery. The English middle classes, mocked and envied, sycophantic and condescending, fearful and confident.

The road dropped suddenly, curving again as the land fell to his right, opposite the house, into a deep, wide bowl of wild-flowered meadow brimming with early-evening sunlight. As he stopped by the gate, he looked across at a poster pinned to an oak tree: a naive drawing of a man in what appeared to be a boar's head, costumed in tattered scarlet and purple streamers. Vivid green letters announced that the Pegman Pageant would be held on Saturday 29 June, three weeks away.

Damp with sweat, his shirt peeled off his back as he stepped out of the car and he felt uncomfortable about his appearance: his face flushed and glistening, hair dank, cotton trousers sticky against his thighs, aware that he must stink. Mopping his face with tissues left a feeling of smeared and crusted skin, and attending to his hair laid a glutinous deposit in the comb's teeth. He walked along the road to a patch of trees and lay in the shade, eyes closed. The village was unrecognizable, no images remaining from that panic-filled race to flee. Giles had been driving by then, and Randall had stared out of the van, everything he saw irrelevant and invisible. This afternoon he hadn't noticed the farm as he drove in – so where was it? Asking might arouse suspicion, but he would buy a map . . . Buzzing aggressively a harvesting bee made him move.

Behind the spearhead railings and the crisp privet hedge that lined them, he could see that money had been planted and cultivated in the garden: a matched pair of tulip trees, rich herbaceous borders, grass shaved smooth. At the foot of six wide steps a small statue of a boy stood in the centre of an ornamental pond, two streams of water flowing like silver drinking straws from the hand at his mouth to form Pan pipes. The house was a mustard-coloured rectangle, four sash windows, upstairs and down, on either side of the central door, frontage decorated with large regular squares embossed with a quatrefoil pattern. A semi-circular conservatory had been added to one end of the house and fir-green wooden barrels filled with marguerites and trailing lobelia stood at the top of the steps. The bell push was set in the middle of an emblematic brass rose.

'Mrs Hetherington?' She had the classic appearance of someone for whom wealth was an inheritance to be prudently husbanded. She wore jeans, espadrilles and a simple striped cotton shirt, understated make-up; only the hair, attractively styled wheat-coloured curls tumbling almost to her shoulders, revealed wealth.

'That's right. Mr Jowett? You found us then.' She had expected an older man, but he could be no more than thirty. He should be taking holidays with a girlfriend . . . or boyfriend? The slender, hesitant face was sexually ambiguous, skin the colour of pale tea, black hair gleaming and longer than was fashionable. She wondered if he had a Mediterranean ancestor. 'I'm afraid I'm going to ask you to drive back to the church and turn right for the cottage. It's about a quarter of a mile away, just past the old chapel. Look out for the white gate. I'll meet you there with the key and show you round.'

'Thank you . . . Can I give you a lift?'

'There's no need. I can take the short cut across the fields.'

He was standing by the side fence when she arrived, gazing across to where a long hump of trees lay like a green cloud on the horizon. The boot of the car was open, matching pencil-grey leather suitcases beside it.

'Good journey?' Standard question, polite enquiry without intrusion.

'Yes, thank you . . . Is that a farm?'

'Where? Yes. It's their land behind the cottage.'

'What's it called?'

'Daylock. My daughter keeps her pony there.' She hesitated,

unsure of a Londoner's rural awareness. 'If you like walking you can go almost anywhere as long as you close the gates and are careful not to tread on anything that's growing.'

'I know.'

'Oh . . . anyway, I'll give you the fifty-pence tour.'

It had been refined over several years of visitors' questions and problems. Electricity meter takes pound coins . . . Instruction book for the washing machine is under the lid . . . Garden chairs in the shed . . . Immersion heater comes on at . . . First rise of the stairs is deeper than the rest, be careful you don't trip . . . It faces east-west so the front bedroom catches the morning sun, if you prefer that . . . I'll bring fresh towels and sheets each Friday . . . It's a summer weight duvet; the heavier one's in the airing cupboard, but I can't imagine you'll need it . . . A man from the village mows the grass when it needs doing, but he won't disturb you . . . There are some local guide books in the sitting room if you want to find places to visit . . . And the balance? Failing to ask for that at the start had led to arguments in the past.

'Sure . . . my bag's downstairs.' He stood aside to let her precede him, an instinctive rather than acquired gesture from this polite young man with vulnerable and intelligent eyes. And he used a bag . . . No, that was jumping to conclusions, but was he seeking solace on his own after an affair with one sex or the other? It wasn't her business. As he filled in the cheque she noticed his hands, graceful as long leaves.

'Thank you.' She tucked the folded cheque in her shirt pocket. Her natural instinct with new guests was to make casual conversation, but he had an air of reserve which made her tread carefully. 'I hope you realize how quiet it is here. I'm afraid there's hardly anything to do.'

'That's OK . . . I was looking for that . . . I'm writing a book.' It was as though he felt the need to tell her, to explain his arrival.

'Oh, you're a writer?'

'Not really . . . I work in a bank.'

'Like T. S. Eliot.'

'Pardon? Oh, yes. I'm not a poet though.'

You ought to be; you look like one. 'So what's it about?'

He replaced the cheque book in his bag. 'I'm not certain . . . A novel.'

She smiled. 'I tried that once, but I couldn't manage the discipline. It was about love, of course. What else is there when you're twenty-two? It was very self-indulgent . . . I'm sorry, I didn't mean . . .' Christ, that was gauche.

'Mine won't be about love.'

'Well, I hope it's an incredible success so I can have a plaque put on the cottage saying you wrote it here. You might make Finch famous.' She felt that her presence was unwanted. 'Anyway, I think that's everything. Let me know if you have any problems. Just pop a note through the letterbox if I'm out.'

'I don't think there'll be anything . . . Oh, what's the Pegman Pageant? I saw a notice.'

'The pageant? That's our big village day. It ends up with a fair on the Pegman meadow – the one opposite our house – and . . . well, it's all very local and bucolic. I'm still trying to work out how I let myself be talked into taking part this year. If you come, you'll see me dressed up as the Lady Marion.'

'Who's she?'

'It's all part of the legend . . . It'll take too long to explain. You'll find it in one of the books.' She glanced round the room, making sure there was nothing she had forgotten. 'Right, you know where everything is and I must get back. Goodbye.'

He occupied himself with unpacking, hanging clothes in the wardrobe, finding a glass for gin and tonic, which he drank while watching television. It helped him to behave like a normal person would, settling in, exploring, putting the lasagne he had brought in the microwave, opening kitchen cupboards and drawers until he found dinner plates and cutlery. He finished eating and went outside, staring for a long time at clouds like brushed raw cotton, colours being pulled down as though slowly melting into the fires of a furnace. It was utterly quiet. Within a few minutes' walk lay the bodies of five human beings he had never spoken to but who were more important to him than anyone he had ever known. The thought was too immense to comprehend.

Later he took a sleeping pill, kept from a prescription years earlier, and only once in the night did a dream-racked cry of distress sound through the open bedroom window. But there was no one to hear.

Chapter Three

Silence and silver light filled St Matthews; silence of emptiness and centuries of hushed voices, light of sunbeams, like lowered steel swords, piercing diamond panes of plain clerestory windows, shining on pale grey pillars and walls of whitewashed stone. The heavy oak north door scraped the tufted mat as Joyce opened it and the clock's half-hour strokes sang muffled from tower to sounding nave. There was money on the pewter plate next to the pamphlets that explained an unremarkable history repeated in countless Suffolk churches, many now more Reformation heritage museums than centres of faith. But Finch, sharing its vicar with three other parishes, maintained a congregation divided between those for whom churchgoing had been a childhood occasion and who wished to preserve some sense of God in a faithless age, those for whom it was a social habit and those who attended because the church had instilled fear in them. Joyce slid the coins through the slot of the small iron box sealed into the wall against petty theft, placed her bag on the table and took out metal polish and duster before turning towards the altar and the brass bits at the holy end; her own ambivalent beliefs could accommodate Larkin's cynicism.

Expecting the church to be empty – too early for tourists, wrong time for prayer, which required booking an appointment with God on Sundays – the bowed figure in the front pew startled her; a man, the back of his head sunk low before the intricately carved arches of the rood screen. Her rope-soled sandals had made virtually no sound and she realized he was unaware of her arrival. She hesitated, not wanting to invade his privacy with weekly housekeeping; whoever it was would probably not stay long, and she could wait in the vestry . . . Then his shoulders rose and fell as he gave a shuddering sigh. Joyce felt embarrassed, unable to decide whether to approach or leave; her Christianity was full of such uncertainties . . . Then he raised his head and turned, as though her presence had reached him.

'Oh, it's you . . . Sorry.' She held up the gingham duster and canister of spray polish as defensive excuses. 'I was just going to . . . It doesn't matter. I didn't mean to disturb you.'

'No . . . Is it all right? The door was unlocked.'

'Of course. We never lock it during the day . . . There's nothing worth stealing and . . . I didn't realize anyone was here. Stay as long as you want.' Across the distance between them it was impossible to be certain, but he could have been weeping. 'I can do this later.'

'But I'm in your way.'

'Oh, for God's sake, we can't keep apologizing to each other. Please stay . . . It's what the place is for. I'm sorry.'

She withdrew swiftly, uncomfortable at having found him so distressed, disliking the flicker of irritation that her routine had been interrupted. That was uncharitable . . . And it would be best if she left the church completely, not lurked in the vestry as though impelling him to go. Outside she faced a hiatus with nothing to do in the unexpected interval. Sitting on the bench near the door would also suggest impatience if he came out and saw her, so she walked away through the churchyard, still carrying her cleaning materials amid the crumbling gravestones. Perhaps her first instinct about him had been right; an affair had ended, new love or treachery slipping through an unsecured door and destroying happiness. But it felt unusual that a young man should turn to the Church – unless that had been part of his upbringing. Or he could be one of the countless who fled back to promises of comfort long since dismissed as superstition. Should she ask if he wanted to speak to Jeffrey? Or would that be an intrusion, exploiting a chance encounter?

After quarter of an hour she cautiously returned; if the polishing was not done that morning there would be no opportunity for the rest of the week, leading to mutterings from the Finch Coven; Kathleen Kershaw could spot dulled metal at twenty paces, and it was a matter of pride never to give her ammunition. He knew she had a job to do, so perhaps he had . . . But he spoke as she was opening the door again.

'It's OK,' he said hastily before she even saw him. 'I'm leaving.' He was just inside, next to the plate on which he had left two pounds for a pamphlet that cost 30p.

'Thank you . . . As I said, come back whenever you want. Nobody should be locked out of a church.' That sounded pious, but she could think of no other way to put it. 'Have you settled in all right?'

'Yes. Thank you. It's very comfortable.'

'Good . . . anyway, I must get on.' Small talk felt inappropriate.

'What's this?'

'Pardon? Oh.' It was the oval slate plaque on the wall by the door which she could rarely bring herself to look at. 'That's . . . it was a long time ago.'

He read the engraved names and inscription again.

Benjamin Porter Godwin. Anne Hilda Godwin. Cheryl Anne Hood. Thomas Christopher Hood. Amanda Rachel Hood. In Memoriam, 11 July 1990. Loving and beloved, they left for God together.

'Who were they?'

She had to control herself. 'Ben owned a farm just outside the village. Annie was his wife and Cheryl was their daughter. Tom and Mandy were her children.' She swallowed. 'They were murdered. Didn't you read about it? Every damned newspaper reported it.'

'I think I must have done . . . It was while I was at Cambridge. Wasn't someone arrested?'

'No . . . I remember trying to rationalize why the thought of no one being punished made it worse. It wouldn't have brought them back.'

'Did you know them . . . Were they friends of yours?'

'Yes. Cheryl especially, but everyone in Finch knew Ben and Annie. They were lovely people.'

He turned back to the wall. 'Two children.'

'Yes. Tom would have been nineteen this year . . . I'm sorry, it's difficult to talk about.'

'I shouldn't have asked. I didn't realize.'

'You weren't to know.' She could see the suggestion of tears in his eyes again. Was that it? He'd lost someone too, and was here to mourn? 'Anyway, life has to go on . . . It's the sort of thing that makes you cling to clichés . . . Oh, dear.' Whatever hurt was very near the surface; he had begun to weep, anguish creasing his face. Joyce's impulse to hold him was stopped by awareness that he was a stranger. 'Come and sit down again.'

She escorted him without touching, as though he were contagious, and for a moment could find no words. Then. 'Look, I have to do this, but come back to my house when I've finished and we can have coffee. OK?' Face hidden in his hands, he nodded and she touched his shoulder gently before walking to the altar. As she started to clean the cross she wondered what she could say, how near she could approach. At least when she looked at him again he was sitting up, still sad but composed.

'Come on then.' She used the brisk, reassuring tone of a mother to a distressed child. Let's talk about something else to take your mind off it. She spoke of the weather, prospects for the harvest, her church duties; as they passed the Godwin graves, stones marbled with shadow, she pointed to some distant landmark to deflect his attention. When they reached the gate he complimented her on her garden, which pleased her. Once in the house, she led him straight through to the kitchen.

'Instant will be quicker. Please sit down.' He took a chair by the kitchen table and looked at the front page of the *Guardian* without interest as she decided that the informality of mugs would be less intimidating than bone china. 'Did you find everything all right?'

'What? Oh, at the cottage. Yes . . . No sugar, thank you.'

'Is that how you keep so slim?'

'I don't know . . . I just am.'

'Lucky you. I have to exercise. Fortunately, I cycle a lot – and go on aerobics binges when I start to panic.'

He smiled, as though any response might sound unflattering, and remained silent as she brought the coffee over.

'Here you are . . . and do smoke if you wish. I noticed the cigarettes when you arrived.' She admired his hands again as he lit one, conscious of their grace. 'Feeling better now?'

He nodded. 'I can't explain . . . about the church.'

'It's not my business.' She indicated his coffee. 'This is just being friendly . . . Have you managed to do any writing yet?'

'Not really . . . It's not easy.' He was looking at the three chains she invariably wore, find golden threads crossing the summer-brown skin at the exposed delta of her throat. 'Have you lived here long?'

'We moved from London in nineteen eighty, the year Rupert was born. It was a good time to buy property, especially in this part of the world. Then the cottage came on the market and we bought it as an investment. We'll sell it eventually, of course, but my husband's waiting until prices go up more. Anyway, letting it through the summer covers most of the costs. Of course, nobody wants to come here in the winter. The east wind can be wicked. Straight across the North Sea from the Urals. What my mother calls a lazy wind – it cuts right through you instead of going round.'

She was conscious of talking more than was necessary and felt uncomfortable. The invitation had been hers, its subtext sympathy, a willingness to listen if that was what he wanted. It struck her how rare it was for her to be alone with a man; Ralph obviously didn't count, and conversations with Jeffrey in the vicarage carried no overtones. She dismissed the thought; this was just lack of practice. So ask him something, be normal.

'Why did you decide to come to Finch?'

'Why not?' There was an immediate edge there, almost suspicion.

'Well, there must be dozens of other places where you could write – I've always thought it would be best near the sea. Have you been here before?'

'No.' His head shook to emphasize. 'I just saw your ad in the

Sunday Times and looked on a map. I didn't want to travel too far from London.'

'Is it what you expected? I mean, I know it's quiet, but . . .' Instinctively she reached across the table and took his hand as she saw what was returning to his face. 'Sorry.'

'It's all right. You aren't . . . I don't know why I chose here. There wasn't a reason.'

Perhaps not a specific reason for coming to Finch, but she was certain there had been a need to get away. Perhaps if she pushed very gently . . .

'Tell me to back off if I'm intruding, but we all wonder about other people and . . .' She hesitated. 'Have you lost someone?'

He pulled his hand away. 'Not like . . . Yes, I have.'

'Oh, that is so awful. Did they die? Were they very young?' She was dismayed as he began to weep again. 'God, that was tactless.' She held up her hands helplessly. 'I was just trying to . . . well, I ballsed that one up, didn't I?' He was no longer looking at her. 'Please . . . just forget I said anything. I'll be back in a moment.'

She walked through to the drawing room, for no other reason than to leave him alone, and stood by the window, caught by his distress, embarrassed by her own behaviour rather than his. She should have been more careful, testing the fragility of his emotions before barging in like . . . like what? The middle-aged, middle-class do-gooder. It was so long since she'd had to express sympathy for another person that she'd forgotten it was a matter of giving them space and following them into it. And . . . She leant her head against the pane.

'And if you'd been a woman or an old man, would I have invited you back here?' she murmured to herself. 'And am I saying this because I'm the one with the case of need here and you, Mr Jowett, are very handy as a fantasy figure? Oh, get your bloody head together.'

She picked up a magazine and took it back with her; thankfully, he looked better and had finished his coffee.

'I wanted to get this. There's a piece in it on this year's Pegman Pageant you were asking me about.'

'Thank you . . . Can anyone go?'

'The more the merrier. You'll be able to see me dressed as a very romanticized medieval lady. I do magic as well.'

'Does everyone have to dress up?'

'No. Only a few of us. It's all part of the legend.'

He looked as though he wanted to thank her, but was finding it difficult. He stood up awkwardly, then they both started as a voice called, enquiring and vibrant, from the garden.

'Anyone home?'

Joyce felt immediate relief. 'Kitchen!'

The woman burst in like a bright bird, flame satin shirt, white skirt with decorative belt of plaited scarlet thongs, tortoiseshell framed sunglasses pushed up into a mane of designer-mop brunette hair, like some courting ornament. 'Hi . . . Oh. Hello.'

'This is . . . I've forgotten your first name . . . Randall. Randall Jowett. He's staying at Windhover . . . Fay Graveney.'

She frowned. 'I've seen you somewhere . . . Weren't you in the supermarket at Bury yesterday morning?'

'Yes.'

'I thought so . . . Anything left in the pot?'

'It's instant.'

'I don't mind slumming it.' Fay turned back to Jowett. 'So. What do you think of Finch?'

'I haven't seen much of it yet. I only arrived on Saturday.'

'There's precious little to see. One wool church, a house where Tallulah Bankhead – you're much too young to have heard of her, and so am I – spent a night for some reason and a Plague Stone . . . Can I cadge one of those?'

'Pardon? Oh. Yes, sure.' He offered the cigarette packet and lit it for her.

'Given up giving up again?' Joyce asked sardonically.

'I've got it down to one a day.' Fay smiled at Jowett through expelled smoke. 'This one's May the fourteenth, 2007.'

'What? Oh. Yeah.' He smiled thinly, then looked at Joyce. 'I ought to go. Thank you for the coffee and . . . well, thanks. Nice to have met you.'

'My pleasure,' Fay told him. 'How long are you staying?'

'Five weeks.'

'Five weeks?' She gave a disbelieving laugh. 'My dear boy, you'll die of terminal boredom.'

He looked uncomfortable, unsure how to respond, then smiled again and walked out through the door and back across the garden towards the church. Fay stood up to watch him and her eyes sparkled as she turned back to Joyce.

'Any time . . . any place.'

'Stop it. You don't mean it – and, anyway, I thought you were committed?'

'Come on, darling, the fact that you've ordered your meal doesn't stop you looking at the menu again, and he's seriously gorgeous. He's here on his own?'

'Yes. I think . . . I'm not sure. I found him in the church. Crying. He may have lost somebody. He's desperately unhappy.'

'Girlfriend?'

'Possibly . . . or boyfriend, of course.'

'Is he gay?'

'I don't know, but the thought crossed my mind.'

'Whichever, who'd leave *him*?'

'I think they may have died.'

'That's it, then.' Fay held up her right hand, palm outwards. 'Keep clear. Aids alert.'

'Don't say that!' Joyce felt unexpectedly protective. 'Perhaps it was his parents . . . or it might not be anything to do with anyone dying.'

'It was something heavy though,' Fay remarked. 'Why else would he want to spend five weeks in Finch?'

'He may just like being on his own. He's writing a book. Anyway, it's none of our business. I asked him back for coffee because I felt sorry for him and that's the end of it. What brings you round?'

'I'm going into Ipswich. Need anything?'

'I don't think so.' Fay owned a badge with the legend 'Born to Shop'; when she put it on, it was like a battle honour.

'What are you looking for?'

'Mainly I'm taking things back. They look so dire when you

get them home. But I must have something for this damned Masonic ladies evening next week. They've got some Lord High Panjandrum as guest of honour and we're on the top table.'

'Why on earth does Oliver belong to them? It's not his scene.'

'Business. If you're not on the square, you're out of the circle. He only goes through the motions.'

'How is he? We waved to each other when he was driving to work the other morning.'

'Fine. Some incredibly rare drawings have turned up in one of his catalogues and we're going up to Christie's so he can bid for them. My part of the treat's tickets for *Buddy* in the evening.'

'Oliver at a rock and roll show?' Joyce shook her head in disbelief. 'He's not real, that man.'

Fay smiled. 'He's not perfect, just a lot more understanding than most of them.' She gulped down her coffee. 'Anyway, I'm off or I'll get caught in the traffic coming home. Thanks. Look after your lost lamb.'

Fay's presence always lingered. She had a life of satisfaction, rare freedom and a husband who loved her more than himself. She was happy – so trite a word for so envied a condition – and complete, with no emptinesses, no self-betrayals. Joyce had once known similar contentment, but found that the memories, which were supposed to bring a glow of warmth, only amplified the chill of now.

So . . . she paused as she put the mugs in the washing-up machine, was that why she'd invited Jowett back? Sympathy for someone also suffering pain an opportunity to raise her own self-worth? She could have waited until she was sure he had left the church and found time for the cleaning in the afternoon. He was not just attractive in the carnal sense Fay had meant, but gentle, sad, needing help. Except in a practical way, nobody she could think of seemed to need her help.

'Dumb bunny,' she murmured, as she closed the door of the machine. 'Let him call the Samaritans.'

Chapter Four

Lambert had walked among the boutiques, booksellers and antique dealers of the Lanes for more than an hour before deciding. Seeing the woman leaving the shop with the Pekinese, a sour-faced puppet waddling on the end of a white leather lead, had clinched it. Parody of a decaying Lady Bountiful – tottering heels, her ageing, fringed silk dress outrageous for daytime, face a parchment mask, rouged and powdered to challenge death – she was obviously from the quarter of Brighton where pensioned warriors, forgotten players and mottled, melancholy gentry lived, troubled over the grandchildren's inheritance as they sold off another piece of silver. The dealer would be understanding as he contemplated the dollar power of American and Asian collectors.

There was no sign of a security camera inside the shop, but the peak of the checked cap shadowed Lambert's face as the owner – badged blazer, regimental tie, disciplined moustache – examined the vase.

'We only moved to the area recently. Near Rottingdean. I passed your shop the other day and was admiring some of the stuff in the window. I must bring my wife in to see that tea set. She's very keen on Spode; her father's something of an authority. I assume it's complete.'

The patter had been refined with practice: the rising executive living in the right sort of village, wealthy in-laws, suggestions that he might prove to be a good customer in the future. It had never failed to smooth the opening moments.

'Yes, everything's there.' A powerful finger banded with a

gunmetal signet ring gently tapped the high relief figure of Aphrodite. 'It's a very beautiful piece. I'm surprised you want to sell.'

Lambert shrugged. 'Neither of us likes Wedgwood, but we can't choose our legacies. I'll have to risk my aunt's ghost haunting me for getting rid of it.'

The faintest smile acknowledged the possibility as the dealer lifted the vase to examine the base again. 'Would you excuse me for a moment, please? I just need to look something up.'

Lambert tensed as the dealer walked into the back, taking the vase with him; this hadn't happened before. The natural thing would be to wander idly round the shop, but if there was a closed circuit camera he wanted to make sure it got no clear shots of him. If the proprietor was checking a police list of stolen goods, could valuables from Tannerslade Farm still be appearing on it after so long? He began to rehearse responses, offended arguments; there must be some mistake, my uncle bought it more than thirty years ago in—

'Here we are.' The dealer reappeared, now also carrying an open catalogue. 'It's extremely rare, which is why I didn't recognize it. See.' He proffered the page with the coloured photograph. Then his eyes narrowed with judicious consideration. 'Yes . . . I think we'd be interested. Did you have a price in mind?'

Lambert gestured vaguely. 'I've always known it was valuable, of course, but . . . six thousand?'

Breath hissed faintly inwards through lips and teeth. 'I don't think we could go to six, sir . . . three perhaps. The market's somewhat depressed.'

Is it ever anything else? Lambert began to play his allotted role in the game of barter. 'I'm not sure. It's not as if we're desperate to get rid of it – incidentally, I'd prefer cash . . . if that's all right.'

The smile was now conspiratorial, a recognition that certain customers – respectable customers in Harris tweed jacket and cords – needed to be financially circumspect. 'That's not a difficulty, sir, although it would naturally have an effect on our offer . . . two thousand five hundred?'

'Seven fifty?'

The fractional pause as though calculating, then the nod. 'Very well . . . but if you're interested in the Spode, we could come to an arrangement.'

'Not at the moment.' That had to be firmly stamped on. 'That's a long-term thing. Perhaps for my wife's birthday. Two seven fifty? Well, I'm in your hands to a degree. Do you have the cash here?'

'Oh yes. Whatever notes are most convenient. I'll just need you to sign a standard receipt.'

'Of course . . . all right. Thank you . . . Twenties will be fine.'

Lambert rubbed sweat from his hands against the sides of his jacket as he waited. But he was nearly there.

'Here you are, sir.' The notes were counted out in front of him. 'And if you would be so good as to sign . . . Do you have identification?'

'Yes, I . . .' Reading the receipt, Lambert casually reached into his inside pocket. 'Oh. My wallet must be in my briefcase in the car and I had to park down at the Hove end. Will these do?'

Two window envelopes, one from American Express, the other from the Inland Revenue, now addressed to George K. Buchanan, Priest's Cottage, Telscombe, East Sussex, done on his word processor; the dates on the postmarks were slightly smudged. Primitive forgery, but easier than a driving licence and it had worked without any problems on previous occasions . . . the dealer, like the ones before him, was not particular.

'Thank you, Mr Buchanan . . . and the date, please. Excellent. Do bring your wife when you're next in Brighton. Good morning.'

After the first sale – four Doulton figurines to a shop in Towcester – Lambert had felt an urge to leave immediately, as though made visible by suspicion, but now it was becoming routine; thousands of antiques changed hands every day without awkward questions being asked. Confident of a fat profit, the dealer would be indifferent to the fact that he might have been lied to. When Lambert never returned, he'd draw conclusions, but by that time the vase would have been sold again. A foreign collector would be ideal, taking it out of England, where even now there was the danger of it triggering someone's memory.

He walked to the Old Ship and into the bar, smoothing down what was left of his hair with the flat of his hand as he removed the cap. Some genetic flaw had struck shortly after he left Cambridge, blond waves ebbing in a matter of months to leave a pattern like haphazard streams on a pink estuary. It made him look, and feel, ten years older, but he'd rejected the vanity of a hairpiece. He ordered a double Scotch and added the day's sale to the total filed in his electronic notebook. Just under fifteen thousand; more than twice as much again needed to reach his target, but he'd often had to sell for less than he would have liked ... What next from the lock-up on the North Circular Road? Ironically, the most valuable thing was the one he daren't dispose of. Turning up at Sotheby's with some story about stumbling across what he thought might be an unknown Constable landscape in a junk shop meant the risk of publicity and the wrong person recognizing it. Perhaps he'd have to take it with him, a souvenir. So ... the Chinese figures? The Toledo sword? Another piece of Georgian silver? The danger of exposure increased as he moved to the rarer items, but time was running out and he wanted to complete his escape tunnel as quickly as possible. Perhaps he should make the final preparations then raise as much as he could in no more than a few days, driving to different towns, accepting whatever he was offered. The passport was the problem; he wanted a British one, which would be accepted unquestioningly when carried by a self-confident white Englishman abroad, but he didn't know who to approach. Plenty of people managed it, though; perhaps the manager of the discreet bank that asked few questions about personal offshore accounts could help.

He went through to the restaurant and was shown to a table

overlooking the promenade. He gave the waitress casual eye signals simply for his own amusement as he handed back the menu, then gazed out of the window, pricked by renewed resentment. Tannerslade had represented the promise of a private income to be spent on indulgence, not necessity.

A man walked past the window outside, laughing and holding hands with a vibrant brunette, taut, honey-tanned skin, her navel exposed between tight, ragged-edged denim shorts, her breasts forced up and out by her halter top. From the surprisingly wide chasm that had opened up between his early and late twenties, Lambert crudely imagined ... Was he in dirty old man country already?

He scowled and crushed out his Hamlet as his meal arrived, remembering meeting Jowett again. He still had the stigma of a loser, but was obviously making it: good job, flat in the Barbican, four hundred pound Timothy Everest suit, sodding hair still intact ... and no petulant, whining child and a wife threatening to bleed him white. Jowett had given up his share of the money, but he'd been a weak sister, blubbering at the time, paranoid afterwards; now Lambert felt acid envy of his freedom.

His own upward curve from Cambridge had abruptly gone into free fall. Salary initially boosted by bonuses and only himself to spend it on, the first couple of years had meant skiing trips, whitewater rafting, weekends with a girl in Paris or some hotel that had caught their attention in a glossy brochure. Lotus-eating days made somehow more scented by the knowledge that he was a killer – not a psychopathic moron, but intelligent, empowered by a secret that only one other person in the world knew and no one else could possibly imagine.

Victoria had been another plump cherry, drop dead gorgeous, incredible in bed – and in the car, on the beach at La Londe, once in her parents' garden. Lambert had never suspected that she was a honey badger – the female of the species went straight for the balls – but he later became convinced she had lied about it being safe to make love that night. She'd become hysterical when he'd suggested an abortion, and later he recognized that a designer child was the latest toy for a spoilt bitch. Darling Daddy had indulged her again, providing the deposit for Gloucester Hill, the trendy north London address his little girl had always wanted, and making it obliquely clear that if Lambert was going to be difficult he had a great many friends in the City, influential people who did each other favours ... like stamping out promising careers. So Lambert had accepted. Marriage had been mentally pencilled in, if not for several years; and at least Victoria met the qualifications.

Then the trap had closed; Victoria obsessed with her brittle social life, neurotic over her looks – virtually manic at the appearance of a single grey hair – paraded Becky like an expensive, pampered doll and was resentful of any complaint about her spending. 'Don't be cheap, darling, if I wear the damned thing a third time everyone will snigger.' And sex – from somewhere out along the seafront, a sensual figure skipped provocatively back into his mind – had reached the stage where it was no longer given, but granted, ending with a 'Better now?' smirk of power. He'd suspected a lover, but a private detective had found no conclusive evidence; in any event, he sometimes thought that Victoria now regarded sex as another bodily function which she required fulfilling less frequently than her husband. A new dress from Dolce & Gabbano or Lacroix was a much bigger turn on. Not that he bought them for her – they came out of Daddy's allowance, while Lambert's salary paid the mortgage and the bills, soon to be bloated by Becky's private school. He resented having missed the frenzied City of the eighties that others told him about, juggling millions on the exchanges, gambling against currency movements, sneering at quarter million pound bonuses. He told himself he'd have been good at that. Now thirty-six thousand a year was poverty country, another weapon for his wife to lash him with.

The morning after the night he'd hit her in fury, she'd gone straight to her lawyer and divorce had been on the table for several months, but her terms were crippling. He could remain in the house, keeping strictly to his own part of it except for playing token attention to Becky, until the solicitors had agreed the money. Every time he tried to force her to retreat there'd been a phone call from her father, warning that he was quite prepared to make Lambert's position worse. So he had played for time, endlessly quibbling about payments as Tannerslade offered the secret escape route, spinning dreams of the day she'd return home and discover the note he constantly reworded in his imagination, three years of growing hatred spat out as he disappeared. There were still places in the world where you could vanish, and the police wouldn't be interested in trying to find another husband who'd done no more than walk out on his marriage. How the hell had he let a woman sink her claws so deeply into him . . . Abruptly, he beckoned the waitress.

'This tastes like shit.'

'Sir?'

'This steak. What is it? Dog meat?'

'I'm sorry, sir . . . If you'd care to order something else?'

'No, I'm not hungry any more. Forget it. Here.' He took a handful of coins from his pocket and dropped them on the table. 'Send your chef on a cookery course.'

He felt better as he walked out, eyes daring a hesitant young duty manager to stop him. Don't piss with me, little boy, I'm way out of your league. He crossed the road on to the seafront, gazing at the pier as he breathed in warm wind. He decided to return to town for a decent meal at the wine bar in the Minories; some of the crowd from the office would almost certainly be there . . . including Kate? Body from heaven and morals from hell. He seemed to be the only man she hadn't come on to – but perhaps she was buyable with a few drinks and the sort of chat-up lines he'd once been good at. He could afford to spend a couple of hundred on personal pleasure.

It was past eleven when he returned home, dejectedly drunk. Kate had been there, but letting some whizz kid from accounts paw her before they had left together, and the evening had become an all-male session of industry gossip, sport, crude jokes and stories of unlikely sexual conquests. Victoria's bedroom light was on, but downstairs was in darkness, and he had to fumble for the hall switch. The morning's post was on the table:

'Congratulations. Our computer has selected Mr Giles Lambert of 17 Gloucester Hill, NW3 to be entered for' ... 'Twenty pounds could save the life of this little girl in the Sudan' ... Postcard of tropical palm trees from Greg and Anna; amazing they'd found time to write it ... Double glazing again ... Credit card statement ... How the hell could one woman spend so much in a month? ... Another letter from Mother; usual moans about being lonely ...

'You've decided to come home then?' Victoria appeared at the top of the stairs, wiping astringent cream off her face. The nightly operation was part of her obsession that her breasts might have fallen a millimetre or her neck had begun to show fatal hints of shrivelling. At thirty-three, she had already started lying about her age. 'You didn't say you'd be late.'

'I got held up.'

'You look as though you need holding up now. Don't wake Rebecca when you go to bed.'

She walked down the landing and he heard her door close. Pain throbbed in his head as he climbed the stairs and went into the bathroom. Sighing with satisfaction he urinated noisily, then looked down. The couple he'd seen on the Brighton seafront came back. What were they doing now? Within ten seconds he'd imagined a great deal, the thought of someone else's enjoyment more vivid than any of his own past experiences. Fantasy sex was always better. He examined his face in the cupboard mirror above the lavatory; defeat stared back, and he hated it. His depressed and muddled brain told him to do something. Now.

Victoria glanced up from reading the *Tatler* as he walked into her room, then laughed sarcastically.

'Oh my God, it's the Hampstead flasher! Put it away before you frighten the horses.' She returned her attention to the magazine.

'I'm sleeping in here tonight.' He was pulling in his naked stomach.

'No, you're not.' She flicked over a page without looking at him again. 'Just piss off and sober up.' Her eyes flashed with

70

anger as he walked towards her. 'Giles! If you don't get the hell out of this room this instant . . .'

'What?' he demanded. 'You're not going to scream; you'll wake Becky.' He lifted the duvet and began to climb in beside her.

'How much have you been bloody drinking . . . Get off!' She tried to get out her side, but he grabbed hold of her hair. 'Ouch! Let go you pig!'

'Oink, oink.' He giggled as he forced her towards him, free hand fumbling as she stiffened with revulsion. He knew she wouldn't physically fight; forced sex was better than risking him damaging her precious looks.

'It's still rape when you're married, you know.'

'Then call the police.' He pushed her on to her back and pinned her down with his weight, trying to kiss her as she squirmed her head away. 'Lie still! You used to like it when I got rough.'

'You're sick!'

'Yeah,' he agreed. 'Sick of you. But this will make it better.'

She pulled a face of disgust as he entered her, then her body went limp as he began. 'Is it in?' she asked, staring at him with contempt. 'I can hardly feel it.'

'Fuck off,' he grunted.

She started to examine her nails. 'Teddy was much bigger than you. And Simon. And . . . well, just about everybody. Georgina had hysterics when I told her how many times I had to fake it with you. Eat your heart out, Meg Ryan . . . Oops! There was something. Not much, but definitely something. Get it over with before I fall asleep.'

'Shut up!'

'Oh, please, darling. Didn't we once say we'd be honest with each other, express our innermost feelings . . . not that I'm having any at the moment. Are you sure it's in the right place? I really can't . . . Oh. Is that it?' She smiled triumphantly as he rolled off her, panting. 'Sorry, I missed my lines.' She began a mocking monotone chant. 'Oh my God, oh my God. Fill me up. Give it to me. Oh, oh, oh. Yes, yes, yes. That was incredible.'

She pushed him savagely and he half fell off the bed. 'Now get out of here before I kick you in the balls! I mean it, Giles.'

A second shove toppled him on to the floor. As he went down he caught his ear against the bedside table, sending a swilling wave of nausea from his stomach to his throat. He suddenly felt very hot as he gurgled and gulped, then looked at her, his focus blurred with tears, before making a clumsy, furious lunge. He'd forgotten how hard she could slap, her long nails adding thin scratches before she leapt away and left him sprawled in sobbing humiliation.

'I hope you enjoyed it, sweetie,' she snapped. 'Because that pitiful fuck's going to cost. You won't believe how much.'

She walked out and he heard her cross the landing to Becky's room, locking it behind her; a spare bed had been put in there in case she was ever unwell.

He scrabbled for tissues in the box on the table, wiping eyes and nose before dabbing them against the scratches, then flopped back, exhausted. Six years ago, he'd murdered five human beings; now one woman could drive him to desperation. He cringed with self-disgust as he tried to comprehend the stupidity of what she had made him do. Had it been the uncontrollable urge of sexual frustration or just hatred of her because that was preferable to detesting himself? All he'd achieved was to give her more weapons to fight him with.

Chapter Five

Isolated and defenceless, Tannerslade Farm appeared ahead and to Jowett's right, exactly how he remembered seeing it the afternoon they had first driven past and taken the photographs. When it had been some sort of daring game, like students planning an outrageous Rag stunt. The fields bore the same crops, the slender poplars still protected the back of the house and the hawthorn sheltered one side of the track that led off the road. Having psyched himself up to walk the half-mile straight that led away from Finch, he knew he would not have the courage to go to the actual house that day. He had to approach it in hesitant stages, each one taking him closer. He forced himself to look at it for as long as he could, overcome with the conviction that someone unseen was watching him, accusing and vengeful, knowing that this was no stranger on a casual afternoon stroll. Five tense paces took him beyond the farm entrance – the gate was open, as it had been before, a trusting invitation to visitors – and he was unable to look back, as though he had nerved himself to cross a fragile bridge over fire.

A public footpath sign stood by a stile on the other side of the road and he paused to check his map, seeking another way back; the path led to the Pegman meadow and the western arm of the village crossroads. He walked through the channel alongside ripening wheat, stalks flattened near where a discarded contraceptive packet lay among poppies and wild garlic. It was humid and still, almost utterly quiet, then he half ducked and whirled in alarm as a black fighter jet leapt out of the empty shining sky above him, its engines roaring like clamouring thunder in deep caves, speed ripping through hovering calm leaving a tremor of savage assault. As he watched, the plane tilted its wings, rapid and arrogant. The bellow grew distant until it was no louder than the fierce drone of an insect, then quietness seeped back.

He had adopted a form of words that he repeated softly to himself as he walked on, four sentences into which he distilled his guilt. *I am sorry they are dead. If there is a heaven, may they be in it. I am ashamed I cannot confess. I wish for a way to forgive myself.* Sometimes he told himself it was meaningless, a robotic repetition, beads of a private rosary trickling through mental fingers, a negotiated agreement for salvation. But without it he could not accommodate the magnitude of what he had done. He sought comfort from the fact that he had been able to approach Tannerslade Farm again, persuading himself that next time it would be easier because somehow he had learnt something.

The wheatfield ended and he went through a gate into Pegman meadow, startling grazing rabbits that rippled into the shadowed protection of a hedgerow. The gate back on to the road was opposite him and he dropped into the bottom of the warmed bowl of captured sun, scented and bee-humming, for a few moments unable to see anything but the rising slope all around him, before starting to climb out. His mind had started to drift, the peace of the countryside betraying him into forgetting why he was there . . . Forcing himself back, he returned to his mantra. *I am sorry they are dead. If there is a heaven* . . . He reached the gate and fumbled with the sprung metal bar, then secured it again before stepping out on the road and turning back towards Finch. Tar softened by the heat, the surface felt adhesive and he stepped on to the verge, unkempt couch and cocksfoot grass brushing his legs. *I wish for* . . .

'Good afternoon!' For a second he was startled; there seemed to be no one visible on the deserted road. Then he saw her, kneeling on a padded cushion by the railings.

'Oh . . . Hello. I didn't notice you.'

'You were miles away. Talking to yourself. Sorting out dialogue for your book?'

'Yes.' He wondered if she could have heard anything.

'I thought so.' Joyce stood up, indicating the narrow strip of earth with a fork held in a canvas-gloved hand. 'I was clearing out some of the weeds. It's not actually our land, but *pro bono publico.*'

'I'm sorry?'

'For the public good . . . I thought you went to Cambridge.'

'I did. But I read English.'

'Well my Latin's only the dog variety.' She wiped the back of her wrist across her forehead. 'What a day . . . I was just going to have a cold drink. Would you like to join me? You look as if you need one.'

'No . . . thank you . . . I don't want to—'

'Don't be silly. It's no trouble. Please.' She picked up a wooden trug and the cushion and waited. She'd said please, and it would feel ill mannered to refuse. They walked through the gate and round the curve of the conservatory, all gleaming glass and basketwork settees, geraniums and some exotic crimson plants. The garden was much larger at the back, mazarine sun umbrellas shading white wrought-iron outdoor furniture beside an ornamental pond. He could just see a turquoise swimming pool beyond the trellis.

'Make yourself comfortable. I'll only be a minute.'

She went across the flagged patio and through the door into the kitchen as he sat in a curved harp-back cast-iron chair next to a beetroot bronze Japanese maple in a terracotta urn. He rationalized why he had accepted; he was tired and hot and the offer of a drink had persuaded him. And meeting her had reminded him that she had known the family, and he felt a need to talk about them. But he could think of no way to lead her to them without making her suspect his reasons. And would it help anyway? A fat chaffinch landed on the table, expectant that Jowett's presence meant food, its head tipped in enquiry, impatiently hopping. As she returned, carrying shining tall glasses on a stainless steel tray, it flew off.

'Lemonade with real lemons. I make it myself.' It was very pale green and the glasses were opaque with frost, as though she

75

kept them in the freezer the way Americans did. Balls of ice like Arctic pearls floated amid slivers of peel.

'Thank you.' He swallowed more than he had intended. 'Great.'

She must have washed her face while she was indoors because the sheen of perspiration had gone; without make-up she looked ... not older, but more mature, ripened. She was wearing canvas shorts, back pocket embroidered with gold and purple tulips, and a loose T-shirt announcing that she was a Friend of the Aldeburgh Festival. An irregular mesh of tiny scarlet veins formed two faint patches on the inside of her thigh; girlish ankles and feet seemed too delicate for such smooth, powerful legs.

'That is so much better.' A faint silver streak of moisture coated the fine down above her lip as she lowered the tumbler. 'Thank you for joining me.'

'It's OK.'

'The fact is, Mr Jowett, I haven't spoken to another human being since breakfast. Country living has its drawbacks.'

'Especially when you're from London.'

'I'm not ... Oh, yes. I told you we moved from there. That was after I married. I grew up in Wiltshire ... but in a rather bigger village.'

'Why are you on your own? I mean ...' He hesitated, unsure if, even how, he should enquire. It was a long time since he had felt at ease with people, and he had mislaid many social courtesies.

Fingers tipped with pale blue nails pushed back a stray lock of hair as though it irritated her or she was aware that it spoilt the curls and spirals of harvest gold.

'Usually my mother's here – she lives with us – but some friends have taken her out for the day. My husband spends the week in London – we have a flat near Camden Market. More a cupboard with pretensions really, but it's a base while he's at work. And the children are at school.'

'Boarding school?' Her lifestyle suggested it.

'Yes and no. Rupert's at Oakham, but Annabel's not a

boarder. She's a day pupil at Margaret Wood School in Bury St Edmunds. It's only half an hour away. She'll be back about five.'

'Do you pick her up?'

'Sometimes, but she's quite happy catching the bus.'

'How old is she?'

'Fifteen . . . Do you have family?'

'Just my sister. She lives in Normandy. Near Rennes.'

'How lovely. Do you go to see her?'

'Not often . . . We're not close.'

And no mention of parents, she reflected. What a lonely young man you are. While preparing the drinks, she had been wondering why she'd invited him in. Another solitary day was insufficient reason; she had adapted to them: gardening, writing letters, polishing silver, attending to church business, planning changes to the house, reading, having coffee at a friend's, chatting to her mother, a constant quiet busyness to avoid just existing in a void she called her life. Had his appearance fulfilled her ridiculous fantasy of the stranger who would appear unannounced, understanding and attentive, offering only uncomplicated happiness? Intellectually, she mocked romantic fiction, but could be tempted by its honeyed artifice . . .

'So how's the writing?'

'OK.' He gestured with his glass at lavender-blue blooms sprawling up the wall of the house. 'That's Lawsoniana, isn't it?'

'Yes.' Joyce felt a spasm of pleasure. 'Do you know about clematis?'

'A bit. Gardeners say they like company. You should plant climbing roses there as well.'

'Really?' She smiled. 'What variety?'

He shrugged. 'I don't know. I'm not an expert.'

But you know something about gardens; perhaps you grew up with one. Did you make it into a hiding place like I do?

'I'll check in my books and choose one for next year. Thank you.' And what will I remember when I look at them? One lonely summer afternoon when I dragged in a passing stranger so that I had someone to talk to?

'This is a lovely house.'

'Would you like to see inside?'

'I didn't mean that. I—'

Frankly, my dear, I'm not sure if you ever know what you mean. 'Bring your drink.' My home may look like gingerbread, but I'm not going to eat you.

It was, as always, flawless: every cushion plumped, nothing out of place, no traces of dust; the sterile show home of a woman with little to attend to but her luxurious cell. He admired proportions, ornaments and furnishings, paintings, decorated plaster ceilings, the sweep of the staircase, the aquamarine sunken bath.

'That's out of bounds.' She indicated a closed door on the landing. 'My daughter's going through the grunge stage. Whenever I look in it I think about calling the bomb squad . . . This is the main bedroom.'

Regency drapes with a deep mauve fringe edged tall windows, blending with wallpaper of pink wild roses on cream, pale violet carpet, mahogany wardrobe, dressing table and standing mirror, circular table with a glass top and a hammered copper bowl containing silk peonies. The empty, impeccable bed with its equivocal atmosphere, created when a woman showed a man the intimate space she shared with her husband. A room that had no purpose in the day.

'And that's it – except for my mother's apartment which we treat as her private territory – and no gift shop on the way out. Would you like another?' She nodded at his empty glass.

'I ought to be getting back.'

'There's plenty.' There was sharp disappointment in the thought of him leaving. 'Unless it's going to ruin the muse, of course. I wouldn't want to be a person from Porlock. You know, the visitor, who interrupted Coleridge, so that he never managed to finish "Kubla Khan".'

He hesitated, as if unable to insist. 'All right.'

Again, he let her precede him down the stairs and into the kitchen where she took a pottery jug from the double fridge and refilled his held-out glass. She realized he was staring at where her breasts pushed out the T-shirt's legend. As she finished pouring his eyes didn't move for a moment, then he raised his face to hers again. This was not just the hackneyed, crude male mind imagining hidden flesh; the look was softened by what she felt was some form of longing.

'I'll get you some more ice.'

'Thank you.'

She kept a bowl of ice-cubes in the freezer and occupied herself with scooping out a handful, then dropping them in the lemonade. 'Let's go back into the garden.'

Murmuring stillness of heat and quiet now infused the afternoon, birds and insects drowsy, growing things suspended in simmering air, shadows fixed, time slow, all movement lazy. There was a sense that it would be wrong to break it with speech. Joyce felt a sudden contentment, and faint tremors of an unexpected and ludicrous anticipation. Jowett didn't look at her, but gazed down towards the dark columns of trees at the far end of the garden, surely seeing other things.

'It's a bath for the soul, isn't it?'

Her voice pulled him back from wherever he had gone. 'What is?'

'A day like this.'

'Yes . . . That's a nice phrase.'

'Use it if you want . . . in your book.'

'I don't know if it's . . . it might not work.' Her speaking seemed to have opened a channel he wanted to explore. 'May I ask you something?'

'What about?'

'Your friends . . . in the church . . . The ones who were killed.'

'Ben and Annie?' She frowned at a blight brought into the afternoon. 'What about them?'

'What were they like?'

'They were . . . Why are you interested?'

'I don't know . . . I just wondered.'

Death, she thought. You are close to it, aren't you? And it's hurting because you've not been hardened.

'As I told you, they were just lovely people. There was nothing special about them, but you couldn't not like them.'

'But they were killed. The children as well.'

She saw the dismay in his eyes and leant forward, laying her hand on his knee. 'Yes. But if you think about it, things like that – even worse things – happen all over the world, all the time. The pain comes when it's someone you know, but . . . God, I'm about to sound dreadfully old. Somebody's death hurts much more when you're young.'

'But they were murdered.'

'Yes, and of course that makes it worse. But . . . I don't know how other people came to terms with it . . . but I decided it mustn't destroy my belief that most people are good. Not perfect, but not wicked. If I lost that, then whoever killed them would have done even more damage.'

'But you must hate whoever did it.'

'I try not to think about them, but . . . hatred can turn in on you.' She smiled slightly as she removed her hand. 'Now I'm sounding philosophical. I don't know what I think about them. They mustn't be allowed to matter. And however much I hated them wouldn't bring anyone back. So you have to let it go . . .'

He nodded, but as if to himself, rotating the glass in his hands, abstractedly watching melting ice swirl and tinkle against the sides. Joyce felt she may have been one of the first people to whom he had tried to speak about what she was increasingly certain was a private grief; his approach had been oblique – five deaths with which he had no emotional connection – but it might give him a perspective on the one that was his own. She waited, then knew he was not ready to continue.

'Anyway, that was a long time ago and this is too lovely a day to think about it,' she said.

Abruptly, Jowett stood up. 'I think I should go now. Thank you for the drink.' His glass was still half full.

'Oh, that was sudden.' She was dismayed. Their meeting should not have ended on so serious a note – and perhaps she didn't want it to end at all, leaving melancholy and regret

80

behind. 'If you want, we could have something to eat. It won't take a minute.'

'No. Thank you.'

She felt an irresistible impulse to tease, to take away the sting of disappointment. 'Oh, Mr Jowett. Are you running away from me?'

'Why should I do that?'

Are you really so innocent or just polite? 'I don't know . . . All right. I'm being selfish. I needed someone to talk to, but you've got work to do.' They walked past the conservatory again, across the front lawn and to the gate; he kept the distance between them greater than it need have been. 'If you go through the first gate you come to, then follow the footpath round the field it brings you out by the old chapel. It's quicker.'

'Right. Thanks again.'

She watched him walk away, never looking back. He held himself very erect, as though disciplined, even guarded, but with none of the confidence of a young and successful man – she had silently admired the red MGF and noted the sumptuous quality of the luggage.

'And why do I suddenly want you so much, Mr Jowett?' The question was a private whisper. 'You can't have got through my layers that quickly.'

Had it been nothing more than an extra glass of wine taken with a solitary lunch, sun-fermented inside her into a caprice, a daydream of delicious passion? He was good-looking, well-mannered, intelligent, made interesting by his uncertainty; she was sure he would be kind . . . Alone and unhappy . . . but why was she wondering what it would be like to be touched by those slender hands? She shook herself. There was that birthday card to send to Ralph's sister, the seam of Annabel's tennis shorts to repair; the proper concerns of a tamed, captured wife and dutiful mother. She must mind her house and not be ridiculous.

Jowett found that he was weeping. She had been so welcoming, an attractive, interested woman whom he should have been able to talk to easily, joke or even flirt with. Then, when they met again, connections would have been made, the distance of strangers reduced, the country of friendship entered. Such idle conversation was something he had lost, another bitter reminder of how unscarred people lived. But her natural and polite interest would be turned to revulsion by the truth . . .

I am sorry they are dead. If there is a heaven, may they be in it. I am ashamed I cannot confess. I wish . . .

I wish I had not been part of the killing of people you loved.

Chapter Six

Jowett read the febrile, fragmented diary written at the end of each painful day, convincing himself that simply having remained in Finch for a week without breaking down, hurling everything into the car and racing back to his hole in London, was a milestone on a terrible road. There had been nothing important, no sudden moment of revelation, nothing that had brought comfort, but he was still precariously there, however frightened and alone.

Sunday: Woken by the church bells, but I couldn't go knowing that other people would be there. I'll do it tomorrow. Drove to Bury St Edmunds, bought food and ordnance survey map. Went into museum, but had to leave when I saw death mask of William Corder, who murdered Maria Marten in the Red Barn not far from here. Took long way back (shouldn't have done). Wrote about Giles, how we met, what I thought of him. Crap film on TV in evening. Day not as bad as I expected.

Monday: Went into the church and was praying (or trying to) when Mrs Hetherington arrived to do some cleaning. She's the type who'd belong to the church. Made myself ask her about the memorial plaque by the door, pretending I thought someone had been arrested. Cracked up when she said she knew them. Asked me back to her place for coffee. She was sympathetic – I've not had that before – but backed off when I lost it again. But she listens, and that's good.

Would it help to talk to her? How? I'll have to think about that. Stayed round the cottage afterwards, read in the garden, then tried more writing, but only about myself. I'm putting off the bad stuff.

Tuesday: Day from hell. Spent hours just walking round the house, couldn't write, felt like shit. Wanted to jack it in, get back to London, but forced myself to wait another half-hour, then an hour, like when I tried to give up smoking. Watched kid's TV; they're still showing things I saw years ago. Finished the gin and went to bed early. Futile session of Onanism, first for several weeks. (Written this Wednesday morning.)

Wednesday: Better. Went into the village and had a ploughman's at the pub. Good beer and nobody tried to talk to me, but there were some looks. They don't get many strangers. Wrote more about Giles in the afternoon. Amazing what came back, like him having a thing about Bette Midler films, and the way he could imitate people's voices. I'm putting too much off. The farm's marked on the map; I've got to make myself go tomorrow.

Thursday: The farm looked exactly the same as I remembered. Felt sick as I walked past. Who lives there now? There was something about a son inheriting. Did he really move in after what we did? I've got to go there – right up to the house – but could I hack it if I met him? Would it do any good? Is anything doing any good? It's like being in a sodding horror movie. Couldn't walk back past the farm, so went across the fields and met Mrs Hetherington again. Invited me into the garden for a drink and showed me round the house. Why? I think she must be lonely, but she ought to have enough friends. Began to fancy her at one point and felt somehow guilty. She told me more about *them*, but I mustn't make her suspicious by asking too much. Nearly a week, but have I got anywhere?

Friday: Good writing day, managed to give all the details. Felt totally gutted when I'd finished, but at least I've faced it head on. Something's got to come out. Beginning to feel the need to talk about it to someone, but I've felt that for years. Who, for Christ's sake? A priest? The Samaritans? God doesn't give any feedback.

Anyway, I'm still here, and that's something. Wondering about returning to the farm tomorrow after it's dark, and getting nearer the house. I don't know what it will achieve, but the idea keeps coming back. I'll sleep on it (I'm sleeping better) and think again in the morning. Nearly finished part one of *War and Peace*, seriously weird way to do it at last.

'Oh Ralph!' Grace Carstairs sniffed the pink dianthus clouded in sprays of gypsophila. 'How do you always manage to remember what my favourite flowers are? Thank you. You're much too kind to your old mother-in-law.'

'And why wouldn't I be, Grace? Come on, let's find a vase for them.'

Joyce made a mock sound of throwing up as she watched them walk into the hall. Hand resting on Ralph's arm, her mother was swallowing another dose of sycophancy not realizing the poison it contained. It was grotesque the way she played the simpering coquette when he turned on the charm, flattering her with attentiveness that she lapped up as he carefully polished the image of the ideal son-in-law – and therefore perfect husband. Joyce had to admit he was clever; flowers one week, an hour chatting in her room the next. Now a morning run to Ipswich to shop, now dropping her off for lunch at Lillian's on his way to golf and stopping for a cup of tea on the way back. Meticulous about birthdays and the anniversary of Daddy's death (his secretary must remind him), and spending the last few minutes on Sunday evening saying goodbye to her before returning to town – and was there anything he could get for her in London? Joyce wanted to scream at the sickening hypocrisy; within a couple of hours of kissing her mother's cheek and telling her to take care, he'd be groping Gabriella as she . . . Joyce physically shook herself to dispel images that bit deep with jealousy and humiliation.

'What a lovely man Ralph is . . . He reminds me so much of Daddy, so thoughtful . . . Lillian's absolutely besotted with him. She never sees either of her sons–in–law from one year's end to the next, poor dear . . . Thank you for marrying him, darling; he's an absolute poppet.'

No he's not, Mummy. He's a bastard and you're too stupid – no, not stupid; too innocent, bewitched by the act, to see it. He's using you. You'd never believe me if I said I wanted to leave your adored Ralph because he's an unfaithful, cruel, manipulative sod. You'd suggest I went to see the doctor, then tell Lillian it must be the menopause – and she'd be on your side. Apart from Fay, nobody knows, and her sympathy doesn't help because I envy her. Do you know what he said to me the night I cracked and told him to get out of this bloody house? He asked me if your heart would be able to stand it, because he'd make damned sure you believed the lies he'd tell you. And he smiled when he said it. That's your poppet, Mummy, that's the man you tell all your friends I'm so lucky to have married. He's keeping you contented because he needs you to stay alive. How old are you now? Seventy-four. And Granny Kitty's quavering heart managed to keep beating for nearly ninety years – so how long have I got left of my sentence? Or do I just go out of my mind first?

She heard Ralph whistling as he came downstairs; a few pounds on flowers and ten minutes putting them in a vase before settling Grace in her chair with a book gave a very good return. She'd stay in her apartment for the rest of the day while he went for an afternoon's networking at Newmarket, coming home when it suited him. He'd lie in on Sunday morning – Grace would say he needed it; her own dear Ronald had always complained that London was exhausting – have lunch, make a few calls from his study, pack the shirts Joyce would have washed and ironed and head back for Camden. When the children were small, she'd arranged family outings, daring him to betray her promises that Daddy would be with them, but after Rupert had left home and as Annabel became more independent that weapon had gone. She'd given up insisting on being taken out to dinner on Saturday nights because they had always deteriorated into resentful, hollow silences, chilled by indifference on his side and loathing on hers. What sort of people don't talk to each other when they are out together in public? Those who are badly married. How Joyce spent her week was irrelevant to him, and he was certain she would never hit back by taking a lover. Mummy would be horrified if he found out and told her – which he would – protesting how good a husband he had been, unable to comprehend how she could be so cruel to them both. Joyce often wondered if there were other women caught in the same trap. Parents lived so much longer now, the wives usually longer than the husbands; was Ralph the only man who'd had the calculating duplicity to see how offering his mother-in-law a dowager apartment would cost him vitually nothing and enable him to put a hammerlock on his wife? Short of killing him – a regular fantasy, frequently with maliciously added pain – Joyce despaired of an escape, yet despised herself for what was being done to her. She even had to continue the pantomime of sharing the same bed with him because Mummy would be appalled at any other arrangement; for her obedient generation of women, a wife not sleeping with her husband was unnatural, and how could her daughter possibly not want to spend the night warm beside so kind and generous a man? In fact, Ralph slept in the adjacent dressing room, functional and soulless as a motel room, while Joyce lay alone in the king-size bed they had chosen together at Harrods, joyously coupled on immediately after it had been delivered and on which Rupert and Annabel had been conceived.

'Are you having lunch?' she asked coldly.

He glanced at his Rolex. 'If it's not too long.'

'It's cold. Ten minutes.'

'Fine. Thanks. Want a hand?'

She looked surprised. 'What's come over you, or are you just trying to save time?'

'Just yes or no.'

'All right. You can lay the table. Thank you.'

It struck her that she was unable to remember when they had last had a real conversation, an exchange of thoughts. On opposite sides of the abyss at the bottom of which lay their marriage, dead dreams and decayed ruins of what had once been love, communication now involved no more than basics: these bills have arrived; I need my evening suit cleaned; don't forget we have to attend Rupert's Parents' Day; Fay's invited us to dinner on . . . Can you make it?; Annabel needs new skis for that school trip; I'll be out of town Tuesday and Wednesday . . . This is the number if you need it; I'm getting Meredith's in to clean the pool; oh, here's a hundred quid for your birthday. Buy yourself something, I've no time to shop in town.

He'd laid out knives, forks and two glasses of water; no condiments, napkins, place mats or the fruit bowl. Immersed in the *Daily Telegraph* sports pages, he appeared irritated as Joyce pointedly disturbed him while she completed the table, but neither of them spoke. She sat down and they began to eat, the only sound that of cutlery against porcelain, cold and metallic.

'What's the new chap at Windhover like?'

Puncturing the silence, the question startled her; as long as the books showed the right sort of income, Ralph never asked about how she ran the cottage.

'Fine. Why?'

'Just wondered. He's staying for several weeks, isn't he? What does he do all day?'

'How should I know?' There was an unexpected feeling of protectiveness, of not wanting Ralph to be any part of it. 'He's paid the full balance if that's what you're worried about.'

'There's no need to get tetchy.'

'I don't get "tetchy" about things any more, Ralph. I'm just not used to you taking any interest. Read your bloody paper.'

'What the hell's the matter with you? I wasn't looking for a fight. I was only—'

'Shut up!' Joyce pushed her plate away fiercely and stood up. Lunching together had long been a farce, but she was suddenly sick of it. 'What's the matter with me? How long have you got? Try everything!'

Seeing him shrug and return to the paper, stabbed more acutely than it had done for months. Whenever she turned on him, he withdrew, beyond attack because he controlled the ultimate deterrent. He didn't look up as she sighed with weary frustration and walked out, tears fretting her eyes.

For once the garden offered her no comfort; its perfection for what? It was only a place where unhappiness could be temporarily masked by colour and scent. She tore off a rose, the pain of tearing thorns unfelt, and began to pull it apart. He loves me not . . . he loves me not . . . he loves me not . . . Christ, get real! You've put up with it this long, you've hammered something out, it can't last for ever . . . just *die*, Mummy! Let me get my hands on his throat and . . . She sobbed violently. I'm sorry. I didn't mean that . . . Yes I did . . . God in heaven! I'm forty-four years old and hate myself for allowing him to make me so unhappy. Will I be old before I have the courage not to give a damn about how I behave and what people will think? Don't kid yourself. By that time you'll have let yourself be defeated so often, you won't have any strength left to fight with. You're pitiful.

From the front of the house she heard Ralph's Mercedes start up and crunch over the gravel; she was usually granted at least a goodbye, however casual. The afternoon and evening seemed to stretch for ever towards the night.

She sat by the pond, picking up tiny stones by her feet and tossing them into the still water, concentrating on the ripples shimmering across the surface, mind emptied because thoughts were too painful . . . He had been here with her the other day and she had felt – not happy, but at ease, in control . . . flirtatious? Inelegantly she sniffed and used the back of her wrist to dab her nose. But he was attractive – and alone – gentle and somehow wounded as well. They shared experience of pain. She leant back in the chair, her mind drifting, her eyes closed against the pulsating sun as it warmed her body. What would it be like to be stroked by those beautiful hands, kissed by those slender lips that she had seen tremble with what she felt must be heartache? Fantasy wove pictures; not just sex, but affection, shared time, comfort ... She moved her images to Cromlix House, the sumptuous country-house hotel in Scotland where she had once stayed. The Lower Turret Suite with its immense canopied bed and long Edwardian dressing mirror that could be positioned so they could watch themselves as ... Walking hand in hand through the estate, amused by rabbits in the twilight ... Talking to other guests over coffee and liqueurs in the plump armchairs of the drawing room after dinner ... Tea brought to them on a silver tray in the morning ... Climbing in the Trossachs above Loch Katrine ...

'Oh, don't be so bloody stupid.' Alarmed, a bluetit fluttered away as she spoke aloud to herself. She sat upright, gazed blankly down the garden, then stood up and went back into the house. He had his own life and was just passing through hers, renting the cottage to write his book. Anything else was la-la land, even though it was ... No. Stop it. Some women might set out to seduce him for their pleasure and amusement – younger ones, certainly – but these were pathetic erotic daydreams that belittled her even further. She turned on the radio and got on with the ironing.

Ralph returned shortly before ten, in time to go up to tell Grace that he had put money on a horse for her and it had won. Thirty pounds to buy herself a treat. Sleep well, I'll see you tomorrow before I leave. Joyce heard him whistling softly as he came downstairs; she was sketching, half curled up on the drawing-room sofa. She turned over the page of the pad as he walked in.

'Jerry and Suzanne were asking after you.' His voice had a sibilant alcoholic lisp. 'She's going to call you. Invite you to lunch.' Only short sentences were within his mental grasp.

'I can hardly wait,' she murmured. Before she'd met Suzanne, Ralph had said she would like her; Joyce had found her an egotistical airhead with a husband who could bore for the universe. Ralph hadn't caught her response as he headed for the drinks cabinet and a nightcap gin.

'What're you drawing?'

'Nothing. Only passing the time.' She closed the sketchpad. 'Anyway, I was just about to go to bed. I assume you're staying up to watch the match.'

'Did you record it?'

'No, but if you remember you put the video on timer . . . It was a draw, by the way. One-all. It was on the news.'

'Shit. You've spoilt it.' He sounded like a peeved child.

'My heart bleeds. Goodnight.' The tiny victory of inflicting irritation made her feel better.

In bed, propped against pillows, she opened the pad again, frustrated at what eluded her. The hair was good, and the jawline, but the eyes weren't quite . . . She erased with a soft rubber, concentrating as she lined and shaded again. She rarely attempted portraits; faces held qualities that called for skills not needed for sketching flowers or old buildings. How did you draw gentleness and that sense of timidity? She held the paper at arm's length, stared at it for a moment, then spontaneously kissed it before letting her head flop back.

'And you walked into my life exactly one week ago,' she murmured. 'Christ, how desperate has that bastard made me?'

She leant over the edge of the bed and slipped the pad beneath it, switched off the lamp and lay down. Sleep finally smothered imagination until she was disturbed by Ralph coughing as he passed through; the dressing-room light came on, then vanished as he closed the door. Defensively hardened against rejection, she was bewildered over why she should suddenly begin to weep.

Menace of cloud-gloomed countryside enveloped Jowett; black shadows within grey, ghost-insect lash of branches across his face, crackle of undergrowth beneath his nervous feet. There were no street lights along the road from Finch to Tannerslade Farm and once he had climbed the fence by the gate to creep along the hawthorn hedge on the other side of the track leading to the house, darkness had drawn him to its centre; he was scared of using his torch, revealing his presence. At one point he froze at the thought of mantraps, vicious half-circles of toothed-steel jaws that snapped together to bite immovably into calf and shin. Surely they were illegal now . . . but if your family had been slaughtered by intruders you would not be bothered about that as you protected yourself. He crouched down and scrabbled until he found a long stick and probed the grass in front of him, night blind and terrified of unseeable dangers, then gasped in pain and panic as he slipped into a dry, shallow ditch, panting as he stumbled.

Looking back at the road, he realized he must be almost opposite the farmhouse and he stepped across the ditch, forcing foliage aside to peer through the hawthorn. Curtains glowed at the window and his eyes, now adapted to night, could make out details. The barn where the old man had been shot was still there, and in his mind he saw again the frantic little girl running to be brutally tossed aside by death; then the woman, just standing at the door until she crumpled and fell. He felt an unexpected sense of detachment, like a warlord surveying a town he had blitzed into silent ruins, broken bodies no longer real people. This was the killing ground, where he had been too helpless with terror to stop Giles' madness and was therefore a part of it.

It was impossible to analyse if returning had helped; could unpunished men who had been guards at Auschwitz or Treblinka achieve anything by seeing again the huts and gas chambers? But that was Cambridge intellectualism, the cloistered mind contemplating the mysteries of human evil. Within yards of where he skulked against the hedge, a man, two women and two children had been slaughtered; that was the hideous reality.

He let the branches close and sat trembling for a few moments before creeping away. He'd been back, but had found nothing there.

Chapter Seven

Head bowed, Joyce found her attention focused on the tapestry
kneeler as the congregation prayed for all those in need. It was
one she had made herself; the angular, stylized figure of a
winged man, a traditional representation of St Matthew. That's
what going to church had come to mean to her: not faith or
fear, but a place where her talents had some use and she had
social value, a balm against loneliness. So sin – or at least what
were becoming constant thoughts of sin – didn't enter into it
any more. The death of God had been widely reported in the
sixties; now everybody was allowed to find Him – or Her – for
themselves. So she could negotiate personal terms. It could not
be wicked to love, or indeed to make love, and if nobody got
hurt it couldn't be classified as sin. It was remarkable how easy a
lifetime of conditioned obedience could now be equivocated
away.

'Give us this day our daily bread . . .' No longer able to kneel
in comfort, Grace sat beside her, head lowered, deliberately
raising her voice when she could not hear Joyce taking part.

'. . . and forgive us our trespasses . . .' she picked up instinctively. And I have certainly been trespassed against. For the rest
of the service, she forced her mind to behave.

'Joyce, I've finally finished that damned bodice. You wouldn't
believe the trouble I had with it! When can you come for a
final fitting?' Pouncing hen-like through the crowd outside the
porch, Sarah Merriman scrabbled in her bag for her diary. 'Oh,
hell. Next three days absolutely hopeless. Thursday evening?

No, scrub that. I've got that wretched woman who wants a dress for her daughter's wedding ... Friday. Morning. Not before eleven, though. If you can't make it then, I've got to go out straight after lunch, so it would have to be the weekend – next thing you know, it'll be the pageant. We'll never get everything done in time.'

'I can make Friday morning,' Joyce assured her. Every year, the Pegman Pageant was a major crisis in Sarah Merriman's life; every year she swore she would never do it again; every year she did.

'Marvellous.' She looked round agitatedly as she scribbled. 'Have you seen Jeremy? He promised to let me know about those loudspeakers he's borrowing from some sports club. It'll be a total farce without them ... Carol! Don't rush off! We need two more knight's costumes, and ...' She plunged through a group of people, panic fluttering about her.

'What a very nice sermon.' Grace sounded contented.

'Yes.' Joyce took her arm. 'A new variation on number seven.'

'Don't be such a cynic. Jeffrey's a marvellous vicar.' They began to walk down the sloping path to the gate. 'I liked the way he related it to how children learn in school. You can understand that. The problem with some of the parables is that—'

Joyce had stopped listening; he had just walked past them.

'Mr Jowett!' He turned, as if startled that someone should recognize him. 'I didn't see you in church.'

'I was at the back ... I'm sorry, I didn't see you.'

'That's all right. This is my mother, incidentally ... Mr Jowett. He's staying at Windhover.'

'Good morning.' Grace offered her hand. 'I hope you're enjoying your holiday.'

'Yes. Thank you.'

'Do you know this part of Suffolk?'

'No. I've never been here before ... It's very attractive.'

'And what have you discovered so far?'

'Not much ... I've not been out very often.'

'But there are wonderful places to visit.' Grace sounded disappointed, as though her adopted county was being slighted. 'Melford Hall is absolutely marvellous. It isn't far.'

'I know . . . I read about it in one of the books at the cottage. Didn't Elizabeth I stay there?'

'I think she did. Are you interested in history?'

'Parts of it, especially the Tudors. I'll try to get over there. Thank you.'

'Mr Jowett isn't just here for a holiday.' Joyce liked the way he was talking to her mother. 'He's writing a book.'

'Are you? Now I'll be able to tell people I've met a famous author.'

'It's his first book, Mummy.'

'Well you must stick to it. My husband and I used to know . . . what was his name? It doesn't matter. But he wrote a book which became enormously successful. I think they even made a film of it. I hope they do with yours.'

He shook his head. 'I don't expect they will.'

'Well, I'm sure it would be better than some of the dreadful things they keep putting on television nowadays. Nobody seems to make *nice* films any more.'

'No . . . I must get back. I've left something in the oven.'

'Oh.' Joyce felt a twinge of regret. 'I was about to ask if you'd like to come back for a drink. Sundays can be miserable when you're on your own.' And I know what that's like, even when there are people in the house.

'It's all right . . . I'm used to it.'

Nobody gets used to it, they just find ways to endure it.

'Will you be here again next Sunday?' she asked.

'I don't know. I don't often . . . perhaps.' He smiled thinly at them both and walked away.

Grace invested Jowett with the standards of her generation. 'What a very courteous young man. Well brought up.'

'He went to Cambridge . . . I met him the other day and he mentioned it.' Joyce was looking to where the drop of the road was taking him below the churchyard wall and out of sight. You can't have known what I was thinking ten pews in front of you. How religious are you? This is the second time you've been in the church. Or are you just seeking comfort because you're unhappy? God, I want so much to— 'What?'

'I was just saying that so few young people nowadays seem to have good manners when you talk to them. They mumble.'

'He's not that young, Mummy. He must be nearly thirty.'

'That's quite young.'

Joyce took her arm again. 'Come on, or you won't have time for your sherry.'

Jowett was terrified someone else might speak to him before he reached the sanctuary of the cottage. Everything had been hypocrisy: accepting a hymn book, nervously reacting to smiles of welcome, pretending to pray, unable to make the responses because it was years since he'd been a regular churchgoer. He'd slipped past the vicar in the porch after the service, not wanting to talk . . . then he'd had to force himself to speak to Joyce Hetherington and her mother. None of them knew it had been a purgatory, an attempt to be with ordinary people, to act like them, because . . . because if he could manage that in that church of all places then it would be easier elsewhere. But if they'd known the truth, they would have turned on him, a loathed figure far beyond their capacity to forgive.

Isolation, his companion for years, seemed greater here. He was an unsuspected leper among the healthy . . . No, stop the bloody metaphors. You're a murderer, lying because you've never had the courage to confess. These are the sort of people whose lives you once mocked for their banality, their lack of sophistication. But they're decent, bringing up families, helping each other, doing no harm – and now you want to be like them, mortgaged to a limited life, boring but guiltless. The simplest ambition of all, and you can't achieve it.

One week . . . and what? Useless prayers, crawling back to the farm in the night, dragging the truth out of yourself on the laptop as if it might do any good . . . You could buy another razor. Great. It'll make all the difference if you do it here, won't it? Are you going to leave a note for Mrs Hetherington to find?

I'm sorry about this, but there were so many things I wasn't able to explain. This is nobody's fault but mine. Thank you for your kindness, I enjoyed talking to you. Please don't let this worry you. Randall Jowett.

His stomach tightened. You can't even imagine confessing to someone after you're dead. Their hatred won't matter then . . . but the only reason they don't hate you now is because they don't know. They're friendly when they meet you, barely thinking about you afterwards. That's what real loneliness means; not just being on your own, but having no existence in anyone else's life. Apart from Ruth, irritated at having to fly over from France for a brother she had hardly anything to do with, and some token representative from the office, who'd be at your funeral? No one. You don't matter . . . except to Giles, who'd be able to relax completely if he heard you were no longer a threat to him. But you're not even that because you've never found the guts to tell the truth.

He was starting to weep again as he closed the cottage door behind him. Who are you crying for? Not them, not even for the children. It's for yourself and the fact that you're an outcast . . . It was good talking to her in the garden, though. Almost like being with a friend for a while – and you don't have any of those. But why did you have to stare at her tits like that? Can't you look at a woman without seeing a body? She's a person, she was interested, you had things in common . . . That's normality. Sod it. Have some lunch and take a walk, do more writing, read some poetry, see if there's anything to blank it out for a couple of hours on television. Get through another day.

'When's the pageant?' Ralph sounded uninterested, checking his diary as he prepared to return to London.

'Not for another two weeks. Why? Surely you're not planning to come?'

'Can't make the parade. Got a foursome arranged. I'll come to the pig roast in the evening, though.'

'Don't put yourself out . . . Stand still.' Joyce scratched her thumbnail across a dried mark on the shoulder of his jacket, wondering why she was still bothered about his appearance. But then both of them occasionally lapsed into long-abandoned habits. She brushed off loosened flakes with her hand. 'There. Won't you be bored? Finch is just an address, not where you live.'

'I keep in touch with people.'

'Like you keep in touch with me?'

'Don't start.' The rebuttal was casual; skirmishes didn't call for heavy artillery. 'I'll just go and say goodbye to Grace.'

The magnetic letters on the fridge door, left over from Rupert and Annabel's childhood, spelt out 'chris conway is kool'. Who was he? No one in the village, so presumably some boy Annabel had met at a disco. Time to think about putting her on the pill, or had that stable door already been opened? Joyce suddenly felt tired of raising children, tired of coping with their increasing resentment, their impatience for escape, while still expecting everything to be done for them – and in this case with a father who agreed to whatever they wanted because that avoided arguments and responsibility. And if they got into trouble – Rupert on crack, Annabel pregnant – it wouldn't be his fault. I was earning the money; it was your job to look after them.

Staring at the fridge Joyce frowned as she heard Ralph come downstairs, shout goodbye and slam the front door. The moment lacked drama. Wasn't there meant to be some burst of revelation, a joyous shout of defiance as she finally rebelled? Standing alone in the kitchen, she suddenly knew she wanted to have an affair and was prepared to do something that could make it happen. She felt the need for a very large drink.

Lambert read to his daughter without affection, irritated by her demands for a bedtime story.

'No,' she corrected, when he missed out a paragraph, 'they go to the market first.'

'If you know the story, why do you want me to read it?' Unable to fight his wife, Rebecca was a soft target. 'It's time for bed.' The child didn't cry, but screamed, denied an indulgence. 'Shut up!'

She slid off his knee and kicked him before running out of the room, shouting for her mother. Lambert swore and went to pour himself another Scotch. The Sunday evening house was like a punishment cell, Victoria casually selecting which spot to torture next. He heard Brigitte, the Australian *au pair* chosen by his wife for being overweight and having a face like a brick, comfort the child and take her up to bed.

'That's done your future visiting rights a whole lot of good.' Victoria sneered as she walked into the room. 'Big man, aren't you? Can't fight me, so you take it out on a three-year-old.'

There was no point in arguing; even when he had a case, she destroyed him. He caught a whiff of something exclusive and expensive as she stalked past and sat in the black leather button-back chair by the fireplace. She crossed her legs, high-heeled shoe dangling from the toes of her right foot.

'Anyway, has what's left of your brain managed to grasp what I said?'

'I need another few weeks to find somewhere. Get the money sorted out.'

'What money, sweetie?' She held out one hand, fingers spread like a fan pointedly admiring the rings heavy and cruel as a jewelled knuckleduster.

'If you're not going to budge on what you want, I need more time.'

'Oh, I'm not budging. You know the figures.'

'And you know they're impossible.'

'Not impossible . . . just calculatedly painful. Like I meant them to be.'

'A court would never give you that much.'

'I don't need a court. Daddy's promised me your balls on a plate if you're not a good boy – and that's without me telling him about you raping me the other night. If I can't squeeze the money out of you, Giles, I'll be satisfied with seeing you in the gutter.' She slid her fingers up and down the stem of her wine glass as she thought. 'But money would be better. All right, you can stay here – and keep well away from me – until the end of August. If you're not out by then, I go nuclear.'

'Do you want to fucking destroy me?'

'You've grasped it at last.' She laughed. 'And you're so easy to break, Giles, so pitifully weak.'

'I'm not weak!'

She stared at him for a moment, then crossed the room and knelt in front of him, turning her face slightly to one side.

'Go on,' she invited. 'Hit me.'

Her eyes dared him, but there was no trace of fear in them.

'And you're not weak?' She stood up. 'Don't kid yourself. I've known it for a very long time.'

Monday morning added Ella Fitzgerald's name to the litany. Dean Martin the previous Christmas, Gene Kelly in February, Greer Garson in April . . . Stars who had glittered in Oliver Graveney's life were constantly going out, and there was a growing sense of gathering darkness. When Christopher Robin Milne had died, with painful coincidence on Oliver's fiftieth birthday in February, it was as though even childhood was being erased. He was conscious of now turning first to the obituaries page of *The Times* to see if someone else he had never met but who had been part of his experience – of his existence – had gone, somehow taking another fragment of his life with them.

He did not fear his own death, but disappointment. He was wealthy, with a handsome home, elegant, intelligent wife and beautiful daughter, but he had not had to struggle for money or privilege; they were among the prizes engraved with his name even before he bid for them. As chairman of Anglian News-papers – taking over from his father after a token period working in advertising and circulation – he felt no more than an older version of the little boy who had all the toys, a silver BMW now replacing the expensive pedal car. His only ability was to make money, the one thing he no longer regarded as having any worth.

'Good God, Julia's getting married again.' Fay held up the invitation that had come in the post.

'I assume it's to Andrew . . . You wouldn't believe me.'

'She's mad. He's absolutely broke.'

Oliver began to fold the *Financial Times*. 'Does that matter?'

'Of course it does. Julia's got three hairdressers and a lifestyle to support.' Fay made a face of impatience. 'I know you liked him.'

'And he understands Julia. I told you that. When is it?'

She looked at the card again. 'Nineteenth of September. At a register office in Newark . . . Do you know where that is?'

'Nottinghamshire.' He took out his diary. 'It's a Thursday. I've got a meeting, but I can cancel it.'

'And what do we buy for a third wedding present?'

'You'll think of something.' He stood up and went to put the paper in his briefcase. 'Are you seeing Jonathan today?'

'Mmm.' The reply was absent-minded as she opened a letter from a friend in Los Angeles, then held up her cheek to be lightly kissed. She twitched her lips affectionately. 'Take care.'

In the early days it had been uncomfortable, both of them learning the rules by which they had agreed to live. Seeing Jonathan meant going to bed with Jonathan, letting him supply what Oliver no longer had any interest in. Now it had become like a Bloomsbury relationship, the husband accepting the lover because he had created the circumstances; it was civilized.

When Oliver had said he no longer wished to sleep with her, Fay had not suspected another woman or that he could be a latent homosexual. Apart from the very earliest times, she recognized that he found little attraction in sex; perhaps because it lacked any intellectual dimension or that he found its messier aspects distasteful. Pregnancy and Emma's birth had given him an excuse to stop . . . and it had never started again. Before Fay's frustration became anger, he told her his decision.

'I'm sorry,' he said. 'But never mistake it for lack of love.'

'But you're still imposing what you want – or don't want in this case – on me.'

'I know. I've thought about that a great deal.'

'And? I'm sure you've worked something out.'

'I think so.' For a moment she thought he was going to take her hand, but he remained on the chair opposite her by the fireplace, carefully maintaining his distance. 'I'm assuming you'll want to take a lover – and I accept that.'

'Thank you. The milkman's going to be a very happy man.'

'Don't cheapen this, Fay,' he warned. 'I've told you I love you, and unless you reach a stage where you no longer love me, which is the last thing I want, I expect us both to behave intelligently . . . I'm sorry, I'm not trying to be pompous.'

'Well, I'm afraid you're not doing very well, darling. It's all right. I'm used to it.' She sipped her vodka and orange. 'Then I have your permission to become an adulteress?'

'No. That involves deception, and we've never done that to each other. If you find a lover, I want you to tell me . . . and I'd like him to be someone I can respect.'

She laughed. 'Ralph Hetherington needn't apply then.'

He picked up her humour. 'I'd be . . . disappointed if it was him.'

'Disappointed? I'd be horrified to think I could be that desperate . . . Pour me another drink. I have a lot to take on board here.'

There had been no purpose in arguing; Oliver never made hasty decisions and was immovable once he reached them. It was ironic. Fay had memories of more than a dozen lovers, but had taken her marriage vows seriously; this was her husband and that part of her life was over. But she was turned thirty and her appetites hadn't gone away. One of her boyfriends had told her she had a male attitude to sex; eroticism was more important than emotions.

But for a long time she had remained celibate, anxious that her choice should not cause damage or hurt Oliver. Jonathan was a solicitor in Ipswich, a friend of friends met at a party, unattached and amusing, instantly on Oliver's wavelength, quoting poetry, exchanging literary anecdotes. A week later, Fay phoned him and said she would be in Ipswich on . . . was he free for lunch? That night, she was fixing Oliver's drink when she told him.

'Do you remember Jonathan? Alan and Jacqueline's friend?'

'Very well. I'd like to meet him again sometime. Why?' She handed him his glass without replying. 'Oh. I see.'

'Is it all right?'

'Of course.'

'Look at me, Oliver. You don't like it, do you? Not now it's happened.'

He shook his head. 'It's not that. It mustn't be. But . . . I may need to adjust . . . When did it begin?'

'It hasn't – well, not in that sense. But it may now.'

'You needed my approval?'

'Yes. That was important. All I've done so far is make a lunch date, but I want to see how much I really like him. If it's enough – and he makes the first move – then . . .' She knelt by his chair. 'Listen. I promise I won't let myself fall in love. Not the way I love you. If I ever think that's starting to happen, I'll end it. Jonathan may become a very special friend, but that's it . . . all right?'

'Thank you . . . I hope he'll not consider me a fool.'

'He'd better not.' She kissed his forehead. 'If he doesn't respect you, then he won't have me. I won't let anybody harm what I value so much.'

It had taken several casual meetings manufactured by Fay – tied in with pretended dental appointments, an imaginary friend in hospital, shopping – before anything happened, and Fay felt an overwhelming delight when Jonathan finally took hold of her hand.

'At last.' She sighed with relief. 'I really was getting tired of driving round the block.'

'What do you mean?'

'My teeth are fine, no one's ill, and even I don't shop this much. Didn't you realize?'

'It crossed my mind a while ago, but . . . I spoke to Jacqueline who said you and Oliver had a good marriage.'

'We do . . . and it has to stay that way.'

'Then why . . . ?' He tried to pull his hand away, but she tightened her fingers to prevent him.

'Please . . . Two understanding men would be farcical. Just finish your coffee, then take me back to your flat.'

He looked confused. 'I'm missing something here, aren't I?'

'Yes, but I'll explain after . . . Oh, for God's sake, ask for the bill. It's all right . . . honestly.'

Now Jonathan had become part of a parallel life, unconnected with Fay's role as chairman's wife. On family holidays in Tuscany she and Oliver would drink wine, perfect their Italian, discuss books and drown together in Renaissance splendour. Contact was no more than holding hands or a *simpatico* brush of cheeks as they said goodnight and went to their separate bedrooms. She would send Jonathan postcards from them both. Joyce, the only other person Fay had told, still recalled controlling her hysterics at the party to celebrate their twentieth wedding anniversary, when Oliver's best man had said theirs was a perfect marriage and everyone had applauded.

Chapter Eight

Joyce told herself it was just another commonplace day ... with an added personal agenda that would almost certainly come to nothing; thinking like that meant there would be no disappointment – anticipation of something happening virtually ensuring that it would not. So she would cycle the three miles to Sutworth Cross for a salad lunch and gossip with Christine, collect her report about the riveting activities of St Osyth's for the parish magazine and then home. And why not choose the slightly longer return that would take her past Windhover? She was free all afternoon, and the stretch through the tunnel of trees would be pleasant. If his car wasn't outside the cottage ... No, that wasn't the point. If it was, he still might have gone out, and even if he was in ... She laughed and rang the bicycle bell for no reason.

The MG*F* was there and three of the cottage windows were open. It would have been better if he had been sitting outside and she could have casually called hello, but there was no sign of him. She braked and stood across the bicycle for a moment, suddenly hesitant. If I don't, I'll always wonder and may regret it; if I do, I'll know – and might not regret it. I've faced tougher choices. She wheeled the bike through the gate and round to the back, conscious of leaving it where it would not be seen by anybody passing on the road.

'Hello? Are you in?' The back door was also open, but she never entered the cottage without permission when someone was renting it.

'Who is it?' He sounded startled.

'Only me. Mrs Hether . . . Joyce. I was on my way home and wondered . . .' She stopped as he appeared out of the sitting room into the passage that led from front door to back. 'I promise I haven't come from Porlock. Just the next village.'

'Oh . . . Hi.' He was wearing a peppermint-green Fruit of the Loom T-shirt and shorts, strong legs dark with hair, bare feet in sandals. 'Come in.'

'Thank you.' The threshold felt curiously like a frontier. 'It was the thought of cycling up the hill that got me. It's absolutely boiling out there. I'm dying of thirst and thought that you might . . .'

'Of course . . . but I've only got beer. Lager.'

'If it's cold, you'll save my life. Do you mind?'

'No, but . . .' He glanced back into the sitting room. 'We can have it outside.'

'Don't bother with glasses. I'll drink it from the can.' To suggest I'm not that old and know how young people behave? I'm confused.

She remained just inside the door as he went into the kitchen, then stepped back into the garden. One deckchair was set up on the grass and she hesitated before sitting in it. As she waited, she tried to rationalize her thoughts. This is nothing more than a return for my hospitality; people who've stayed here before have invited me in for a drink . . . Liar. The sight of the glasses disappointed her slightly, as though he was too conscious of her status, of her age.

'I'm afraid I've taken your chair.'

'It doesn't matter.' He handed her the drink and sat on the grass. 'Which is the next village?'

'Sutworth Cross . . . Well, it just about qualifies as a hamlet. I had to visit someone.' She didn't say why; for an inexplicable reason, she didn't want to mention the church. 'Were you writing?'

'Yes, but it's all right. I was finding it difficult.'

'Writer's block, I expect. I wonder if Dickens ever suffered from it? You'd never think so. If he'd had a word processor,

God knows how much he'd have churned out.' She sipped the beer. 'Mmm, this is very good. Have you been working all day?'

'Yes, but I'm going to the Wheatsheaf later for something to eat. I had lunch there the other day.'

'The Shoulder of Mutton's better. Ask for Maggie's special.'

They were both aware that they had little to talk about; they knew almost nothing about each other and what Joyce had calculated was an age-gap of at least fifteen years was barren of meeting places. As before he seemed reluctant to talk about his book and the humdrum chronicle of what she had done since they had sat together in her own garden was irrelevant. Authors crafted openings in such circumstances; the reality was mental fumbling, uncertainty and fear of embarrassment. She stared at him until he felt the attention of her eyes and looked back; the contact held neither the blankness of strangers nor the warmth of friends. He looked away again, and she knew nothing would happen unless she made it happen.

'Don't you ever get lonely? Writing must be so . . . solitary,' she said. Go on; your turn.

'Not really. I live on my own.'

Thank you for that. 'But that's because you choose to?'

'Yes.'

'I can remember when I could choose. I just made wrong decisions.'

'We all do.'

They returned to silence, like skaters moving cautiously back to the safety of the shore when they saw dark water swirl beneath ice. Distantly, the church clock chimed four; she would have to be home by five-thirty, the end of another afternoon of waste. But if neither of them could find words, she would have to leave within a few minutes, and their fear would have built a barrier. So they would just drift out of each other's lives . . . Joyce reached down and placed her glass on the ground. He must have half seen the movement, but did not look at her again, even when she stood up.

'I wasn't really thirsty,' she said, and waited. He sighed, but whether from relief or apprehension she couldn't decide. Come on, I've taken a step for both of us; either follow me or make me feel foolish by walking away from this. I can cope with that. He ran his fingers up and down the can, watching them smear the film of condensation.

'So perhaps I ought to leave now.' Jesus, am I that unattractive? Are you another one who's going to put me down?

He shook his head, but still did not look up at her. Joyce felt an urge to explain. She sat down again, making him look at her.

'Can I call you Randall? Thank you. I've never done anything like this before, and to be honest I can't completely understand why I'm doing it now. But it's not just because I've got a lousy marriage. If that was the reason, I'd have done it ages ago. OK?'

He nodded, but remained motionless. Joyce plucked a long stem of grass from the lawn and began to twist it in her fingers.

'I can't leave my husband, because . . .' She sighed. 'Eight years ago my father died and my mother came to live with us. She's turned seventy now – and she thinks Ralph is wonderful. But he's been having an affair in town for years. She wouldn't believe it if I told her – well, even if she did, she'd probably say it must be my fault. And she'd be devastated. Really. It would . . . well, breaking her heart's over the top, but it would hurt her dreadfully.'

'So what can you do?'

She shrugged. 'Nothing . . . until she dies. Obviously I don't want that – I love her – but it's the only way out.' Unexpectedly, she smiled. 'And she comes from a very long-lived family.'

'Why are you telling me?'

She could no longer resist laying her hand over his. 'Because I want you to know why I'm here, and . . . well, I've cut off all my lines of retreat now, haven't I? Have I embarrassed you?'

'No. I'm . . . I enjoyed talking to you before. In the garden. It was good.'

Joyce squeezed his hand. 'I enjoyed it too. That's why I came today. To talk to you again and . . .' She looked down. 'I promised myself I wouldn't lie to you. I would like us to talk more, but ... well, I'm just so grotesquely out of practice at this sort of thing. Sorry.'

Fearful of rejection, however sensitive, she remained totally still until he turned his hand and tightened it on hers as he stood up. Her mind was blank as they walked into the house.

Upstairs their movements were hesitant, arabesques of cautious exploration. Joyce drew the curtains, heavy orange cotton turning white-painted stone walls amber, and spent a moment ensuring they were completely closed; when she turned he was standing by the bed awaiting permission, and remained motionless as she unbuttoned his shirt. There was a scar, a pale flaw shaped like a tiny bow, just beneath his collar bone, and she ran her fingers across it gently, concerned that he had been wounded. Rupert had a scar from the day at the playground when he had ... She placed his hand on her hip, then looked at his eyes as she pushed the shirt off his shoulders. Any time, any place, she remembered. Fay would have been excited by now, expectation flared, clothes spilling off her body.

His hand remained where she had put it; no exploring movement of fingers, no pressure. As she kissed him, she made a little pleading noise in her throat. Help me, this is difficult. If you don't want me, I can't do this on my own. I've forgotten the rules for playing the tart – and I don't want you to want a tart – but you have to want me; I need your matching hunger. All right?

She stepped back and breathed in deeply, putting her shoulders back as she took off her shirt and twisted both arms behind her flicking metal hook and eye apart. They've suckled two children, but they're not shot to hell and I can just about remember when I used them to tantalize and provoke. It's a long time since I did this other than simply to get undressed ... there. Still worth seeing, still worth fondling, arousing, kissing. There are dozens of men who'll never touch them, but would love to if I would let them; it's a privilege I'm granting you. There haven't been that many before ... Christ, do I have to do everything here?

She felt perspiration on his palm as she took his hand again, placing it over warm smoothness broken by the puckered thimble of flesh. She pressed herself against him, trapping his hand as she kissed him again, throat-song now deeper, urging with promises; then he trembled and his fingers squeezed as though in relief.

'Come on,' she whispered. She wanted to pass the point where a voice that said no became one demanding yes. To where hesitation and surprise and the delicate dances of approach became the tempo of gasping urgency, inflamed, irresponsible. She comprehended only their bodies, clawing the muscles of his back, rigidity entering softness, of desiring the end and not wanting it to finish, of nothing else existing. To the final exquisite rush to a primitive height and a slow, spinning fall back to awareness.

So great a reckoning, she thought, in so small a room . . . and so swift, so desperate on both their parts, gratification grasped at as though it would vanish in an instant. They both still had their watches on. How different from fictional passion, playful and perfect, repeated ecstasy, lust without complications. Reality was clumsiness, a creaking bed, a fleeting twinge of cramp in her calf, that terrified moment of wanting to stop and flee back before complete surrender. Reality was trying to think of what to say.

'Thank you.' A phrase open to mean anything. Thank you for the pleasure, for finding me desirable, for not being brutal or hurting me.

'I'm sorry.'

Please, not that. Suggesting this was your seduction makes me the stupid middle-aged woman who lost control; I was in the driving seat first.

'I'm not.' Why did men always need flattery? 'You're very . . .' A little laugh to leaven . . . 'very satisfactory. Come here.'

She cloaked her body with his again and felt the dampness of tears against her chest. Stroking his hair, she noticed the time; Annabel would be back from school soon. Back to boring but dependable Mummy, who would ask about her day, nag about

110

her room. Who cuddled her when she was unhappy, washed and cooked; who had once been young, but wasn't now.

'I really ought to go.' Regret was echoed in retreating caresses. Sleeping together really meant what should happen after sex, in the indulgent latitudes of an uncomplicated affair or the comforts of a good marriage. Remaining in bed, relaxed bodies slipping into slumber of contentment, lightly touching, waking up with the warm realization that someone was still there; affection, love and renewed delights. Sleeping together was not permitted when one's daughter was due home.

'Yes . . . all right.' She felt pleased as he kissed the palm of her hand, a tiny token of affection. 'Will you be able to . . . ? If you don't want to, I'll understand.' His tone suggested he would be hurt.

'Well, one of us has got to be sensible about this, but . . .' She grinned. 'Frankly, I'm pissed off with being sensible. Right now, I'd like to spend the next three weeks in this bed with you and we'd have pizzas delivered. I hope you're not shocked.'

'No, but you mustn't think that—'

'At the moment, my darling, neither of us should think,' she interrupted. 'So I'm not going to.' She got up and started gathering her clothes in the order she needed to put them on. 'I can be here again tomorrow, about seven-thirty. I won't need to be home until late. All right?'

'Yes.'

'Good.' She thrust her feet into her sandals as she rebuttoned her shirt, examining face and neck in the dressing-table mirror. 'Just one house rule. Nothing that leaves marks.' Relax; I want this to be fun, not involvement. She stepped back to the bed and kissed him lightly. 'Now get back to your writing. I know my way out.'

And such sex brought the wicked, secret amusement of waving to someone she knew as she cycled home, the sudden wetness at the apex of her thighs against the leather saddle, the sense of having broken away, of folly without regret. For a moment she thought that it should not be repeated; she had experienced the forbidden and could now get on with her life.

111

But she had promised to go back and was already imagining how it would be now that the first barriers had been breached; no fear, no guilt, eagerly, without haste . . . and God, he'd been so big—

'Hi, Mum!' Annabel was walking towards the house, body leant to one side to balance the red and black Headbag pulling on her shoulder, one ankle sock slipped down. 'I'm starving.'

'What did you have for lunch?' Joyce braked and stepped off the bike, wheeling it along beside her.

'Nothing. It looked awful. Have we got any low-fat cheese?'

'What do you want with it?'

'Water biscuits . . . and I've got to be at Wendy's by six o'clock.'

'What about homework?'

'It doesn't have to be in until next week. Where've you been?'

'Just over to see Christine . . . And hang your clothes up properly.' This to a figure retreating towards the stairs; from the bedroom came the thump of Kurt Cobain and Nirvana.

She spooned cottage cheese, the current diet of choice, on to a plate, then scooped out a blob and licked it off her finger. Guess what Mummy's been doing this afternoon. With Mr Jowett, who's renting the cottage. In the bedroom, on her back. That's right. Mummy was being screwed and was enjoying it, and . . . She closed her eyes. And thinking about it here is bringing it home, where it shouldn't be. Macavity slid through the cat flap, trotted across the floor and rubbed against her legs, purring for attention. Feed me, like you feed them.

'Is it ready?' Annabel reappeared so quickly, she wouldn't have had time to hang up her uniform after changing into jeans and sweatshirt, but Joyce felt it would be hypocritical to criticize so small a disobedience.

'What do you want to drink with it?'

'Diet Coke.'

'God help your stomach. Anyway, I'm going to have a shower.'

'Fine.' The magazine she had brought down with her was more important.

'Back home by eight o'clock, right?'

'Sure . . . Can I go to a club in Ipswich on Saturday?' The rest ran out in one carefully rehearsed sentence. 'I mean it's all right . . . There'll be a whole crowd of us, and we could hire a mini bus . . . Keith can drive . . . and it closes at one o'clock, so I won't be home that late . . . and Sara says they're very strict on the door, they don't let yobbos in . . . and there's no drugs or anything like that . . . Is it all right?'

You were little once, and it doesn't seem that long ago. I can always remember walking into the sitting room and seeing you in your playpen, smiling in look-at-me triumph because you'd managed to stand up on your own for the first time. Now you're going to follow Rupert, who's already started going away, so it will be just me and Daddy and Grandma. And you'll think I'll be happy – if you ever think about me at all.

'See what Daddy says.' There, I've opted out of my responsibility; Ralph will say yes because he doesn't care. Betrayal is my thing at the moment – but at least I may have stopped betraying myself.

Telling herself that the sun must be going over the yardarm somewhere in the world, Joyce fixed herself a long vodka and lime and took it up to the bathroom. She examined her body before stepping into the shower, as though it were novel to her, as though it mattered once more. She dried herself and smoothed on lotion by the window, opened to swallow steam, then stood sipping the drink and letting the faint late-afternoon breeze cool her. Beyond the trees a crayoned bank of purple-brown cloud stretched across a sapphire backcloth, and the feathered vapour trail of a jet spread into a delta of chalk; the ordinary had become vivid.

'I committed adultery this afternoon,' she said. 'Christ, I'm talking to the bloody sky because there's no one else I can tell.'

She walked through to the bedroom and put on a tangerine cotton dress, grimacing slightly at the suggestion of tautness across her hips. It didn't matter. Tomorrow evening they would

113

be able to take their time, have space to stroke, explore and arouse. What a very short distance it was between obedience and daring, between captivity and the excitement of freedom.

'And will I start feeling guilty about this, Mr Randall Jowett?' She smiled at the question. 'Not that I give a damn at the moment.'

In the cottage Jowett stared at the laptop screen, what he had written unseen. It had not been lust but a reaching, a recognition of loneliness; she had granted him kindness. And she had known *them*, been their friend, loved them. She was a bridge to where he might find absolution. For a few ecstatic seconds in that room the rope had snapped and the still bleeding albatross had fallen away; now it was back, but he had fleetingly known the sensation of not bearing it. He began to write again.

They walk with me constantly, those whom I never met, but know. They no longer accuse, but ask why, and I can give no answer. Sometimes I feel they wish to forgive – that they even have forgiven – but I cannot hear them saying it. Remorse is like a wilderness that has no visible horizons beyond which you can travel . . . unless you find someone to lead you there.

Chapter Nine

Stark black jacket and white blouse rigid as a chastity bodice gave Christine Sheaffer the appearance of a highly trained and methodical secretary, an impression reinforced by the silver propelling pencil poised to take shorthand notes, pad balanced on one slender knee. Fair, silky hair inherited from an Austrian father was wound like a scarf across the back of her head and she wore minimal pale make-up; she masked her Saxon beauty, as though it were a gift she chose not to use. Opposite her, across the desk, were Inspector Peter Haggard and the disturbing bulk of Sergeant Harry Pugh, examining a grubby handkerchief as he dabbed his chin to see if a shaving cut had stopped bleeding. His name was a pronounceable corruption of Iorwerth, which actually translated as Edward.

'How much do you know about the case?' Haggard asked.

'It's among the most serious murder inquiries this force has ever conducted — and we didn't get a result. Some of the team have told me about it — it's still talked about, of course — but I don't know any operational details.'

The response was typical; no false affected knowledge in an attempt to impress. Newly arrived from a successful two years with drugs, she listened to experienced officers, accepted as much as she dismissed, appreciated it when she received the right sort of treatment. Resistance to women still lingered in CID — especially to a woman with a sociology degree who could write a thesis on sexual harassment — but Sheaffer defied it. And she was hungry for metaphorical stripes, further rungs on her career ladder.

'I'll fill you in on the basics,' Haggard said. Her pencil began to scamper as he continued. 'There were about seventy officers involved at the height of the investigation, but we all ended up running down blind alleys. The Godwins were good people, churchgoers, well liked, no known enemies. We couldn't find motives among any members of the family, and most of them had alibis anyway. The only thing that ever looked like a lead was a chap called Billy Marsh, who came up when we checked for anyone with form in the area. He'd done eighteen months for aggravated robbery and GBH and the rural patrol officer reckoned he was mixed up in drug dealing on Finch council estate. But he had an alibi as well. After we pushed him a bit, he admitted he'd been fishing illegally that afternoon with a couple of mates and they backed him up. We had nothing to place him at the scene and we didn't find anything when we searched his house. Otherwise, we had no positive suspects. There was one set of fingerprints we never eliminated, and impressions of two pairs of trainers on the sitting-room floor – so we know there were at least two of them. I can't think of any line we didn't pursue, but finally we ran out of TIEs.'

Sheaffer glanced up. 'TIEs?'

'Trace, implicate, eliminate,' Pugh grunted. 'What do they call them in drugs?' Sheaffer said nothing.

'Anyway, the press got bored when we didn't pull anyone in, so the publicity dried up and the inquiry inevitably ran down,' Haggard continued. 'The last thing that happened I'm aware of was in 1993, but that turned out to be nothing more than an outbreak of neighbourly vindictiveness.'

'Wasn't there a confession?' Sheaffer queried.

Haggard laughed. 'How long was it before Bertie Kerridge turned up, Harry?'

'An hour after we announced it – said he'd wanted to finish his dinner first. Bertie comes with the territory, Chris. He started his hobby by swearing he'd shot Kennedy.'

Haggard sat back. 'And that's the guts of Suffolk Constabulary's biggest failure. Several boxes of files and God knows how much computer space will finally tell you the same thing. Questions at this stage?'

Sheaffer flicked back a page of her notebook, resting the pencil tip against a line of hooks and circles that ended with a question mark, a small cross where the dot would normally have been.

'Are we absolutely certain this was a robbery that went wrong? Or could it have been a murder and the stuff was taken to disguise the fact?'

'Good point.' Pugh sounded faintly surprised. 'We looked at that, but you still come back to motive. These were good people. Who'd want to kill them?'

'Who benefited?'

'Ben Godwin had left money to various relatives; quite a lot in some cases. And of course Trevor inherited Tannerslade.'

'Where he's still living.' Sheaffer shook her head. 'I've always thought that was seriously weird.'

'So did we at first,' Haggard said. 'But you've got to remember the Godwins have been at Tannerslade since the Flood. It's always been handed down to the eldest son. Trevor said he wasn't going to let a couple of savages with a gun destroy that.'

'So he lives in the house where his parents, his sister and her children were killed?' Sheaffer still sounded disbelieving.

'Somehow. It can't have been easy for him.'

'It still could have been a motive.'

'But it collapses the moment you look at it. Apart from the fact that everyone told us how much he cared for his parents, he ran a successful market garden business in Stowmarket and wasn't on his beam ends. He reckoned it could be years before he got Tannerslade – old Ben was healthy enough – and he was building up the business for his younger son to inherit when his brother got the farm. They were only schoolkids at the time. Tim must be about twenty now.'

'What about professionals?'

'Another blank. We asked for unofficial inquiries to be made in Essex, the Met, West Midlands, Greater Manchester, Merseyside,

Glasgow . . . you name it. The fact that two children had died might have made someone talk, but nobody knew anything. Personally, I never thought they were full-time villains. There was too much intelligence behind Tannerslade, Chris. Virtually no clues at the scene and no prints on those shotgun cartridges. All from the same weapon, so five shots meant it must have been reloaded twice. Normally, you'd expect to find a thumb-print on the metal end where they were put in the barrels. OK, so they wore gloves at the time of the killings – but none of those cases had anything on them. Which meant they were even careful enough to wear gloves when it was loaded beforehand. Then they just disappeared. Somebody planned this bloody well.'

'But why Tannerslade?' Sheaffer asked. 'There must be dozens of other potential targets in that area.'

'A county magazine had run a piece about the Godwins a few months earlier,' Pugh said sourly. 'What was in the house; the fact they lived alone. All a villain needed was a couple of quid for a copy.'

'Irresponsible.'

'A free press . . .' Haggard commented. 'And Ben and Annie co-operated with them. They were too trusting to think what it might lead to. Perhaps we should be relieved there are still people with enough faith in goodness to think like that.' His mouth twisted slightly.

Sheaffer hesitated. 'You say all the family had alibis, but we held the daughter's husband for questioning. David Hood, wasn't it?'

'Yes,' Haggard agreed, 'but—'

'We didn't push that bastard hard enough.'

'He was in the clear, Harry. No motive, and he was in York at the time. Two canons at the cathedral confirmed that.'

Haggard had known it would only be a matter of time before Pugh's resentment at their failure surfaced. Hard as the rock out of which his valley fathers had hacked coal, blacksmith-broad, forearms like pigs' thighs, the Welshman had been the angriest of them all at Tannerslade, yelling at Preston, who led the inquiry, when he had been ordered to take a couple of days off to get some sleep. Haggard had been worried that Pugh would be the one to find the killers and what those terrible hands would have done. But it had been bad for all of them. It was Mandy, who had looked so agonizingly like his niece, whom Haggard remembered most vividly. But this little girl had not been laughing, demanding that Uncle Peter show her his handcuffs; her dead eyes had been staring at sky she would never see again, her face like a child playing some game in which you were out if you moved. And nobody in that farmyard had made any of the usual protective jokes about murder; Jack Gotobed had turned his back so that the press pack could not take a picture of him weeping.

'Any more questions, Chris?'

'Not at this stage, sir – except why you wanted to talk to me about it.'

'I'll come to that in a moment, but first you should know there's been a development.' Haggard opened a file. 'A weapons collector in Somerset has contacted us. He bought a seventeenth-century German headsman's sword from an antiques dealer in Bristol – sort of thing they used for executions – and was showing it to somebody who remembered the alert we put out after Tannerslade. The police down there have checked it at our request and it's definitely the one Ben Godwin owned. A nick in the blade matches the description he put on the back of one of the photographs we found.'

'How did the dealer get hold of it?'

'Somebody walked in off the street sometime last December with a story that he'd inherited it. He asked for cash.'

'Any description?'

'Not much of one after all this time. Late thirties, possibly older, well-spoken – certainly not local, possibly London or the Home Counties – five ten . . . He might remember more when we talk to him. Mike Davenport's gone down there.'

'So they've finally started selling?'

'We finally know they are,' Haggard corrected. 'A lot of the stuff from Tannerslade wasn't that identifiable. I'm no expert, but I imagine one Dresden shepherdess looks much the same as another. They could have been shifting stuff for years, but something's only just been spotted. We're putting out another warning to the trade to see if anything else turns up.'

Sheaffer wound out another few millimetres of lead from the pencil. 'And where do I come in, sir?'

Haggard closed the file, tapping the contents into place on the desktop. 'We've heard you've just moved to Finch. Where exactly?'

Sheaffer began to understand. 'A cottage on The Street – at least that's what it said in the estate agent's bumf. Most people would call it a rabbit hutch in the middle of a terrace. It needs a lot spending on it, which is why I got it cheap.'

'Met Dave Truman at the Shoulder of Mutton yet?' Pugh asked.

'I think I've seen him, but we've never spoken. Why?'

'He used to be in traffic. Remember me to him.'

'I'll do that.' She turned back to Haggard. 'But what do you want me to do, sir?'

Haggard leant forward across the desk. It was nearly twenty years since he had been the police national bantamweight champion, but, less than half the width of Pugh, he remained all compacted strength.

'Tannerslade still rankles around here, Chris. You must know that. We want it cleared, and not just to close the books and have some judge compliment us at the end of the trial. This one was personal for a lot of us. So anything that might give us a lead we're prepared to try.'

'And now I've moved to Finch . . .' She left it for him to continue.

'Precisely.' He tapped the file. 'There isn't enough in this Bristol business to justify us going back to the village and asking questions at this stage. It would raise people's hopes and all we've managed to do so far is disappoint them.'

'But you want me to make inquiries?'

'Inquiries is a bit strong . . . but keep your ears open.'

'Do we have any reason to think they came from Finch?'

'No – we don't know where they came from. But you might hear about somebody who's . . . I don't know. Bought themselves a new car when everyone thinks they're broke.'

'If they were as intelligent as you say, would they be that stupid?'

Haggard remembered what Bingham in drugs had told him; Chris Sheaffer thinks fast on her feet and remembers everything you tell her.

'Fair point, but something might surface. Maybe you'll hear about someone who's been going away regularly without any obvious reason. It's a long shot, but sometimes they get results.'

'How much authority do I have?' The question was sharply interrogative. Sheaffer always wanted clear orders.

'You're an officer in this force. That's your authority. So use your intelligence . . . but this needs instinct as well. You grew up in a village, didn't you?'

'Yes. East Soham.'

'Then you know what it's like. After a while you become part of the community. You can't hide the fact of your job, but eventually they'll just accept you as someone who lives there.'

Sheaffer looked dubious. 'Villagers keep newcomers at a distance. It takes time to be accepted.'

'We're not in a hurry, Chris. You might not come up with anything, but we wanted to brief you. All right?'

'Yes, sir.' Sheaffer closed her notebook and slipped the pencil into an inside pocket. 'I assume you know I'm starting three weeks' leave on Friday? I want to get the place straight and decorate it.'

'Yes, I know. It will be a good opportunity for you to meet people.'

'I want to read the files as well.'

'You won't get through them all in two days,' Haggard warned. 'But you can fillet out the important parts. You can skip most of the statements from the locals. They won't tell you anything.'

'Thank you, sir.' She stood up. 'Harry.'

Pugh took out a pipe charcoaled with use as he watched her

pass the window of Haggard's office on her way back to CID operations room; Sheaffer would have complained if he'd lit it while she had been in the room and the Chief, newly converted to the anti-tobacco lobby, would have supported her. There was a faint hissing crackle as he sucked the thick flame of an old-fashioned petrol lighter into the bowl as though trying to drag the fire into his mouth.

'What makes you think she'll crack it?' The words emerged through an acrid cloud of impatient smoke.

'I'm not saying she will,' Haggard replied. 'But we didn't crack it, Harry, and we don't lose anything by bringing her in.'

'What's she going to do? Get someone to talk by flashing her tits at them?'

Haggard laughed. 'You never change, Harry . . . but perhaps you'll think better of her if she does come up with something.'

'Money on it?'

'No thanks.'

'So how much faith have you got in her?'

'Enough to let her try.' Haggard looked straight at him. 'I want them as much as you do, boyo. You ought to know that.'

Pugh stared back, then nodded. 'OK, Peter. No bet, but there's five pints for you from me if she does it.'

'And what does she get?'

'I'll teach her all the dirty versions of every rugby song I know.'

Teeth clamped on the stem of the pipe, Pugh grinned, then left in pursuit of the comfort of hops.

Chapter Ten

Joyce found the complications of deceit amusing. Dozens of people in Finch would recognize her Honda Accord, so how could she leave it parked outside the cottage for several hours? But her plans for the evening demanded it. She wanted to take food – cold salmon, asparagus and baby new potatoes, fresh strawberries – to eat with the Piesporter, quieter appetites satisfied in easy companionship before hungry devouring. And it mattered that he should see her in soft satin and high heels, that she should look desirable. So it meant using the car, even if . . . Sod it. The more blatantly she parked, the less suspicious it would be – assuming that anyone would suspect Joyce Hetherington, voluntary teacher for slow infant readers and former Mother's Union president, of rolling naked with a handsome young man, delirious and sinfully gasping. She felt a slight chagrin at the thought that probably no one would imagine it; but she would feel shameless satisfaction if they ever found out.

Perhaps he'd left the front door open to allow a breeze through the cottage; but perhaps it was a welcome.

'Hello? Where are you? It's me.'

'Oh . . . sitting room.' Surprise in the tone? Relief? Apprehension? But sitting room was right for what other visitors called the lounge, suggesting a good family, people who behaved well. He did not come out to greet her and she found him lying on the sofa under the twilight-washed window, arm resting along its back, bare feet again, lavender chinos, woven cotton sports shirt. Joyce was instantly conscious of how the late tawny sunlight and pale shades emphasized his black hair and tinted

123

skin, and of looking at a man in that way again after so many years.

'I hope you haven't eaten.'

'Only a sandwich. Why?'

She patted the lid of the wickerwork basket. 'I've brought supper for us. Stay there.'

She was grateful he hadn't instantly started mauling her, even though she would have responded; she wanted fulfilment to be reached gradually, not grabbed at like something available and cheap. In the dining room she opened the basket and spread the table with the linen cloth she had brought; everything was ready on plates and in dishes, protected by thin plastic film; crystal wine glasses were wrapped in fabric napkins. It felt like setting out a superior picnic, wine on an engraved silver coaster, cutlery gleaming.

'Come and look,' she called.

He gave the first real smile she had seen from him as he entered the door. 'How did you do all this?'

'Magic – and about two hours preparation this afternoon . . . Damn!'

'What's the matter?'

'I've forgotten . . . It doesn't matter, it's silly, but . . . hang on.' In the kitchen she searched in the cupboard under the sink for candles and matches supplied in case there was a power cut; only one candle was whole, and the battered pewter candlestick had been bought from a charity shop.

'Not exactly moonlight and roses' standard,' she apologized as she returned, guarding the flame with her hand, 'but the best we can manage. There. Would you like to pour the wine?' Please smile again; I want this to be happy. She felt an overwhelming appreciation as he held the chair for her, then sat opposite, thrusting the opener into the cork.

'I've missed you,' she said. 'It's been a whole day.' I need you inside me again so much, but I'm stupid enough to want to be wooed.

She placed her fingers on the base of the glass to steady it as he reached across, levelling the bottle. He should have been a craftsman, she thought, a sculptor or potter, beauty flowing out of those delicate hands. Crystal touched and chimed like the faintest of bells and she dipped her head in acknowledgement.

'Had a good day? With the book?'

'Yes.' They began to eat. 'And you?'

'Oh, my days are all like each other . . . I'm meant to be at a meeting to discuss the Pegman Pageant tonight. I told Annabel . . . I said it would probably go on till late.' So we've got hours now. Just talk to me for a while.

'This is very good.'

'Thank you. I took a cookery course once, but this is very basic.'

'I didn't expect it.'

There's a great deal going on here that neither of us expected. How aware of me are you? Does this dress make me look sexy? Are you wondering what I'm wearing underneath it? Have you been fantasizing about me? I have about you. 'I panicked at one moment that you might hate fish.'

'No . . . and I love asparagus.'

For a few moments they ate in silence.

'Will you tell me something?' she asked.

'What?'

'I haven't thought about anyone else but you since yesterday. I can't remember thinking of anything else . . . So what have you thought about?'

'You.'

'Well, you would say that, wouldn't you?' It was a very gentle teasing. 'I handed you that one.'

'I was afraid you wouldn't come back.'

'Ooh, clever.' The teasing deepened fractionally. 'You're a smooth talker.'

'I mean it . . . I can't explain . . . You'll laugh if I say I love you.'

Not laugh, just feel a spasm of dismay. 'You can't. You're very sweet, but we hardly know each other.'

'Does that matter?'

It certainly hadn't mattered yesterday, but he was adding

unwanted dimensions. Was he like her brother had been, unable to keep control, insisting that almost every new girlfriend was a lifelong passion . . . until it ended and the next one came along.

'Let's just agree we're very fond of each other. I'm not interested in analysing it . . . Tell me about yourself.'

'What about myself?'

Oops, that was defensive. 'Anything. Where you were born. Your family. Being at Cambridge. Your job. Your favourite colour. What music you like. What you read.' I need a crash course; this thing won't allow us much time to discover each other. 'I want to know who Randall Jowett is.'

'There's nothing special about me.'

'Nor me.' This is like drawing teeth. 'Come on.'

He pulled the bowl of strawberries towards him and picked up his spoon. 'I was born in Bedford. My father owned a stationery firm. He and my mother died a few years ago.'

'I'm sorry.'

'It's all right . . . I've got an older sister. Ruth . . . I've told you that.'

'Yes. In Normandy. Do you go and see her?'

'Not often . . . We've grown apart. I work for the Hong Kong and Shanghai Banking Corporation as a currency dealer and I've got a flat in the Barbican. That's it, really.'

You'd give more information about yourself on an application for a credit card. OK. Back off for the time being.

'My turn, then. I was born in Wiltshire – as you know – and my brother's a headmaster at a school in Warwick. My father was a doctor and joined a practice in west London, which is why we moved. I wanted to be one too, but the nearest I ever got was private secretary to the chairman of a pharmaceutical company. You know everything else. Lived in Finch nearly twenty years, two children . . .' She paused and looked straight at him. 'And, of course, a bastard husband I've stopped loving. But I don't make a habit of what happened yesterday.'

'I didn't think that.'

Then what did you think? Not that you're irresistible to women, thank God. You're too uncertain of yourself for that

126

... Now finish your bloody strawberries – and don't suggest coffee.

Joyce made the first physical contact, walking round the table and placing her hands on his shoulders, coaxing him to turn his head so they could kiss, then easing him up. She put her arms round his neck, fingers over her wrist to lock them and tilted her head, looking at him quizzically.

'Does it really matter why?' she asked. The question was for both of them. 'It certainly doesn't at this moment.'

Hunger of deliberate delay surged through her and she kissed him again, lips apart as though letting him bite into soft fruit. Her spine cracked faintly as his arms tightened, then his fingers were scrabbling at buttons running down the back of her dress. She became intent on seeking his nakedness, hands still fumbling with his belt as she stepped back slightly, rotating her shoulders to allow the dress to fall. Too impatient to wait for him, she thrust off her bra straps, shaking her breasts free as his belt came loose. She had refused endless requests from forgotten boyfriends and Ralph because she didn't want to, but ... Jowett slid his fingers into her hair as she knelt.

'Let's slow down,' she whispered as she pulled away. 'Believe it or not, I don't want to hurry. Just lie here with me.'

The rug smelt dusty – and was really too thin for such activities – but he was a pliant lover, giving gentle strokes as he removed the last of her clothes, mouth soft on her nipples, pausing with her to enjoy simple closeness and a sense of savoured time.

'We'll be comfier in bed, darling,' she murmured as their caresses became impatient, and he suddenly did something spontaneous, lifting her off the floor without effort, throwing back the hair she had playfully pulled over his face as he carried her out to the hall.

'Ouch!' she protested as her head bumped against the door frame.

'Sorry.' He turned sideways and she felt giddy as he swung round the turn of the stairs and into the bedroom. He was panting as he laid her down.

'Get inside me.' Arms and legs grasped him fiercely as he entered her, forcing him to stay still. 'Wait, darling . . . slowly . . . oh, that is so good.'

It was like holding a child close against her, gently rocking with him, deep sensations in warm, gripping channels spreading throughout her body, swelling the comfort of embrace. She imagined what she had long ago felt with other men – even Ralph – that the bed was some ultimate private place, a garden of total indulgence. His face was in the pillow beside her and she took hold of a handful of hair, pulling his head up so that she could look at him. His eyes looked apprehensive, as though this should be forbidden. She smiled an invitation then opened her lips, pressing him down to let other flesh mingle in wetness. Then it was happening too soon, but . . . Far off, she heard the bedhead tattoo against the wall as a burst of golden heat blossomed in trembling chambers. Arms and legs lost all strength and she was falling away from him so that she lay like a helpless starfish, battered and hurled on the sand by the sea. Then she belched.

'I'm sorry!' Her hand flew to her mouth as she laughed. 'That never happens with Glen Close, does it?' He was slipping out of her and she was aware of his weight, bony kneecap digging into her thigh as he slid aside; they lay and stared at the ceiling like exhausted runners seeking to recover what had been spent. A settling blackbird's song was drowned by the noise of a passing car, then outside her closed eyes it was very quiet . . .

'What time is it?' She was startled into sudden consciousness.

'It's OK. You've only been asleep a few minutes.'

'Thank God.' She relaxed. 'I'd forgotten that sort of sleep . . . Did I snore?'

'No,' he lied.

'Good. I don't want you to think me unladylike.' She laughed again. 'Although I've hardly been behaving like one.' Limp and passive, his hand contained no response as she took hold of it. 'I'm not going to say that was the best sex I've ever had – but it was the best for a very long time . . . I trust that you've got no complaints?'

128

His fingers squeezed slightly. 'It was the best for me.'

'Flatterer . . . but it will get you somewhere.' She sat up. 'I want another drink. Stay there. I'll get it.'

There was a delicious naughtiness in remaining naked as she went downstairs, seeing herself in the mirror as she poured the wine, a satiated woman, blatant and released, hair tousled, hunger gorged.

'Oh, Joyce Davinia Hetherington,' she murmured to her reflection. 'What would they think at Cheltenham Ladies' College?'

Upstairs, Jowett closed his eyes as a shudder racked through him. Surely this was a greater lie, the deceitful smiling mask that hid the monster's face. But trying to analyse it only deepened confusion. After her kindness and sympathy had warmed him, she had become the knowing woman, tempting because she was both experienced and forbidden . . . but there was much more than that. She offered him a connection with what he needed to touch; his ghosts had been her friends. So you fucked her . . . No, not that! They would all hate me in this village if they discovered who I am, but if one of them can share love with me, then . . . then it's better. I've repaid something . . . haven't I?

'Here we are . . . Oops!' Wine slopped over the edge of a brimming glass and splashed on the floor as Joyce came back into the bedroom. 'Help me. I need another pair of hands . . . Here. Take this one. Thanks.'

Walking carefully, they stepped back to the bed and sat beside each other, pillows propped up to lean against.

'I assume you've switched off for the moment,' she said.

'What do you mean?'

'You know. I can hold on to what has just happened for hours, but men have a memory cell missing about sex. You're only able to remember the pleasure for about ten seconds afterwards. Women get used to it.'

He looked down at his glass. 'I wasn't just . . . you know . . . there was more to it than . . .' He shook his head.

'Oh, please!' The protest was mocking. 'Are you trying to say you weren't just fucking me? I do know words like that. Don't treat me like the lady of the manor who thinks it's really all too sordid.' She squeezed his penis playfully. 'I have been around the circuit a few times . . . but not for a while.'

Joyce frowned as he pushed her hand away. 'For heaven's sake, you're not feeling guilty about this, are you?' Hastily, she put her glass on the bedside table and took hold of his shoulders. 'Don't be silly! I'm not . . . I *wanted* you! I don't know why, but that doesn't matter. It's . . . Oh, come here.'

It was like comforting a child again, but now distressed, not warm and contented in her arms. She felt tears against her skin. Please, all I was looking for was someone who'd . . . want me in return. Just for a while. Neither of us needs this, it's too bloody dramatic. Gently, she pushed him away from her, still holding him, staring in concern at his face.

'Can we just lighten it? You're so . . . Oh, Christ! I'm sorry. The first thing I thought about you was that you might have lost someone. Is that it? I didn't mean this to hurt you.'

'It's nothing like that.'

'Then what is it? Can't we just . . . ?' She ventured a small grin. 'Enjoy it? I'm not going to start making demands . . . promise. It's not a bad deal, is it?'

'No.' He swallowed. 'I'm sorry, I just . . . got confused.'

'Well, there's nothing confusing about me, my love. I may be a standard issue frustrated woman, but I'm not carrying any baggage.' She raised his head so she could see into his eyes. 'I hope I'll always remember you, but all I want for the time being is for you and me to make everything but babies. Don't start looking for things that aren't there. All right?'

She waited, then nodded when he told her it was. 'Good. Now let's finish this wine just to prove it can raise the desire without ruining the performance.' Briefly but fiercely she kissed his mouth. 'I want to find out how many of the things I used to do I can still manage.'

As she drove home, Joyce prayed that Annabel would have gone to bed; beneath her clothes she felt ravaged, convinced her body emanated odours that her daughter would detect and recognize. It had been hard work, but she'd finally made him laugh and . . . had she really lost control so much at one point that surely half the village could have heard her? Outside the house she remained in the car, knowing that the moment she went back inside the evening would be finished. She wound down the window and breathed in warm night air, craning her neck to peer at shredded moonglow cloud and one visible star . . . No, don't throw romance at me, God. He's young, sensitive, disgustingly good-looking, got some hang-ups I can't understand and – she smiled to herself lasciviously – and can make my eyes open very wide indeed. I don't need anything else.

Chapter Eleven

Trevor Godwin wept, suddenly and without effort; it was a long time since it had happened and he tried to identify what had triggered it. During the first two years, troubled, protesting ghosts had ambushed him in every room of the house, as though they had been dragged away so violently that they had not had time to take all of their personalities with them. In those days he had cried a great deal, weak until his anger had returned, stiffening his determination not to be broken. The first recorded Godwin had farmed these fields before Shakespeare was born, and the direct inheritance from father to son was traceable from Cromwell's Commonwealth. Europe, out of which enemies had once come, now sent endless paperwork, regulations that dictated his yields and governed his prices; but it was only the latest change in a process in which the Godwins had been permanent. As a child his father had told him that Tannerslade Farm would one day be his, and he had promised it in time to Tim; savagery could not be allowed to destroy something so valued, passed on in blood trust. If it succeeded, he would have failed.

He realized that his tears had been prompted by nothing more than the grandfather clock, bought in Bury St Edmunds in 1877 as a wedding gift for Jacob and Henrietta Godwin. Normally unheard, for some reason a single tick had cracked one of the many dams built in his brain to hold back memory and a boiling cataract of images had poured out, the torrent dazing him: the metallic grind of the ratchet as his father had wound it every Friday evening before dinner; checking his

132

watch against it while waiting to leave for church on the morning of his marriage, self-conscious of his morning suit; the day four-year-old Tim had inquisitively opened the front, lifted the iron weight off the pendulum, then screamed in alarm as he dropped it. And the look on Tim's face ten years later when Trevor had sat and gently told him that Grandpa and Nana were dead. And Aunt Cheryl. And boisterous Thomas. And chattering Mandy, who had told everyone that she was going to marry her handsome, adored cousin when she grew up.

Coming downstairs Janet Godwin saw him, rigid, eyes seeing nothing visible but all the horrors that imagination insisted must have happened. The helpless panic, screams, despair, pleas for mercy, the terrifying knowledge that here was death come . . .

'Black dog?' She stroked his hair softly as she reached the last step. 'It's a long time since he walked. What was it?'

Godwin shook himself. 'Something stupid . . . the clock. It's all right.'

She hugged him briefly, then they pulled apart; each had learnt that physical contact at such moments spawned emotions that could overwhelm and plunge them back into grief still with the power to tear open deep wounds.

'Take a beer out to the boys. They're practising in the garden.'

'How long until lunch?'

'About twenty minutes.'

Godwin heard them exchanging insults as he walked between the apple trees to the stretch of grass where family games of cricket had been played since before he was a child. As he appeared, Matt was running up, colt-like, trying to put spin on a worn, flaking ball; Tim saw his father and drove it fiercely.

'Catch, Dad!'

Three cans of bitter fell with a clatter as Godwin instinctively threw out his right arm, flinching as the ball slapped into his palm.

'Oh, well held!' Tim sounded surprised that he had moved so quickly. 'Want to be twelfth man?'

Godwin tossed the ball back to Matt and retrieved the beer.

'You can't be that desperate. Here. Be careful it doesn't spray all over the place.'

They took the cans, holding their hands over the top to stop the hissing squirts as they opened them, then sat on the grass. Godwin reflected that it was now rare they were all together; Tim was away most of the year at agricultural college and Matt would be going to read business studies at Newcastle in September if his A-level grades were good enough. But he and Janet were becoming irrelevant to them anyway. The boys' lives revolved around friends whose names Trevor could never remember, nights out in Ipswich or London, cricket, girls who appeared at Tannerslade once and were never seen again. Soon it would just be him and Janet, the Stowmarket flat replaced by a farm with a black dog.

'How are you getting to the match?'

'Mike's collecting us.' Tim picked up his bat like a sword. 'I'm going to massacre that bastard who trapped me with a leg break last season.'

'Don't wave that thing around like your prick again, then,' Matt said, and ducked as his brother shook the can and aimed the spray at him.

'Where're you going afterwards?' Trevor asked.

'Probably to the Shoulder of Mutton.'

'Are you coming home after that?'

'We'll see what turns up. Maybe.'

What had once been conversations were now question and answer sessions. With the shallow confidence of youth, the boys no longer needed a father to tell them things.

'I saw that MGF again yesterday.' Tim, as usual was talking only to Matt. 'It's got to belong to someone who lives round here.'

'What did he look like?'

'Couldn't see him properly. Lucky bastard.' He turned to his father. 'Twenty-first birthday present?'

'We'll see. They're expensive.'

'Tell you what. I'll save a couple of grand towards it. Any chance then? Come on, you can afford it.'

'You had the Cavalier for your eighteenth.'

'Cavaliers are for sales reps, Dad. And the heating system's buggered . . . Didn't you get an Austin Healey for your twenty-first?'

'Yes, but I didn't get anything for my eighteenth. That didn't count when I was your age. You want two bites of the cherry.'

Tim shrugged. 'So I like cherries. That MGF is awesome.'

And he did his familiar trick of turning away, irritated at not being instantly promised – if not actually given – something he wanted. Too affectionate towards the first-born of another generation, his grandfather had planted those seeds. Tim had become the arrogant Godwin male, privileged in land and family money, but envious for more, the dynast hungry for his inheritance. Conceited before mirrors, he had never been humbled and rarely defied.

Brighter than his brother and less self-assured, Matt was the more gratifying son, accepting the laws of primogeniture with-out rancour; he would achieve something for himself, while Tim would only inherit what others had won.

'I'm going to have a shower.' Tim stood up, leaving the empty beer can lying on the grass.

'Lunch is nearly ready.'

'I'm not hungry.'

'Mum's doing it for all of us.' Trevor injected a rare note of reproval, silenced in the years immediately after the murders, and now difficult to bring back.

'No problem, Dad. I'll eat.' And he was gone, jumping to fingertip a high branch as he passed beneath it, bending to pick up a windfall apple and throw it at a grey squirrel scampering away, confident and casually aggressive. For a few moments they remained silent, as though relieved to be free of his presence.

'Black dog turned up again just now,' Trevor said quietly.

'Shit.' Matt's sympathy was immediate. 'How bad?'

'Not too bad. But it's been a long time and I wasn't ready.' He was conscious of deliberately not mentioning the incident while Tim had been there. Tim's reaction to anything about the murders had always been anger, fuelled by resentment at being denied vengeance; accustomed to denial, Matt carried his pain softly.

'It's the anniversary soon,' he said. 'Perhaps that's it . . . What are you and Mum doing this year?'

'We'll be here again. It never really helped going away because it was all still waiting when we came back.'

'I'll be around as well . . . We'll do something.'

But Tim would not be at Tannerslade on the eleventh. On the first anniversary in 1991 he had abruptly raged through the house, smashing one of the panes in the french doors before racing out screaming, returning hours later and locking himself in his room. Trevor had excused it as the bewildered greenstick grief of the young, but had later recognized it as selfishness, a fury that something had been taken from him – not from his parents and brother, but him personally.

'I'd better have a shave.' Matt collected his brother's discarded beer can as he stood up. 'I won't be long.'

'OK.' Trevor rested his arms on bent knees, then raised one hand to wipe away a trickle of tears. His road of mourning seemed to stretch ahead for ever, haunted by known ghosts and faceless killers. Murder had infected all the corners of his life, and any pleasure – including love-making with his wife – was darkened, memories of good times shrivelled in the shadow of the worst thing. He also carried the irrational conviction that somehow he should have prevented it, that he had failed to protect them. Although the black dog bit less often now, it took time to shake free of its tearing teeth.

Deafening under the low smoke-tarred beam and plaster ceiling of the Shoulder of Mutton public bar, the chanting grew louder, amplified by stamping feet and fists banging on table tops, screams of disbelief from the girls. In a space to himself in the middle of the saloon bar, Tim eased the long bell-ended glass tube at a steeper angle above his head, gulping as the liquid poured out, eyes watching the ball, big as a grapefruit, trembling in his grasp at the far end. If he allowed that reservoir to spill over too suddenly, the final contents of a yard of ale would become a tidal wave impossible to swallow, drenching him in defeat. Encouragement and jeering warnings grew louder, but his mind was focused only on the ball and its contents. Lowering the tube to take breath meant failure (the beer had to be drunk without stopping), but everything depended on this last, delicate manoeuvre . . . liquid trickled from the corners of his overflowing mouth, then there was an enormous cheer as he raised the glass like a trumpet in triumph, gasping for air.

'That's twenty quid and you pay for the beer, right?'

'I should have bloody known better.' The team captain handed him the money. 'I never thought you'd do it after how much you've jugged tonight.'

'Just settling the dust,' he panted. 'I think I'll have a chaser. Whisky, Maureen. Double. OK? I'm just going for a piss.'

The lavatories were on the far side of the yard and the moment he stepped into the night air he knew he had to reach them quickly. He half fell through the door of a cubicle, vomit spluttering from his mouth and splashing over the edges of the pan. Hands pressed against the narrow walls, he groaned and started to sweat.

'Jesus.' He tore off a handful of lavatory paper and wiped his mouth, feeling nausea rise and fall in his throat before spitting out its sticky residue. Cupped handfuls of cold water revived him, but in the mirror over the basin his face was ashen.

Crowded and raucous, the bar was heaving with heat, smelling of cigarettes and beer. Behind the racket of voices the juke box belted out Oasis at full volume. There were scattered cheers as Tim returned, waving boozy acknowledgements as he collected his whisky.

'You look dreadful,' Matt said. 'Come on, I'll get you home.'

'Bollocks.' He reached into his back pocket, pulling out the money he had won for drinking the yard of ale and slapping the notes on the counter. 'Let me know when that runs out, Maureen.'

His eyes went glazed for a moment. 'And give me that picture, will you? That's it . . . the one of Grandpa. I want to look at it.'

The barmaid took the framed photograph down from the wall behind the bar and handed it to him. It showed Ben Godwin presenting a darts trophy he had sponsored. Tim held it carefully, then rubbed the knuckles of one hand across his eyes before raising the picture and kissing the glass.

'Love you,' he murmured softly. 'Never leave me.'

Chapter Twelve

'Is Polish allowed?' Joyce rearranged the plastic tiles on their wooden support. 'If I put 'zcelkas' in front of that 'a', I'll score about three hundred. It's on a triple word.'

'I didn't know you spoke Polish.'

'I don't – but neither do you, so you can't argue that it's wrong.'

'The rules say only English . . . in the dictionary.'

'Spoilsport.' She put out her tongue at him. 'I'm miles behind.'

'You're the one who wanted to play.'

They were sitting up in bed, the abandoned family Scrabble board from the collection of games left in the cottage between them on the crumpled duvet. She had gone straight to Windhover as soon as Ralph had left for London, telling her mother she had to attend another pageant meeting. Love-making had been almost instant and for Joyce exquisite, but she had wanted them to share something innocent as well.

'Then I give up.' She jerked the board into the air, scattering the tiles. 'It's not fair. You know too many words . . . Can I read your book?'

'No!'

She frowned at the force of his refusal. 'Why not?'

'It isn't finished.'

'That doesn't matter . . . What's it about?'

He thrust away her hand reaching for him. 'Nothing . . . It's just writing. Private things.'

'Am I in it? Is that why you don't want to show me?'

'No . . . it's just . . . It doesn't matter.' She was startled as he abruptly grabbed hold of her. 'Again?'

'Why do you need to ask?'

She winced as his fingers dug deep into her flesh, as if he were desperate to escape into her, unable to understand his anger.

His father's image in her mind, Sheaffer was startled by the resemblance when Trevor Godwin opened the door. But photographs she had seen of Benjamin Godwin had shown an old man whose features retained the vigour of youth; his son was the painful *doppelgänger*, what could have been an almost boyish face scoured with decay and age-cloaked by coarse steel-grey hair. She wondered what he had looked like before the summer of 1990.

'Yes?'

'Mr Godwin? I'm sorry to trouble you. My name's Christine Sheaffer. I wonder if I could talk to you.'

He frowned. 'What about?'

She showed her warrant card. 'I'm with Suffolk CID . . . But this isn't an official visit.'

'Then what is it?'

'I could explain better inside . . . if it's convenient. I can always come back.'

'No . . . All right.' He stepped aside, indicating the door on the far side of the kitchen. 'Through there.' He kicked off his rubber boots before following her.

Sheaffer identified locations she had seen in photographs as she walked ahead of him. Mrs Godwin sprawled across the doorway leading out to the yard, Thomas in here, next to the cooker, Cheryl Hood on the Persian rug by the sofa. She avoided it when Godwin invited her to sit down. She had taken care over her appearance: casual russet-coloured trousers, cream blouse, flat shoes, long hair tied in a pony tail. A visitor who presented no threat, not someone interfering, inexcusably reviving memories. But that was what she wanted to do. This was the first direct approach she had decided to make; she could persuade herself it was no more than letting the Godwins know of her existence, but the agenda was to probe, to test some of her thoughts.

'What's this about?' Godwin's voice carried a pessimistic trace of hope. 'Has something happened?'

Sheaffer was prepared to argue later that she had been given no orders not to tell him anything. 'Yes, but we don't know how significant it is. Somebody's sold a sword that matches the German one your father owned. In Bristol. We're trying to trace them.'

'Why haven't I been told about this . . . or is that why you're here?'

'Not really, but I thought you should know. If we do find whoever sold it, I'm sure you'll be officially informed.'

'Then why have you come?' Puzzled resentment was starting to show. 'I've not met you before, have I?'

'No. I've only been with CID a few months.'

'So why've they sent you?'

'I think you know Inspector Haggard?' She waited for the nod. 'I've just moved to Finch, and he thinks I might be in a useful position to hear things.'

'Like what?' Godwin had slumped back in his chair. He was wearing two pairs of socks, the inner one showing through a hole in the outer on his left foot.

'I don't know, but Mr Haggard briefed me on the inquiry.'

'The inquiry.' He gave a very small, bitter laugh. 'Of course. The one that's still marked unsolved after six years.'

'Mr Godwin, I understand this is very painful for you, but—'

'Do you?' The interruption accused. 'I mean really understand. How old are you?'

'I don't think that . . . Twenty-eight.'

'Married?'

'No.'

'Ever been? Do you have children?'

'No.'

'But you still understand?' The word was cynically emphasized. 'No. I don't think you do.'

Sheaffer controlled her reaction, telling herself he was allowed to be patronizing. 'I hope you know what I mean, Mr Godwin. And you also know that the police have done everything possible and—'

'Yes, yes, yes. I've heard it all before. It will never be closed, you'll get them eventually. I must never think you've given up. What is this, Miss . . . Sheaffer, was it? Some new customer relations policy? Show them they get value for money from their taxes.'

'No, sir.' Sheaffer had anticipated anger, but it was coming sooner than she had expected. 'We're just doing everything we can. I'm not promising anything, but—'

'Then don't waste my time! I only want to see the police in this house when you come to tell me you've found those bastards. How the hell you do it I'm not interested in. Right?'

'Trevor, what on earth's going on?'

Sheaffer turned to where Janet Godwin had appeared from the hall.

'Ask her! She's going to miraculously solve it.' Godwin stood up angrily and walked out of the room. The two women remained silent as they heard him cross the wooden floor of the kitchen and leave the house.

'Police?'

'Yes. I was trying to explain that—'

'You chose a bad time.' Janet Godwin wiped her hands on her apron. Working hands hardened by washing, husbandry of the garden, attendance to poultry and horses. Her face was stone pale, what must once have been pretty scarred by endurance and sorrow; tendrils of silver were threaded through the copper-brown bell of hair. Sheaffer instinctively knew she held the strength at Tannerslade. 'It goes away, then comes back without warning. The other day I found him in the hall, just staring into space and . . . Would you like a cup of tea?'

'Thank you. If it's not any trouble.'

'Nothing's trouble when you own a farm. Come into the kitchen . . . I'm sorry, I don't know your name.'

'Christine Sheaffer. I'm a detective constable.'

She nodded an acknowledgement and Sheaffer followed her.

'I don't know why, but it's somehow easier talking in here.' Contents already partially heated, the kettle started to wheeze almost the moment she switched it on. 'Move those carrots off the chair. Now, what's this about?'

She made the tea as she listened, and passed a mug to Sheaffer before sitting opposite her across the long scrubbed pine table. Through the window behind her the afternoon was overcast, but the shell of cloud would withhold rain that the parched verges and crops needed.

'It doesn't sound very official,' she commented.

'It's not . . . but it might produce something.'

Hands clasped around the warmth of her mug, Janet Godwin smiled sadly. 'A lot of things might have produced something, Miss Sheaffer. But they never have, so finally you stop hoping. Why should you do any better?'

'Please call me Christine . . . I don't know that I will.'

'But you want to, don't you?' Janet looked at her closely. 'Would they promote you if you did?'

'It's not like that.'

'Isn't it?' She held her hand up. 'I'm sorry. It's just that . . . well, cynicism is as good a protection as any. Trevor'll probably feel guilty about how he behaved later. I'll talk to him.'

'There's no need . . . May I ask you something?'

'If you wish.'

'I . . . this isn't my business, but why did you stay here?'

'I married into a tradition.' The reply was simple. 'Our son will inherit it.'

'But would *you* have come to live here if it had been your choice?'

She shook her head. 'And I'd leave tomorrow if I could persuade Trevor. But I know I can't. Why do you want to know?'

Sheaffer looked down at her cup. 'I just find it difficult to understand how he could stay here.'

Janet Godwin leant forward, forcing Sheaffer to raise her eyes. 'You think he had something to do with it, don't you?'

'No! I just . . . I didn't mean . . .' She had.

'It's all right, you're not the first. Some of your colleagues obviously thought that, and there are evil tongues in Finch who'll say it to you in an "Of course, I'd never believe such a thing" sort of way. It doesn't offend me – unlike my husband, I'm long past being hurt by anything to do with this – but don't waste your time on it. There's no need to apologize.'

Sheaffer looked at her. 'You keep him going, don't you?'

'Yes. For better and for much worse than anyone can ever imagine. What else can I tell you?'

'Did you suspect anyone?'

'No.' Janet Godwin took the corner of her apron and wiped away a mark on the table top. 'It was impossible to imagine why anyone would have done it. Nobody had a reason to hurt any of them, and if they'd just been burglars, why kill them all, even little Mandy and Thomas? My father-in-law was a brave man, but he would never have risked the lives of his family by resisting men with guns.'

She finished her tea. 'Is that Welsh sergeant still with you? Hughes, was it?'

'No. Harry Pugh.'

'That was it . . . Does he still suspect David?'

'Cheryl's husband? He had an alibi.'

'That didn't seem to make any difference to him. He kept asking about the marriage break-up, if they'd had rows, if he'd ever hit her.'

'Had he?'

'Never.' The stressed denial was reinforced in her eyes. 'The marriage had just died, the way they sometimes do. But everybody was desperate for someone to be punished. The village, the police, the newspapers – and us, of course. Poor David was caught up in that, even while he was burying his own children. That was dreadfully cruel.'

'Do you ever see him?'

'Not often now; he moved to Scotland. But we still write to each other.'

'What's he doing?'

'Feeling guilty about every day he lives. He said that in one of his letters.' A coarsened knuckle wiped the corner of one eye. 'You're scratching a lot of surfaces, Christine.'

'I'm sorry.'

'It's all right. It happens all the time. Anyway, I don't think I've helped you very much.'

'I didn't expect . . . I just wanted you to know I was here.' Sheaffer sensed she should leave. Contact had been made. 'I'm sorry I upset your husband.'

'He'll be all right later . . . Whereabouts in Finch are you living?'

'The Street. It's called Tradewinds for some reason.'

'I know it. A retired Royal Navy captain lived there. What was his name? It doesn't matter.' She stood up. 'We'll probably run into each other in the shops . . . You'll let us know, won't you? If anything happens, particularly with this Bristol thing.'

'Of course.' Sheaffer followed her to the kitchen door. 'Can I ask you to keep this confidential? Obviously people are going to discover what my job is eventually, but I'd rather they didn't know what I've told you. About being asked to listen out for anything.'

'If anyone asks, I won't even tell them you're with the police . . . but they'll find out. Believe me.'

Sheaffer looked towards the track leading from the road. 'I wonder if anyone saw them when they drove up? From the house.'

'Mandy could have done. Her body was in the yard, so she may have been out playing. But there was no reason why it should have alarmed her. Just another visitor.'

'Someone she knew?'

'Possibly. Perhaps even someone she went to welcome.' Janet Godwin sniffed slightly. 'May I ask you something in return? If the police do find whoever did it, would it be possible for me to talk to them?'

Sheaffer looked uncertain. 'It could be difficult. But why?'

'You don't often get the chance to meet someone who destroyed almost everything you love.'

Chapter Thirteen

Joyce reflected that a scarlet MGF did not arrive, it made an entrance. The drive had been exhilarating, sitting close to him in the cabin as the car swept through the countryside; it made her feel young again, the effortless power of the engine a snarling echo of all the energy she had once possessed. And as she stepped out in the pub car-park, skirt riding up her thighs, face flushed, she noticed a woman walking past look at her, part surprised, part envious. She felt an instant desire to flaunt; look what I've got. She knew it was juvenile, but there was foolishness in her. She ran her fingers through her windblown hair and grasped Jowett's hand as he joined her, laughing as they walked towards the restaurant entrance.

'I've just shocked her rigid.'

'Who?'

'That woman behind us . . . Don't look. Put your arm around my waist . . . That's it. I bet she's forty shades of green.'

'Why should she be?'

'Don't be such an innocent. It's because I'm having a second chance. She'd like to have a lover.' She pulled his head towards her and kissed him. 'God, you make me so happy.'

Jowett felt a vivid surge of what she meant, his torment fleetingly swept away. It was as though everything that was crushing him had been briefly lifted. She was happy, and it might not be impossible to hope that . . . Then it passed as quickly as it had come, escape abruptly cut off. The day had created it; her suggestion that they go out together, miles from Finch where they would not be recognized. They had driven

146

south, to where the land flattened into Essex water meadows and exposed wide skies.

She was capricious, teasing, savouring freedom as though she wanted to grasp every essence of it. He had never been with a woman in such a mood. Girlfriends of years before had squandered such times because they were plentiful; Joyce was like a child with a precious treasure of bright pennies. So little time ago, when they had first met, she had been no more than the businesslike owner of the cottage, polite but formally distant; then she had eagerly given him her body – and was now an enraptured lover. How had it happened? He had not encouraged it – Finch was a place for remorse, not love – but he had not resisted. And amid the bewildered pleasure lay the fear that he would hurt again.

They ordered mussels with French bread, and two huge bowls arrived piled high with grey-blue shells.

'I used to pick these off the rocks in Devon when I was little.' She pulled open a shell and plucked out the cream and brown flesh. 'What's the collective term for mussels? Like a pride of lions.'

'I don't know . . . but I know what it is for apes. An astuteness.'

'You're joking!'

'No, I'm not. I read it somewhere.'

'How bizarre. Let's make some up.' She thought for a moment. 'An envy of bridesmaids. Your turn.'

'OK . . . er . . . a mendacity of politicians.'

'A frustration of virgins.'

'An ethic of journalists.'

'Very ironic.' She laughed. 'Just a minute . . . a dribble of babies.'

'A resting of actors . . . an entrance of doormen . . . or an advance of publishers.'

'Stop it! I give up! You're too clever.' She reached one hand across the table and locked her fingers between his. 'How about an amazement of lovers?'

He stared at her. Or the amazement of such easy laughter, of a mind freed from guilt and permitted to play again, the sense of having found a way back to all that had been lost, the disorienting gratitude. And the agony of her trust, of never being able to be honest. Of knowing there was no way to avoid pain.

The empty bar of the Shoulder of Mutton was gloomy. Coins stuck on with beer bronzed the timber surround of the fireplace, and snapshots of drinkers and pub partygoers formed a patchwork of colour on one wall. Next to a sepia photograph of a Victorian landlord beside a stagecoach, a calendar advertising Finch's one garage still showed Miss April, naked and pouting, amid cherry blossom. Sheaffer hit the button bell on the counter; aching all over, she wanted a drink and something to eat. Her hair felt gritty as she ran a hand through it; the headscarf had been inadequate protection against plaster dust.

'Wondered where you'd got to.' Appearing through the door from the kitchen, Dave Truman resembled a figure coloured by a child, cloud of white hair, apple-red face, yellow waistcoat checked with orange stripes over a green shirt. He was holding a mug of what looked like deep brown paint. 'Not much food left.'

'A beef and salad sandwich'll be fine . . . and a pint of shandy with three pounds of ice in it.' She stretched, rubbing one shoulder. 'He must have stuck that bloody paper on with Superglue.'

Truman gushed beer into a glass. 'I heard Dougie Thomson offering to come over and give you a hand yesterday.'

'He wasn't just interested in stripping walls. He was chatting me up the first day I came in here.'

'If he knew what your job was, he'd run a mile.' Truman topped the glass with lemonade and put it in front of her. 'If you want an easy collar, you could pick him up for poaching any time you want – but you didn't hear that from me.'

'I'm not interested . . . thanks.' She swallowed gratefully. 'I met Janet Godwin in the shop this morning.'

'How was she?'

'For her, she looked very well. She's invited me to go with them to the pageant on Saturday. Says it'll be a chance for me to get to know people.'

'Everyone'll be there. I'll be running the beer tent again.' Truman finished whatever liquid the mug contained. 'Just don't start suspecting everybody you meet.'

She pulled a face at him. 'All right. You spelt it out the first time we talked. You're positive they weren't from here.'

'If I owned one, I'd bet the farm on it. This village would have found them long ago.'

'So why did Peter Haggard and Harry Pugh brief me?'

'Perhaps they don't agree with me. Don't forget I was in traffic, not CID. My only contribution to Tannerslade was at one of the road blocks we set up. Waste of time, but the Chief wanted people to see we were doing everything possible. All I did was catch a joker with a van-load of stolen video recorders.'

'So you think I'm wasting my time as well? Or is someone waiting for me to step out of line so they can hang me and leave me to spin in the wind?'

'Not Peter Haggard. He doesn't think like that.'

'What about Harry? He thinks a woman's place is in bed and she should only be allowed up to get the coal in.'

Truman laughed. 'So young and so cynical.'

'It's protective covering.'

'I know what you mean – my daughter taught me. But I don't think you're being set up. Peter and Harry know enough to play their luck. There was a case a few years ago which was cracked by a beat copper, because he stopped off to buy fish and chips. The murderer was in the shop and panicked when he saw the uniform. It isn't all Sherlock Holmes and forensic, Chris. Hang on, I'll organize that sandwich.'

Jowett ran his fingers over the sharp facets of the lead crystal tumbler as though they were diamonds; she had bought it for him in the shop at the National Trust house they had visited. It was a long time since anyone had given him a present. His sister sent token money at birthdays and Christmas, and there was nobody else who would even think of it. He had protested at the cost, but she had ignored him. In return, she had asked him to buy her a book of Elizabethan romantic sonnets and had read them aloud as they had driven back to Suffolk, stopping when she spotted a ruined priory and they had made love on the grass in the afternoon sun. He could not remember such contentment – even before the murders, and there had been a few moments during the day when he had managed to forget them.

But the aftermath was hard and cold as the glass.

'You've put on weight!' Four pins gripped in her teeth, Sarah Merriman complained as though this was yet another disaster deliberately designed to ruin the pageant.

'It's fine,' Joyce assured her.

'Only as long as you don't breathe. It was perfect when we tried it last week. Let me see.' She knelt down and tugged at the waist of the dress. 'Good God, woman! You're not pregnant are you?'

'I hope not.' Not so soon, even with no thought of precautions.

'Well, I haven't time to let it out. I've got to finish six more dresses tonight.'

'I'll deal with it. I used to be quite good at dressmaking.'

'Why didn't you tell me that before? You could have done it yourself.'

'I offered, but you said no.'

'When did I say no?'

'Weeks ago. When I agreed to play Lady Marion.'

'Rubbish! I don't do it all on my own for the fun of it.'

'Yes, you do, Sarah, and we all love you for it.' She raised the little woman to her feet and kissed her. 'Now, go home and deal with everything else you have to do. I'll take care of the dress.'

She was reluctant to let go. 'I suppose I could . . . Let me just check your waist again.'

'No! If I've put on weight it's my fault, so I'll sort it. No arguments.'

Carrying her carpet bag of fabric, pins, needles, endless cottons, tape measure, pinking shears – and, according to village legend, a tailor's dummy and full-size sewing machine – she allowed herself to be ushered out.

'I can come back first thing in the morning. Just call me.'

Joyce laughed as she closed the door behind her, then felt her waist experimentally. Sarah had got her measurements wrong again. It didn't matter. She would not have to wear the dress for long – and her mind would be on other things.

Chapter Fourteen

Darkness and terror lay in the story of the Pegman, but it had been purified; even his name had been changed to sound less threatening, more romantic. The reality lay in ancient records that spoke grimly of the Pigman, a solitary swinekeeper who had tempted children to his hovel in the woods to show them secret and unspoken magic, until three mothers had stolen out of the village one night and killed him in vengeance. But in the legend, wickedness became mischief and abuse was turned into goblin games until the fair Lady Marion, daughter of the lord of the manor, had put a charm on him and he had become a pig himself to be roasted in high style; revenge became celebration as he was eaten. Now each year a noisy pageant of children paraded through Finch to the meadow where the Pegman awaited them in flying fronds of ribbon, and there was a wild chase until the Lady Marion cried out her spell and dangers were banished from the shadows in the trees.

Commotion and people filled The Street, spectators applauding from the pavement or waving from upper windows as floats went by; flatbed lorries transformed into forest and castle, spaceship and pirate island with coloured crêpe, tissue and ribbons. At the front a shining brass band played and a shrill Pied Piper led more than eighty children from Finch and the villages around, all dressed as elves, soldiers, rabbits and cats, figures out of fairy tale and pantomime, Batman and Star Wars and this year's favourite Disney characters. Harlequin girls cartwheeled; a clown pulled his red-ball nose from his face and emerald smoke blew from his hat as it snapped back; men in stetsons split the air with starting pistols; a fat Mother Hubbard wobbled with laughter as she ran from a pursuing, flapping penguin; coins tinkled into plastic buckets and the crowd gasped, startled and delighted, as a maroon tore into the sky and exploded against the sun.

Following the children, as though making sure none should be lost, rode Lady Marion in her Norman-windowed plyboard court, attended by maids and escorted by Boy Scouts, cardboard-costumed and wooden-sworded into a company of knights, silver-painted and bannered by St George. Her white muslin skirt swirling, she turned to either side, hand waving as though casting spells of goodwill, chiffon streamers floating from the high point of her conical hat. As the float reached the crossroads, she stopped for a moment; Jowett was behind the crowds on the corner opposite the church, partly shaded by trees, alone, looking straight at her. Her arm arched in a wave only for him and she shook her head as though something unbelievable was happening; private magic amid tinsel fantasy. For the past ten days he had been the only thing that mattered for her.

'God bless you, Lady Marion!'

She turned as a woman called from the other side of the road, caught up in the excitement, in the make-believe world. Evelyn Kenin, the postmistress, whose daughter was pregnant again by her alcoholic live-in boyfriend, was escaping permanent disappointment and a sense of failure in a carnival of happy children. Joyce threw a rose to her and the procession moved on.

At the gate a huge hand on a pole was raised in greeting, and stalls, striped tents, Victorian wooden swingboats and a bulbous scarlet and yellow castle in which to bounce and tumble, ringed the meadow. Beer was tapped from barrels and beneath a copper beech a pig slowly revolved on a spit, skin lacquered with ladles of apple juice, flesh spitting and dripping fat. Arrows flew at ringed butts and ponies gave rides; pennies were being rolled; a roaring man in the stocks was being splashed by water-soaked sponges, bells tinkled on the legs of Morris Men. Joyce leant down to take the hands of two of her knights and stepped from her float, watched by a wide-eyed boy, thumb in his mouth, too young to disbelieve.

'This bodice is bloody hot!' she complained to Fay, who had walked in among the crowd following her.

'You can hardly go topless, darling. Marion's meant to be a virgin. Stay here; I'll get you a drink.'

Joyce looked back at the people thronging through the gate into the meadow. Nobody was alone; husbands and wives, groups of teenagers, grandparents, lovers . . . but Jowett was. She instantly took in everything about him she could see – sleek hair, the shirt she had taken off him the first time, black jeans, bare feet in black leather sandals. He was walking towards her and she felt an urge to wave again, but stopped herself in case someone noticed.

'Hello. Did I look completely ridiculous?'

He shook his head. 'You looked great. It was fun.'

She stepped closer, speaking low and secretly, lustful and urgent. 'The Lady Marion wishes you to attend her in her bedchamber, My Lord. And if you dare to refuse, she will order one of her knights to cut off your head.'

He seemed embarrassed. 'I thought your husband was home at the weekend.'

'I told you, he's going back to town tomorrow evening. And I want it to be in my bed this time. There's no problem, you can . . .' Her eyes flickered past him. 'Bless you; that looks magic.'

Fay was behind Jowett, holding two plastic glasses of iced mineral water.

'You remember Randall, don't you?' Joyce said.

'Of course.' Fay handed Joyce her glass. 'Has living in Finch driven you mad yet?'

'No. I'm enjoying it.'

'And how's the book? You did say you were writing one, didn't you?'

'Yes . . . It's OK.'

'Is this a research trip?' Fay gestured at people passing them.

'Are we all going to end up as characters? If we are, I demand to be the heroine.'

'It's not that sort of book . . . Where can I get one of those?'

'Beer tent. If you're quick, you'll beat the crush.'

There was no logic in Joyce's sudden desire to let Fay know about Jowett as he left them, but a need to share it with her, to invite envy. Her voice dropped and she stepped closer.

'For God's sake don't scream in disbelief, but there's something I want to tell you.'

'You're screwing him?' Fay blandly sipped her drink.

Denied her drama, Joyce was dismayed. 'Christ, is it that obvious?'

'No, or I'd have seen it sooner. But you'd better learn to control yourself in public, darling. When I came back you were looking as if you wanted to eat him. How long?'

'Obviously not very.' Joyce sounded rueful. 'It's happened indecently quickly.'

'Well, you had to work quickly. He won't be here for long.'

'You're not shocked?'

'Hell's teeth, no. I've been waiting for something like this for a long time. You'll have a summer to remember when you're old. If I were married to Ralph, I'd have done it years ago. Which of you started it?'

Joyce sighed. 'Me . . . and I've never been here before. Now I can't bloody think straight.'

Fay kissed her cheek. 'I like your taste. I said he was dishy, and you deserve it, so enjoy. What do you know about him?'

'Very little. He hardly talks about himself. He works in a bank, his parents are both dead, he's got a flat in the Barbican, went to Cambridge, speaks good French. That's about it.'

'Girlfriends?'

'There must have been, but that's never mentioned.'

Fay shrugged. 'Then gather ye rosebuds . . . How long before he leaves?'

'Another two weeks . . . but I don't want him to.'

Fay frowned. 'You do realize it's going to run its course,

don't you? I mean, he's definitely tall, dark and have some, but don't start dreaming. How old is he?'

'Twenty-seven.' Joyce looked uncomfortable. 'It terrifies me that I could just about be his mother.'

'Only if you'd started awfully young.' Fay squeezed her hand. 'Just keep your head . . . He's coming back.'

Joyce hid her face in her glass, telling herself to keep control, as four small knights appeared to escort her.

'I'm on parade,' she told Jowett, then turned to Fay. 'Look, Randall doesn't know anyone. Can you stay with him for a while?'

'Of course. Oliver's around somewhere. We'll take care of him.'

Jowett took Joyce's glass as she left them, back in character, smiling, bowing graciously, accepting a posy from a child as she walked among the crowds.

'What's this chase thing?' Jowett asked.

'You'll see.' Fay glanced at her watch. 'It's in about half an hour. Let's find my husband.'

The meadow was now filled with noise: the wheezing music of a steam organ; the cries of children; the clanging bell of a town crier calling attractions. Jowett felt isolated, unrecognized evil dressed like any other man . . . and with a woman in the meadow who desired him. Coming back to Finch had brought more confusion and new guilt forged out of betrayal and lies. He found Oliver's attentions difficult, his courteous questions like an oblique interrogation in which he might fatally reveal something. Fay he couldn't understand; her smiles were too warm for a stranger. She seemed determined to make him part of a place in which he did not belong . . .

'Trevor! Janet! How lovely to see you.' She embraced the woman and held her hand out to the man in simultaneous greeting.

Jowett felt an inexplicable tension streak through him, as though he should recognize these people.

'This is Randall, who's staying at Joyce's cottage, and we're looking after him in case he gets lost.' Fay turned to Jowett.

'Trevor and Janet Godwin . . . and Tim and Matt.' She grimaced as the boys joined them. 'Will you two ever stop growing?'

The name brought back the face, last seen years ago on television, much younger than his father's, but formed from the same mould. All four were looking at him enquiringly as Trevor held out his hand.

'Hello. Nice to meet you.'

Unable to speak, Jowett touched the flesh of flesh he had watched die, unaware, greeting him.

'And this is . . . I'm sorry, I don't think we've met.'

'Oh, this is Chris.' Janet Godwin was apologetic. 'Chris Sheaffer. She's just moved into Captain Woodville's old house on The Street.'

'I thought Tradewinds was falling down,' Fay said. 'Or do I mean sinking?'

'That's why I got it cheap,' Sheaffer replied. 'I'm spending my holidays fixing it up.'

'You should apply for a grant or something. I don't know if—' Fay broke off and Jowett flinched as the strident blast of a hunting horn ripped through the air. 'It's the chase! Come on.'

Mind in torment, Jowett was taken with them all to join the circle of spectators gathered round the rim of the meadow's bowl. At its deepest point stood what looked like a crude square tent, its sides painted to resemble blackened wattle and daub, a dark, menacing place in the cup of bright green. A ragged arc of children had formed in front of it, with the town crier leading them. He rang his bell and soprano voices rose in chorus.

'Who lives in this house?'

They all took one step of fearful excitement forwards, and the chant was repeated, louder.

'Who lives in this house?'

A second pace and again the shouted question, now shot through with gleeful terror.

'Who lives in this house?'

Long familiar with the ritual, the chattering crowd had gone quiet and the third shout was followed by expectant silence. Then one side of the tent burst open and a huge figure appeared, swine-headed and swathed in flapping folds, arms raised as it bellowed the reply.

'THE PEGMAN!'

With shrieks and squeals the children scattered as the Pegman began his lumbering, frantic pursuit, stumbling as he nearly caught a victim, then turning with a roar to pursue another, snarling at cardboard knights who challenged like darting hornets. The crowd booed as he knocked one down, then cheered as another thrust a toy sword into him. Everyone had become part of the chase that would end in white magic.

'I've seen you somewhere, haven't I?'

Jowett stared at Tim Godwin's question, a voice from reality. 'No. I've never been here before.'

'I've still seen you.' The repetition was impatient, as though irritated at being contradicted. 'And it was round here . . . Hang on! Have you got an MGF? Bright red one.'

'Yes.'

'That's it. You were driving through the village. Christ, you lucky bastard. What does it do? You know, how fast?'

'Top speed's a hundred and thirty. I've never done it though.'

'Shit, I would have.' He took hold of Jowett's arm. 'We can do it now.'

'What do you mean?'

'There's a couple of straight stretches of road near here. Come on. Anything's better than this.'

Around them the crowd erupted in cheers as the Lady Marion appeared and began to cast her spell. The Pegman danced and protested in fear, then fell and lay on his back with his arms and legs in the air. Jowett found he was unable to resist Tim pulling him away.

'Nobody'll miss us.' It was more command than assurance.

Outside the field Finch felt deserted, empty and detached from the meadow and its activity. The noise faded as they walked back to the church and turned towards the cottage.

'It's a family thing going to this Pegman bollocks. My grandfather organized it for years and we're still expected to be there.'

Jowett didn't look at him. 'I didn't know that.'

'You would if you came from Finch. Everyone knows us . . . Haven't you ever heard about the murders?'

'No . . . not really. But there was a plaque in the church and . . . someone told me . . . I'm sorry.'

'You can't do anything about it . . . Hey, look at that.' He walked ahead as they reached the cottage. The car's hood was down and he reached inside to feel the six-spoked steering wheel. 'This is seriously cool. How much was it? Twenty grand?'

'Just under eighteen.'

'Jesus, I've got to have one of these . . . Can I drive it?'

'It's only insured for me.'

'Balls . . . OK, I wouldn't risk it if it was mine. Come on.' He climbed in the passenger side. 'Turn right out of here then left at the T-junction. There's more than a mile of straight after that.'

The engine snarled awake, then hummed as Jowett reversed out of the cottage entrance. He was conscious of Godwin's bulk filling the seat behind him, legs too long for the foot well, fingers covetously stroking the paintwork of the door. There was a sense that what was happening belonged in a fantasy as dark and unbelievable as the Pegman's story. But this was what he'd wanted; to face those he had hurt and to find out if it would help him. He turned at the junction, into where the road ran arrow-straight ahead.

'Go for it,' Godwin urged, and was thrown back into his seat as Jowett dropped a gear and accelerated. 'Yeah! This is incredible!'

The needle arced past one hundred as Jowett moved up to fifth and throttled again, sun-heated air like a blast from a furnace. Above the engine's scream, Godwin was shouting the speed.

'Hundred and ten . . . fifteen . . . twenty . . . twenty-six . . . go on! Why the hell are you . . . Shit.' The needle dropped back as the road ahead curved and Jowett braked. 'Turn round and really push it this time.'

They topped one hundred and thirty on the second run, but Godwin insisted on doing it twice more before they began to return.

'Jesus, that was incredible.' He turned to Jowett, connected by a shared experience. 'What are you doing in a shithole like Finch?'

'No reason . . . It was just somewhere quiet. Away from London.'

'Too bloody quiet . . . Hey, what are you doing tonight?'

'There's the pig roast.'

'Christ, I'd forgotten that. I'll have to put in an appearance . . . but we could leave early. There's a great pub in Ash Sounder. Real ale and you should see the tits on the barmaid. With a car like this we could pull anything we wanted . . . and we could take them back to your cottage. How about it? Yeah?'

'I can't.'

'Why not?' Godwin looked uncomprehending. 'You're not bent, are you? You're wasting your time with me if you are.'

'No, I just don't . . . I've got things to do afterwards . . . work.'

'On a Saturday night? You're very sad. You can't mean it.'

'It's important . . . The office sent me some papers.'

'Guys like you are dead by the time they're thirty. OK, that's your problem. Any chance of another run out sometime? Or have you got a schedule?' The question was flecked with sarcasm.

'No, I've just got to get this thing cleared for the morning.'

'Good. Tell you what, do me a favour. Come up to the farm next week. Tuesday afternoon, OK? I want my old man to see this. I'm trying to talk him into buying me one. We live at a place called Tannerslade. Just follow the road, opposite the church, signposted to Dencom Water. You can't miss it. On your right. Yeah?'

'OK.' As he turned into the cottage drive Jowett knew he would need time to understand for himself why he had immediately agreed. 'Look, I've got to make a couple of phone calls. I'll follow you in a few minutes.'

Godwin grinned. 'You're a workaholic . . . but it's a great car. See you.'

Faintly, Jowett could hear the laughter and noise that filled Pegman meadow, the multitude of voices a muffled, chattering sea unseen beyond a headland. Less than half a mile away it inhabited another, somehow brighter, place, and the lonely silence in which he stood was alien to it. He was the outsider at the feast; heads turned sharply as he arrived, enquiring and guarded. We're all friends here . . . but who are you? Are you one we should welcome or fear?

He did not want to go back, but if he didn't she would wonder what had happened to him. And now he'd met them there, the son and the grandsons, made contact with one of them. That was why he'd come to Finch, to touch and discover what touching brought. Hiding had never been the answer.

Like virtually all of Finch that afternoon, the sunlit road up the hill from the cottage was empty as Jowett walked like a dark pilgrim towards the celebration place where the children had been saved.

Chapter Fifteen

'I don't know! One minute he was standing next to me, then he vanished.' Fay took hold of Joyce's hand as her eyes scanned the crowds in agitation. 'Calm down. He hasn't run off with anyone.'

'But where would he go? What's happened?'

'Stop it,' Fay told her sternly. 'Keep this up and you may as well ask Jerry to put out an announcement over the loudspeaker to let everyone know you've got a thing going with him. He'll be back.'

'Where from?'

'Jesus!' Fay's grip tightened. 'He's taken a couple of girls back to the cottage – does that make you feel better? What's the matter with you?'

'I . . .' Joyce's teeth pressed against her lower lip. 'All right. Let's go and . . . Oh, hello.'

A couple with a little girl had walked up to them, the child sucking her thumb for reassurance, gazing wide-eyed at the fairy-tale figure from the safety of her father's arms.

'Here you are,' the mother said. 'This is Lady Marion. You wanted to meet her.' The child buried her face in her father's shoulder. 'Don't be silly.'

'What's your name?' Joyce coaxed and smiled at the shaking averted head. 'I've seen you at church, haven't I? Did you boo the Pegman? When you're bigger, you can be in the chase. It's great fun.'

Small eyes peeped hesitantly, responding to her kindness but still unsure.

'Would you like to try my hat on?' Joyce's hair sprang loose as she lifted it off. 'Look, it's the same colour as your dress.'

'Go on, Melanie,' her father urged. Tiny fingers reached cautiously as the mother raised a camera . . .

He was back, standing only yards away. It was all right, he'd not . . . Joyce was unable to comprehend her reaction. The child was still waiting, but Joyce momentarily froze, nothing else existing except the fact that she could see Jowett. He was talking to a woman she didn't recognize. A young woman, gleaming waterfall of blond hair, tapered jeans, shirt knotted above her waist . . . sickeningly beautiful.

'T'ank you.' The offered gift withheld, the child seemed to feel the good word was needed to deserve it.

Joyce stared, as though aware of her for the first time, then recovered. 'That's right. Here, I'll put it on for you.' Why did her voice seem to be coming from somewhere else? 'There . . . You can keep it.'

'Oh, Melanie, aren't you lucky?' The mother stopped Joyce as she turned to go. 'Please let me take a photograph.'

'Of course.' Joyce stood by the child, holding the hat in place. 'Take care of it. It's magic.'

The camera clicked, and Fay's lips pursed as she saw how quickly Joyce left them and joined Jowett.

'Hello. Where've you been?'

'Out in the car. That chap . . . Mr Godwin's son . . . asked if I'd take him for a run.'

'Tim? You shouldn't have gone along with it. He gets every damned thing he wants as it is . . . I'm sorry. Who's your friend?' The ice maiden with bright blue eyes and a mouth like—

'Oh . . . er . . . Chris. She's just moved into Finch.'

'We'll probably meet sometime, then. Would you excuse us a moment?'

'Of course.' Sheaffer registered the hand that grasped Jowett's, leading him off like a child, then walked away.

'And when did you run into Miss Scandinavia?' Snapped out the moment there was no one near enough to hear, there was accusation and fear in Joyce's question.

163

'What? While you were doing the chase. I met her with Fay. Why?'

'Did she come with you and Tim in the car?'

'No. I met her again when I got back. We were just talking. What's the matter with you?'

'I was worried.'

'What about?'

'I thought . . . Christ, I don't know what I thought.' Joyce felt exposed, unable to understand her anger towards him. 'Have you got a cigarette?'

'I didn't know you smoked.'

'I don't very often. But I'd like one now.'

'I didn't bring any with me.'

'Terrific . . . all right, it doesn't matter.'

'Are you OK?'

'I'm fine . . . forget it. I'm just pissed off with all this nonsense and this dress is bloody uncomfortable.'

'Why don't you take it off?'

'Here?' It was an opening to restore something that her behaviour was damaging. 'Darling, we don't want to frighten the horses.'

'I didn't mean that.'

She had to force herself not to touch him. 'I know you didn't. Anyway, it's nearly over. I can go home and . . . I didn't mean to get mad at you, it was just . . . You are coming to the pig roast, aren't you? Fay and Oliver will be here again, so you'll have someone to talk to apart from me.'

'Yeah. I'll be there.'

'I'll see you this evening, then. Anyway, I'd better do a last circuit.'

Fay was looking over at them both as they separated; she'd been unable to hear anything they had said, but there had been an urgency, even hostility, in the way Joyce was speaking and the way she had stood. Jowett watched as Joyce passed through the remaining crowds, patting a dog, kissing some couple she knew, skirts held wide as she curtseyed to a group of people who applauded. Thoughtfully, Fay walked over to him. 'Have you enjoyed yourself?'

'What?' His attention was snapped away by Fay's question. 'Yes. I like old traditions. Thank you for . . . you know . . . showing me round. Joyce . . . Mrs Hetherington . . . says you and your husband will be here tonight.'

'Yes. It's primitive, but amusing.' Fay plucked a stray strand of grass from her shirt. 'Joyce tells me you're leaving in a couple of weeks. Do you think you'll come back?'

'I don't know.'

'We've certainly got plenty of peace and quiet for writing . . . Excuse me, my husband wants me. See you this evening.'

As she joined Oliver Fay caught a glimpse of Joyce, her long skirt raised as she walked up the slope towards the gate on the road near her house, almost as though she were running away.

Joyce dashed upstairs and into the bathroom, panting as she locked the door and leant her back against it as if to secure privacy. The panic about Jowett's absence had been senseless, her rebukes and questions about another woman irrational. He wasn't hers to own, but, greedy and demanding, she wanted to own him. No, something more intangible than owning. Have, take pleasure in possessing, feel wanted by, share pleasure with, be part of his life, laugh with . . . love.

'Christ.' She pushed herself away from the door and pulled down the zip at the back of her dress and let it fall so that welcoming cool air stroked her body. In the shower cubicle she held her head back as stinging water pelted her skin, cupping her hands to wash her face as steam misted about her. I'm forty-four and he's twenty-seven; I've adored what we've done, but he's going away in two weeks and that's it. I am too old – and supposed to be too intelligent – to start behaving like a besotted teenager. She stopped the shower and stepped out, towelling herself dry with a fierce impatience. Stupid, half-witted, thick, idiotic . . . Abruptly she sobbed, gripping the towel in frantic fingers as if to grasp something real. The thought of ending it was intolerable and allowing it to continue was terrifying.

★

Garden flares set up around the crackling pig were lit as twilight seeped into the heated evening; blossoming orange flames that spun curls of ghostly smoke and cast quivering shadows. Big-band swing beat out of loudspeakers, unheard over chatter and laughter. Children squealed with delight as they rolled down the incline of the darkening meadow and scrambled back to the top again. Ralph was with Joyce now, eating roast pork, rye bread and warm salad off plastic plates next to Fay and Oliver and Jowett on travelling rugs beneath the trees.

'Who supplied the pig?' Ralph asked as he chewed.

'Trevor,' Fay replied. 'The family always does.'

'Didn't know they kept pigs.'

'They don't. He buys it from someone.'

'Good business to be in at the moment, pigs. No BSE scares. Only eat beef now if it's Aberdeen Angus. Know it's safe. Decent of Trevor, though. He's a diamond, that man.'

His voice was slightly fuzzy; he'd started at the golf club, had insisted on a top-up before setting out and was now drinking beer. Joyce looked past him to Oliver, his pale face and thinning fair hair catching the flames, grey eyes observant and intelligent. He and Randall would get on so well . . . in fact they did already, discussing literature, comparing life at sixties Oxford and eighties Cambridge. Then Ralph interrupted, asking Oliver about advertising deals.

'We do discounts for the group and for bookings on five editions or more. Otherwise, it's what the rate card says.'

'Come on, the rate card's just the starting point. Even Murdoch's lot can be talked down.'

'We don't operate like that. Why are you interested, anyway?'

'Got a client who's thinking about using the provincials.'

'Then call my advertising people.'

Ralph grunted. 'We could always use local radio. You can't rip people off just because you've got a bloody press monopoly.'

'I don't rip anyone off, Ralph. I just run an efficient company.'

Joyce felt embarrassed; Oliver was a friend – to her, a good friend – but Ralph had a distasteful gift for turning any conversation into a display of boorish aggression. Oliver turned to Randall again, asking if he had read Pat Barker's Great War trilogy, deliberately cutting out Ralph whose taste only reached macho airport blockbusters. After a few moments Ralph stood up and walked away, greeting someone with boisterous enthusiasm as though his evening had been made by meeting them.

'Hello. May I join you?' Holding a plastic plate, wine glass and paper napkin, Sheaffer had appeared behind Oliver. 'I was looking for the Godwins, but they don't seem to be here.'

'They never come,' Fay said. 'Pull up a toadstool. Did you meet Joyce this afternoon?'

'Only briefly.' Sheaffer sat down as Jowett made room for her on the rug and smiled at Joyce. 'You were Lady Marion.'

'They'll rope you in for it one day,' Fay warned.

'Miss Merriman has already asked me.' Sheaffer smiled. 'She seemed very keen.'

'The pageant looms very large in her legend ... You'd be perfect though. Traditionally, she was a blonde.'

'I said I'd think about it.'

'She'll take that as a definite yes.'

'Do you live alone?' Joyce asked.

'Yes.' Sheaffer caught a trickle of grease on her lips with her napkin.

'Haven't you got a boyfriend to share it with?'

'Not at the moment.'

Fay tapped Joyce's ankle with her shoe. 'Help me get more drinks.'

Joyce began walking towards a trestle table covered in wine bottles, but Fay took her arm and led her to where they were alone outside the ring of flares.

'What is it?' Joyce asked.

'Partly, I wanted to stop you grilling that girl before you made a fool of yourself. And I want to talk about what's happening to you.'

'I don't know what you mean.'

'Yes you do, darling. You're in over your head with Randall.'

'Don't be ridiculous.'

167

'Don't say that and immediately turn away from me ... You're frightened that you're in love with him, aren't you?'

'No ... yes.' She looked straight at Fay. 'Help.'

'You want logic?'

'I don't think it'll work, but try me.'

'OK. You met him – what is it? – three weeks ago. He's dishy, polite, intelligent, sensitive and probably magic in the sack. But you told me this afternoon that you still know hardly anything about him and he's a hell of a lot younger ... Do you need diagrams?'

'I know all that. Grant me some intelligence.'

'Then show some.' Fay was impatient with concern. 'For God's sake, this could all be an act! He's writing his book when you wander in, take your clothes off and say pretty please. You're probably one of his characters by now. An attractive lonely woman in a lousy marriage gagging for him. It's cliché time in fantasy land.'

'It's not like that.'

'You mean you don't want it to be.' Fay shook her head in frustration. 'Please! There's nowhere for it to go.'

'I said logic wouldn't work.' Joyce sobbed slightly, then swallowed. 'You've got Oliver and Jonathan, and I'm in a sodding strait-jacket with Ralph and my mother!' She grasped Joyce's hands as they fell away from her. 'Look it's not the sex ... all right, that's part of it ... but it's because I misunderstood my needs. I thought I could find myself, have a life again by fighting back. What I didn't realize was that I really wanted someone to love me.'

'And does he love you?'

'He told me he does.'

'And you believed him?' Fay arched one eyebrow.

Joyce sighed. 'Not really. He said it the first time we made love ... but today I realized I love him. Too bloody much.' She gave a small grin. 'So what's logic got to do with it?'

'Oh dear.' Fay shook her head. 'All right. I'll be around when you land, but you may have to crash and burn.'

'Is it totally hopeless, then?'

'Think about why you're asking me that . . . Come on. Let's get those drinks before you become paranoid about him inviting that blonde back to the cottage for a nightcap.'

Sky purple was deepening through indigo to black, the plump pig a butchered carcass, the flarelights dwindling, occasional silhouetted figures slipping away, fading voices calling good-night. Oliver and Jowett were now discussing overseas investments. Fay sat, her skirt covering crossed legs, watching Jowett's face; Joyce sat facing away from them, gazing into the gloom, conscious that Sheaffer was still there, silent and listening.

'. . . but would you recommend it?'

'Not to make money. You'll be lucky to come out with four per cent.'

'I'm not worried about that. I like the things they invest in. I'll speak to my broker. Thank you.' Oliver looked at Joyce and his wife. 'You two are very quiet.'

'We're dumbstruck at the feet of such wisdom,' Fay said impishly, then turned to Sheaffer. 'What made you move to Finch?'

'I was brought up in a village. I like the quiet.'

'That's why Randall's here. It helps the creative process. He's writing a book.'

'Really?' Sheaffer looked at him. 'What's it about?'

It was the inevitable question; Jowett wished he'd never mentioned it, found another reason. At least he now had an answer prepared.

'It's difficult to explain. If it's ever published, you'll see what I mean.' Perversely it was true – and sufficient excuse to deflect.

'You must let me know when it comes out,' Oliver said. 'I'll want to buy a copy.'

'He'll expect you to sign it,' Fay added. 'Actually, we'd all like one, then we can show off if you win the Booker prize.' She finished her wine. 'Anyway, it's getting chilly. Take me to my carriage, I'm hideously bored.'

Jowett felt instantly depressed. At some point in the previous hours his mind had closed off the past and there had been soft undercurrents of contentment. The evening had seemed detached from reality, an enchanted pastoral scene in a play, a village

Arcady ... but it had only been men talking sport and cars, cracking jokes as they drank beer, women discussing their children and social lives, a teenager being sick in the bushes, a faint stench from the portable lavatories, greasy litter. No enchantment; just a night out in a field eating pig. And now it was over.

He stood up. 'It's been a great evening. Thanks.'

'You must come and have a drink with us while you're here,' Oliver said. 'We're the house next door but one to Joyce. I still think you're wrong about Forster, incidentally.'

'He'll talk books for ever if you let him,' Fay warned. Jowett smiled, uncertain how he should respond.

'I'll see you to the gate,' Joyce said. 'I might find Ralph.'

And really I don't want you leaving with this much younger woman who lives alone.

'I'm sorry I've hardly spoken to you, and we can't talk now,' Joyce found it difficult to wait until they were out of earshot. 'Here.' She pressed a folded square of paper into his hand, moving away immediately.

'What is it?'

'Directions for tomorrow night. Nobody will see you.'

He closed the note in his fingers. 'You're sure it's all right?'

'Of course it is. Rupert and Annabel are both away on school trips and Ralph always leaves for London by ... Christ, there he is. I'll have to go. Goodnight, darling.'

She turned towards where she had seen her husband and Jowett walked on alone, waiting until he was out of the field and past the church before reading the note by the light of a streetlamp.

Take the path at the back of the cottage and follow it round the field until you reach a holly hedge. The gate in that opens into our garden. Ralph usually leaves at six, but wait until seven, just in case. If there's a handkerchief on the ground just inside the gate, come back later. I'll have supper ready for you. I love you. Joyce.

PS Better burn this. Or am I getting neurotic?

*

'You're very thoughtful.' Oliver stepped to one side to let Fay pass as he opened the front door. 'What is it?'

She switched on the onyx table lamp. 'Top secret this. OK?'

'Of course.'

'Joyce is having an affair with Randall. She told me this afternoon.'

'Good God. He's—' Oliver stopped himself. 'No, that's irrelevant. But they hardly know each other.'

'They do in the biblical sense . . . and now she says she's in love with him. But she's a learner driver on this course.'

'So do you think she is? In love?'

'Love?' Fay was checking her hair in the hall mirror. 'I don't know. Certainly obsessed. What worries me is that she'll get badly hurt. What did you think of him?'

'I liked him. Bit reserved at first, but once he started talking he was very good company. It crossed my mind as to why he's here on his own.'

'Mmm.' Fay sounded dubious. 'Joyce's original theory – before she got involved – was that he was getting over something. Could have been a love affair; could have been someone dying.'

'Whichever way, he'd be vulnerable.'

'Yes . . . like Joyce. It's a gruesome twosome.'

'What does she know about him? I found him . . . evasive in some ways. He didn't want to talk about himself.'

'That's struck Joyce too, but . . . well, it's a pleasant change from Ralph.'

'Do you think he suspects?'

'Don't be silly, darling. Ralph's too bloody conceited – and he's got too much of a hold over her. But there's no reason he should ever know, so that's not the problem.' She sighed. 'Joyce probably needed an affair – and deserved one – but not like this. I should have found someone for her.'

Chapter Sixteen

Warm night breeze seeped through soft billows of net curtains at the open window as Joyce lay beside Jowett; her head supported on her bent arm, she was twirling locks of his hair into black twists with her free hand. They were both naked. He'd been concerned about her mother being in the house, but Joyce had assured him she would go straight to bed after watching television in her apartment and hear nothing. Even so, she had muffled her cries of ecstasy.

'Have you got a middle name?' She frowned in irritation as a curl refused to stay in place, licking her fingers and wetting it.

'I've got two. Howard Unwin. The Unwin's a family surname. You?'

'Davinia,' she murmured, concentrating. 'I keep very quiet about it. You're privileged . . . Damn! Your hair's impossible.'

'What are you doing?'

'Trying to turn you into a Greek god . . . Lie still. Are you Greek? Well, something like that. The first thing I thought when you arrived was that there might be Mediterranean in you somewhere.'

'My father's grandmother came from Florence.'

'So I was right . . . and I adore Florence.'

'You'd say that if she'd come from anywhere.'

'Not anywhere. I'd draw the line at Workington . . . There.' She sat up and examined him. 'Now, let me think. My mythology's rusty. Apollo?'

'He tried to rape Daphne.'

'Lucky Daphne.'

172

'But Gaea turned her into a bay tree to stop him.'

'Unlucky Daphne.' She rubbed the false curls away affectionately. 'I love it that you know things like that. Ralph could only
name a Greek if he played football or ran a restaurant in Soho
. . . Hell, I didn't want to mention him. Sorry.'

'It's all right.'

'I wish it was . . . I've got a challenge for you. Who said,
"Marriage is an unsuccessful attempt to make something permanent out of an incident"? Come on, my clever English
graduate.'

'I don't know. Wilde? Shaw?'

'Too obvious, and both wrong.'

'How about Saki? Mark Twain?' She looked gleeful at the
prospect of defeating him. 'Was it a woman? Liz Taylor?'

'It should have been, but no.' She laughed and pulled his ear.
'One more guess or there's a forfeit.'

'What is it?'

'I'll think of something.'

'Was it someone famous?'

'Relatively famous . . . Big clue there.'

'OK . . . erm . . . I can't think . . . Tolstoy.'

'No! I win! It was Albert Einstein. I told you relatively was a
clue. Right. Forfeit.' She thought for a moment. 'Go down to
the garden – exactly as you are – and pick me a rose.'

'But I've got nothing on.'

'So? It's not cold.'

'Somebody might see me.'

'Not in the back.' She rolled away from him. 'On your way.
Be careful of the thorns.'

'It's ridiculous.'

'It's fun.'

And I want fun, you idiot; I want you to let some light into
this. Come back with the rose between your teeth and make
love to me again – but without the bloody angst afterwards . . .
Christ, I wish you didn't make me feel you were the other half
of me.

'What colour?'

'There are yellow ones edged with pink on the bushes just beyond the pool. Solitaire. They're my favourite at the moment.'

'OK.' He swung his legs on to the floor. 'Won't be long.'

'I'll still be here.'

Jowett felt blankly elated as he went downstairs, but accusation came at him out of the darkness as he cautiously stepped into the garden. Their love play had let him momentarily escape guilt. But he had not come to Finch for affection, for night games with a willing woman. To enter a garden naked for amusement was a blasphemy, a desecration ... His sudden choked sob sounded loud and made him afraid. For a frantic moment he wanted nothing more than to escape. Trembling, he sat on a patio chair, the metal cold against his skin. He would have to go back to the bedroom, warm and dimly lit and ... tell her? No. He didn't have the courage. So he would have to find the rose, take it to her, slip deeper into the web of lies, continue to deceive.

He felt he was passing beyond confused lust towards feelings he could not remember knowing before. She was intelligent, attentive, giving; the relationship was taking on dimensions of – crossing the lawn past the pool, the definition eluded him – of friendship. A casual, too often meaningless, word, but suddenly valuable. Giles Lambert had been the last person he had used it towards.

The rose stem was tough, and he had to pinch fiercely between thumb and fingernail to sever it. As he turned back to the house he saw her framed by the curve of curtains at the bedroom window, watching him. He held up the flower and she waved, secret signals in the sleeping night.

'Here you are. One rose.'

'My hero.' Joyce was back in bed. 'You looked like some mythical wood creature out there. Thank you. I'll press it in a book and keep it.'

'You're a romantic.'

'I used to be. And I'm becoming one again. Come here.'

*

174

Half awakened by the cough of a car starting, Joyce sat up abruptly as she realized it was light.

'It's all right,' she assured Jowett as he stirred beside her. 'It's only five-thirty. My mother won't be up for another two hours.'

'I still ought to go. Someone might see me.'

'Worried about my reputation?' She grinned. 'You're right, though, but just a few more minutes. Just cosy together.'

They lay holding hands, both staring at the ceiling, listening to the soft start of day. Jowett felt exhausted and wanted to be alone to think. He twitched as Joyce sighed deeply.

'God, I wish you weren't going away . . . Can I come and see you in London?'

'Do you want to?'

'Do you want me to?' She felt a pang of dismay when he didn't agree immediately, then lay on top of him, breast held teasingly above his mouth. 'Will this help you to make up your mind?'

'Would you leave him?' Lips brushed her nipple as he spoke, then he looked concerned as she rolled off abruptly, sobbing as she lay with her back to him.

'That's cruel. You don't mean it.'

'Yes, I do.' He sat up and stroked her shoulder. 'But you've told me about your mother.'

'Oh, terrific!' Suddenly angry, she thrust his hand away. 'It's so damned easy to say then, isn't it? It's like tormenting an animal that's tied up. You know I can't leave him, so you're perfectly safe asking me if I can.'

She turned to him, face filled with pain and resentment. 'Be honest, darling. I've been a great holiday lay, haven't I? You'd probably have preferred someone younger, but there was no danger of any complications with me.'

'No. You mustn't think that.' He seemed unable to meet her eyes. 'There's a lot you don't know about me.'

'You've not told me very much. You've got a thing about older women?'

'No. Just about you.'

'Me? Why?' She sighed in bewilderment. 'I'm not special. I'm not the world's greatest intellect and God knows there are more beautiful women. One of us has to keep some perspective in all this.'

'You said you wanted to come and see me in London.'

'And you didn't reply when I asked if that was what you wanted.'

'I do want you to come.'

'Don't look away when you say it . . . Oh, hell!' She flopped back on the bed. 'It's hopeless, isn't it? Bed's just our escape. It's not reality.'

He sat up. 'I would like you to come . . . to London. I mean it.'

'Stop being so sweet. It hurts too much.' She shook her head. 'Come on. It really is time you left . . . but I'll come to the cottage this evening and we'll talk then. OK?'

She watched him dress; then she put on a floppy T-shirt that covered the top of her thighs. 'For decency's sake. I'll see you out. We're not in any danger of being spotted, unless the milkman arrives early.'

They crept downstairs and through the french doors on to the patio. Brilliant sun glittered off the dew, all colours were very pale and there was the shimmering, soundless stillness of things reawakening in limpid silver mist.

'What a morning!' Joyce spun round, bare feet leaving prints on night-damp stones. 'Lift me up as high as you can.'

'Why?'

'Because I want you to! I want to touch that sky. Don't ask me to bloody analyse it!'

He clasped his hands on the sides of her hips and she held her arms straight up as he raised her, hair cascading as she bent her head back as if worshipping. For a few moments they remained perfectly still, then she looked down at him.

'I love you, Mr Randall Jowett.' There, she had said it.

He eased his grip and she slid down, arms falling on to his shoulders, then kissing him as though she wanted to swallow him whole. It had all lasted less than a minute, but Joyce felt she had never been happier in her life.

'Off you go,' she whispered. 'I'll get through the day somehow.'

She watched as he walked down the garden, pausing to wave as he closed the gate and disappeared behind the hedge. She breathed deeply as one hand flicked away tears . . . then jumped as she heard a slight sound from behind her. Standing just inside the french doors, face rigid with disbelief and accusation, her mother was staring at her. Neither moved nor spoke before Grace Carstairs drew her dressing gown more tightly across her body, turned away and walked out of the room.

There were no rules for the first move. Occupying herself with polishing the silver, Joyce angrily prepared arguments. Simply carrying on with her day as though nothing had happened was tacit defiance, a warning sign to keep away. And if she did insist on talking . . . Frankly, Mummy, it's none of your business. If you hadn't got up at such a ridiculous hour and come downstairs – if we hadn't given you a home in this house – you'd know nothing about it. If this concerns anyone, it's me and Ralph. You've got your independence, leave me alone with mine. I'm an adult with my own children to look after, not your little girl. I don't need your self-righteousness, asking me what Daddy would have thought. That's irrelevant. Don't dare spoil this. She grimaced in irritation, trying to reach into the crevices of the claret jug's engraved handle. This is my goddamed life and—

'I'm going out for a while.' Her mother was in the kitchen doorway, walking stick in one hand, cotton gloves in the other. Joyce wondered if the hat was meant to be making a point. 'I need some fresh air.'

'OK.' Indifferent, Joyce returned to the polishing. 'I'm going out later myself.'

'I won't ask where.'

'It's only to Bury for shopping.' The jug was put aside, one of the pair of fluted Georgian candlesticks started on. 'Can I get you anything?'

'No, thank you.'

'Have a nice walk then.'

Drawing on one glove, Grace remained in the doorway. 'Perhaps we'll be able to talk later.'

Joyce shrugged. 'I don't see any need.'

'Well, I'm afraid that I do.' Inflamed by resistance, Grace's outrage was emerging out of controlled calm. 'I know that people have what are called open marriages these days, but . . .'

'It's not like that.'

'Then it must be what we used to call being unfaithful. When the cat's away.'

'It's not that either.'

'Then I don't know what to call it . . . Surely this can't be from me.'

'Spare me the spurious guilt, Mummy. You don't mean it. Just forget it, all right?'

'Forget it? Forget the fact that I saw my daughter with another man at six o'clock in the morning? Half naked and kissing him like a . . . I don't know what the word is now, but when I was young we'd have said a common trollop.'

'A common trollop?' Joyce laughed. 'Can't I be a lesser spotted trollop?'

'If that's going to be your attitude, there's obviously no point in discussing it.'

'No there isn't.' Joyce turned to face her. 'There's an awful lot you don't know about me, Mummy, and a lot you wouldn't believe if I told you. Now, enjoy your walk.'

Each glove was smoothed meticulously. 'There's one thing I must make absolutely clear. I expect you to tell Ralph.'

'That's my business.'

'But now you've made it mine. If you don't tell him, I will.'

However inevitable, the threat still triggered resentment and dismay. Joyce slammed down the candlestick.

'Mummy, will you please mind your own damned business! I'll deal with this. Just . . . leave it alone.'

The gloves were on like gauntlets. 'Joyce, you've accused me of not understanding, but you clearly don't understand me. Unless Ralph knows, I will now also be deceiving him. I'm not prepared to do that – any more than I would ever deceive you. I'm not insisting that you ring him immediately, but I expect you to talk to him at the weekend. After that, if either of you wants to discuss it with me, I'll be only too happy to help if I can. In the meantime, I want you to know that I'm . . .' For the first time, her voice stumbled. 'I'm very upset. I expected better of you. I'm going to St Matthews. You may not mean it when you pray, but I do.'

That stung. 'I'm sorry, Mummy, but—'

'I can't believe you're as sorry as I am.'

Joyce stared at her reflection in the shining metal as she heard the front door close and the sound of sensible shoes on gravel. She blinked and bit her lip, then began to polish again. A love that had begun forty-four years before, a love she had never questioned or doubted, was being scattered.

And convinced Ralph had been betrayed, her mother would tell him, because that was where her sympathies lay. Would she believe it if Joyce told her about Gabriella? Ralph would simply deny it – I can't understand, Grace; she's no more than one of my colleagues at the office; Joyce is being completely irrational – and how could she prove his behaviour? Her mother had only seen her.

And Randall was at the cottage, knowing nothing, waiting for her to arrive. It wasn't fair that he should be mixed up in this. She sighed and crossed the kitchen to the wall telephone.

'Fay? Hi. Me. I need to talk. Can I come over?'

'What's happened?'

'It involves the shit and the fan.'

'Oh . . . I'll have a drink waiting for you.'

Jowett felt disoriented as he drove up the track of Tannerslade Farm, as though the sequence of events that had brought him there – meeting the Godwins, agreeing to Tim's request to show his father the car – had never happened and it was impossible to understand how he could be going back. But it had been a way into the farmhouse again, another step through the maze of his emotions, like undergoing flagellation to exorcize sin. There were times when he wondered how much control he still had over parts of his mind.

'Hi! You came! Great.' Tim appeared at the kitchen door before he had turned off the engine. 'Hang on, I'll get Dad.'

Jowett heard him calling inside the house, then he reappeared. Trevor and Janet Godwin followed him, looking puzzled.

'Just look at that, Dad! That's what I want.'

Godwin turned to Jowett. 'Did my son ask you to come?'

'Yes, he—'

'Well, I'm afraid he's been wasting your time. We knew nothing about this until now. He doesn't seem to accept the fact that I have no intention of buying him one.'

'Shit!' Tim was disbelieving. 'That's it? You won't even get in it?'

'Don't use language like that in front of your mother! And don't try using other people to get your own way. I'm sorry Mr . . . Jowett, isn't it? This is a family matter and you shouldn't have let yourself be dragged into it. Excuse me, I've got a lot to do.'

Godwin walked across the yard and climbed on to a tractor, engine spluttering and bursting into noise as he swung it round and rumbled down the track to the road. His son glared after him, then walked back into the house without a word.

'Tim!' Janet Godwin sounded horrified. 'Oh, that was unforgivable!'

Jowett felt trapped. 'It's OK . . . Perhaps I shouldn't have come.'

'No, but . . .' Embarrassed before a stranger, she had a need to explain. 'I'm afraid our son is spoilt, Mr Jowett, but that was appalling. Please accept my apologies. On behalf of my husband as well. I can't . . . Will you come in for a moment? Would you like a cup of tea? Or something cold? Please.'

He suddenly saw how near she was to crying, pleading with

her eyes, holding her body as though coaxing him into the house. She wanted to make amends.

'Thank you.' Her smile of relief was painful. He followed her into the kitchen.

'Tim will be sulking in his room. I'll talk to him later. What would you like? Coke? Orange? Or dandelion and burdock? You've probably never heard of that. It's an old country drink—'

'Coke's fine. Thanks . . . Do you mind if I smoke?'

'Not at all. There's an ashtray just behind you.'

He was being made welcome in the house. There was a framed photograph on the Welsh dresser, a smiling elderly couple dressed as if going out to a formal dinner . . .

'Here you are.' Calmer now, she still wanted him to understand. 'It was kind of you to spare your time – you weren't to know what Tim's like – but Trevor can be . . . You see, something happened . . . a long time ago . . . I sound as if I'm making excuses for him, but—'

'You mean the murders.' Jowett heard his own voice from a long way off.

'Yes . . . You know about them?'

'Mrs Hetherington told me. I'm very sorry.'

'It's all right . . . and that makes it easier. Perhaps you can understand. It's still with him, and . . .' She tried to smile. 'I'm apologizing too much, aren't I?'

'You don't need to. It's OK.' Jowett sipped his drink. 'It can't be easy for any of you.'

'No. It's the anniversary next week as well. Always a bad time. I assume you read about it.'

'Yes, I . . . I must have done. I don't remember the details though.'

'It was Trevor's parents, his sister and her children. They just slaughtered them . . . I'm sorry, I shouldn't be talking about this.'

He looked down at his glass. 'How do you feel about them? Whoever did it?'

'What?' There was resignation in her thin smile. 'I expect that's the sort of question writers ask. Everybody brings their own agenda to this.'

'I didn't mean it that way.'

'I don't mind. It's more honest than the way some people ask. As if they're fascinated, but won't admit it.' She sighed. 'What do I feel? Not hate any more. I'm long past that. But we don't know who they were or why they chose this farm. They just came into our lives one day, out of nowhere, and destroyed them. It makes you fatalistic. I've never hurt anyone – or if I have, I didn't mean to – so what was it? A punishment? What for? Where was the God I was taught to believe in that afternoon?'

Her voice dropped as she spoke, almost as if she were talking to herself. From the hall, a clock chimed.

'Anyway.' She came back. 'That's why we don't behave very well sometimes. But it shouldn't be turned on other people. I'm sorry.'

Jowett didn't take his eyes off her. He wasn't hated.

Chapter Seventeen

Fay was the friend to run to in panic and dismay; over Riesling, cold chicken and Caesar salad, she became an audience as Joyce began to feel a wayward excitement. As she talked, her apprehension became defiance and a growing sense of resentment towards anyone who dared to criticize or reproach. Randall and everything he meant to her was the reality she wanted and deserved; nothing else was relevant because finally it concerned nobody else. Her mother was interfering, Ralph despicable, Rupert and Annabel welcome to all the independence they wanted as long as they recognized that she had rights as well. Finch, Suffolk, the entire world could keep out of it. She was prepared to throw away the life she had created and start over again – with him, because he was now the only person who mattered. There would be protests, condemnation laced with po-faced cant – and secret envy – but they would simply ignore it, perhaps even feel pity for the narrow, mean people who remained prisoners of their little minds as they broke free to make something new. And when all the petty wars were over, they would still have each other, laughing and crazily in love . . . then Joyce Jowett? Why not? She would wear—

'Well, it's certainly a watershed, but it needn't be a major disaster area, darling.' Fay slid Joyce's refilled glass across varnished pine. 'Just point out to Grace that Randall's leaving soon and you'll never see him again. I think she'd back off. The last thing she wants is you and Ralph splitting up.'

'You can't mean that.' Joyce stared at her in disbelief.

'Can't mean what? She's got a very comfortable home and if

183

this morning hadn't happened, nobody would have been the wiser, so . . .' She seemed suddenly to register the protest in Joyce's voice. 'Hold it right there. What are you thinking? You must see you've got nowhere to go together.'

'Haven't we?'

Fay stared as though Joyce were denying her own name. 'Of course you haven't. I know you told me you're in love with him, but for heaven's sake that's going to pass, and—'

'Have you been listening to me?' Joyce demanded. 'I mean have you *really* heard anything I've said?'

'Yes, but . . . Oh boy.' Fay refilled her own glass and spluttered as she gulped down more than she had intended. 'Excuse me, darling, you'll have to bring me up to speed on this. What do you imagine you're going to do?'

'Isn't it obvious? I want to go to London with him. I want to live with him. I was just thinking about what it would be like to marry him.'

'Oh, Christ.' Fay reached across and took hold of her hand fiercely. 'Now listen to me, darling. You are out of your tiny mind.'

'Then there's no point in talking, is there?'

'Oh, there's every point, because if you can't see it, someone's going to have to hammer it home to you. If Emma came to me in a state like this, I'd slap some sense into her.'

'And you'd do that to me?'

'Metaphorically, yes. Believe it.' Fay's sympathy had become anger. 'For God's sake! Where do you want me to start? How about the fact that you know sod all about him, you could be the twentieth older woman he's screwed and I wouldn't drop dead in amazement if he turned out to be married. He could be lying to you through his teeth.'

'No, he's not.'

'You mean you don't want to think that. What would you be telling me if this was happening in reverse? That I should ditch everything I've got for some toy boy who'd floated into my life and bonked me when I asked? When did you first go to bed with him?'

Joyce pulled her hand free. 'That's not important.'

'God, was it as recent as that? If you pulled him the night he arrived, it can only have been . . . When did he come here?'

'On the . . . it started on the eighteenth. I went to the cottage and—'

She wanted to talk about it, to relive the first time by telling what it had been like, how she had felt, how the second time had been even better, of her terror at falling until she realized she didn't care and—Fay's interruption was caustic.

'The eighteenth? So that's twelve – correction, thirteen – days ago. Are you asking me to believe you've found the love of your life in less than a fortnight? What am I meant to do? Tell you how ecstatic I am? Dream on!'

'I thought you'd understand.'

'Then you're mad.' Her eyes filled with sudden sorrow and fear. 'I love you so much, Joyce, but you're frightening me. This is going to hurt you very, very badly. I know it.'

'So you won't help me?'

'Help you do what? Throw yourself over a cliff? After you told me on Saturday how you felt about him, I was worried you were heading for some heartache and was on standby with the TLC and bandages. But this is . . . God, it's unreal.'

'Fine.' Beyond reason now, Joyce felt bitter at betrayal. 'It would have been good to have someone on my side, but I appear to have been wrong expecting it to be you. Forget it. I'll hack it on my own.'

She stood up, and they stared at each other, Joyce resentful, Fay appalled.

'Don't you ever dare say I'm not on your side. Please, sit down.'

'What's the point?'

'Because I don't want us to quarrel. I've said my piece. Just tell me what you're planning to do.'

'So you can start shooting me down again?'

'No. Promise. And I won't try to stop you. I assume the first thing you're going to do is talk to Randall.'

'I have to. Perhaps he'll . . .' Caught by renewed sympathy,

Joyce's voice broke across tears. 'It might be best if he goes back to London now and I sort out the mess here. I don't want to drag him into it at the moment. After that, I'll go and see him in town and we can talk.'

'When did you decide all this?'

'I don't know. This morning? It certainly crystallized it. I think it's been . . . coming on.' She opened her shoulderbag and took out a handkerchief, mopping her nose as she sniffed and swallowed. 'I just love him so bloody much. Don't think badly of me for that. You've never had to start from where I was.'

'Does he love you? I know I've asked that before.'

'Oh . . .' Joyce smiled as she shook her head. 'If we'd still been arguing, I'd have got angry and said of course he does. But . . . I think he could love me more. That's what I'm relying on. Colour me stupid.'

'I don't have that much colour.' Fay sighed. 'Can't you see that? No, you can't. Let me know what happens . . . Will Grace ring Ralph at the office?'

'No. She'll wait until the weekend and expect me to tell him. By then I'll have got my head more together. What I've been working on is how to convince her what Ralph's really like.'

'There I can help. She might take it from me.'

'We'll see . . . Thank you.' She returned the handkerchief and pulled the drawstring tight. 'Anyway, I'd better go. How's my face?'

'Minor repair work. Use the downstairs loo.'

As Joyce came back into the hall, Fay was standing by the open front door, expelling cigarette smoke out of the house.

'I'd hate to drive you back to forty a day,' Joyce said. 'I thought you'd stopped buying them.'

'I keep a pack for four-alarm emergencies.' She stubbed it out in the ashtray on the table beside her. 'One thing. Randall's got to start being upfront. I've no proof he's ever lied to you, but it doesn't make sense that you've got so close and still know hardly anything about him. If I'm allowed a piece of advice, for

Christ's sake, don't jump into bed with him again until you know a lot more.'

'All right . . . Do you like him?' She needed to know that; if friends saw attractions in him, she would feel less isolated.

Fay paused. 'Yes. Really. He's . . .' She smiled. 'He'd probably bring out my maternal instinct.'

'Oh, shut up!' For the first time, Joyce laughed. 'I've got enough hang-ups about this without you joining in.'

'I didn't mean it like that. He's vulnerable, which makes him gentle . . . Has it struck you that he's the exact opposite of Ralph?'

'Oh, yes. If he wasn't, would this have happened?'

They kissed, then Fay hugged her tightly. 'Good luck. I'll worry like hell until you tell me what he says.'

It was half-past two and Finch was deserted, still and silent houses soaked in sun. As Joyce reached the crossroads, from somewhere far off a train ran a thread of sound through the heat-humming quiet, then there was just the wooden clap of her Scholl sandals as she walked down the hill. She wished she'd worn high heels, however uncomfortable and impractical . . . because they would have made her look more desirable? Perhaps that was the subconscious reason – but Fay had been right, this was not the time for sex. Unless, after she had told him, for comfort and reassurance – a form of love-making they had not given each other so far. But there were things she had to know first, fragile bridges she needed to test. Would he prove treacherous, that appealing hesitancy no more than a device to seduce foolish women? Would he be the coward who fled from outraged husbands? Would he cynically persuade her into bed for a final indulgence before leaving without even a note, later boasting to his friends in London about the pushover he'd met on holiday?

Or would he meet her and be happy for them to move on together?

The car was not parked outside the cottage and she remembered telling him she would come later in the evening; perhaps he was shopping. She thought of going home, but she had a spare cottage key on her keyring and it was better to wait here than have to face more accusations from her mother. She called his name as she opened the door, in case there was some other explanation for the car's absence, then went into the front room and flopped on the settee, safe in their private place, rehearsing how she would begin to explain. There was a paperback of *The Mill on the Floss* on the floor, spine broken with use, and she picked it up, smiling at the notes scribbled in the margins, looking in the front where he had written his name and college. What had made him read it again? Was it set in Suffolk? Didn't George Eliot always write about the Midlands? He'd know.

As she put down the book, she noticed a grey nylon bag partly hidden behind the floor-length curtain, half recognizing it, but knowing he had never shown it to her. Then it registered; she had one just like it, for the Compaq Contura Ralph had given her when he'd upgraded. She picked it up and hesitated; despite repeated questions, he had never been prepared to talk about his novel, but . . . it could become another link between them. One day she might check his books, correcting, querying, discussing what he meant, arguing if she thought he was wrong about something. Perhaps she'd be able to help him – if he wanted the ingredients of a recipe for a story or needed some information that only she knew. How a woman might think if . . . but was he writing a novel? She thought he'd said so, but wasn't certain.

She unzipped the bag and took out the word-processor, plugging it in to the mains, as she always did with her own to save the battery, then opened the lid and pressed the maroon on-off switch and the F3 button to edit. On the pale blue screen, a single file appeared in the menu: PENITEN. She called it up and saw that in full it was Penitence. A fashionable single-word fiction title; or a factual examination of religious contrition, a philosophical critique? He was clever enough to be capable of any of them; his mind delighted her. And would the writing reveal something about the Randall Jowett she needed to reach? He never wanted to discuss it with her, but surely she was entitled to ... Unless he suddenly returned, he need never know. It was the most personal thing in the house connected to the man she had fallen in love with, the man she wanted to commit her whole being to. She began to scroll through the pages.

Awareness returned with a vicious pain that streaked up her leg. She cried out as she stumbled, fell and lay confused for a moment. A sharp arrowhead of flint on the footpath had got inside her sandal, stabbing into the flesh of her sole; her feet were stained with grime. She whimpered as she pulled the stone out, then desperately looked around for her bag, for something to stem the trickle of blood. She had nothing with her, but there were patches of dock growing next to where she lay and she used the leaves, thinking that if they cured nettle stings they would contain no poison; she remembered reading that people once wrapped butter in them to keep it fresh.

A hedge rose above her, but there were no visible landmarks to show where she was. Pressing the leaves against the wound, she saw her watch; ten past six. It was impossible to know how far she had walked, but her legs ached and a blister was swelling near the cut. How could she not have felt that? Her mind refused to function, and she began to panic. Nervous breakdown? Amnesia? Insanity? Her memory was chaotic. She could remember her name and those of her children ... Being sick after drinking Retsina on holiday in Greece ... Her best friend at school had been Maureen Littlechap ... Seeing the Kennedy Center for the Performing Arts from a cab at night in the rain ... joining the Brownies ... Buying a hat for someone's wedding ... Running a cake stall ... Swearing when she spilt coffee over a letter she had just finished typing ... The embarrassment of sudden toothache while watching *La Traviata* ... It was as if everything she knew about herself had exploded and only random, unconnected fragments remained.

'Joyce Hetherington,' she said aloud. 'Joyce Davinia. I live in

'. . . in . . . a village. In Suffolk. Rupert and Annabel. I think I'm forty-four.'

She pulled back the dock leaves, grimacing at drying blood caked to the dirt beneath them. She used her fingers and saliva to smear the worst away, but it needed cleaning and antiseptic. She felt too exhausted to walk again, but would have to; it was unthinkable that anyone should find her in such a condition . . . Finch. That was it. The house is called Four Elms. Why? Did I call it that? Are there four elms? There must be. What's happened to me? As she wept in despair and terror, mosaic pieces of memory began to float back, in no order, but faster and faster. Ralph . . . of course . . . It was Kit's wedding . . . I was Sir Malcolm Glenholm's secretary . . . Mummy's called Grace . . . I had a studio flat in Baron's Court . . . The girl who lived opposite was a dancer . . . My first car was a Fiat . . . Fay Graveney . . . and Oliver . . . I'm allergic to penicillin . . . My brother once took me to Twickenham to watch the All Blacks . . . I vote Conservative . . . I can't stand small dogs . . . I have a lover . . . he's called . . .

From the cornfield behind her a cloud of startled rooks flapped upwards like torn black petals as she screamed in grief and desperation.

Jowett saw her handbag on the floor by the doorway of the living room. He shouted upstairs, then went into the garden looking in the shed and behind the apple tree before going back inside.

'Where are you hiding?' He listened for muffled laughter as he went upstairs. 'Come on. I know you're here.' It was typical of her to want amusement. There were times when she acted as if she were a much younger woman, even a girl.

'Come out when you're ready, then.'

He put away the shopping, constantly expecting her to creep up behind him and place her hands over his eyes, demanding him to guess who it was. The playful innocence of such moments brought him more comfort than the sex; they offered a normality he had lost long ago.

'Tea?' He called, loud enough for her to hear wherever she was. 'I bought some biscuits as well.'

He made two cups, then began to feel puzzled when she still did not appear. If she'd had to rush home for some reason, surely she would have taken her bag, even left him a note? As he carried the cups through to the front room, he wondered if he should telephone ... For several moments, he stared, convincing himself he could not possibly have left it there for anyone to see. He never did; it was habit. But now it was on.

I didn't fire the gun – Giles told me it was unloaded – but I saw two of them killed and heard the others. The little girl wasn't afraid. She just ran towards him, and I feel sick that I couldn't even shout a warning to her. If I'd managed to save her, perhaps I'd have been able to stop him. But I was a coward, and I still am. I don't have the courage to kill myself, so I've spent six years in hell. Now I'm back here.

I try to remember good things I've done, but none of them matters. I've given money to charity, including a donation for a little boy to have an operation in America. I helped to save his life. Is that something? It doesn't feel as though it is, but if I saved one life, then . . .

The cursor rested on the last word at the bottom of the screen. She must have read Giles' name, how they had met, planned it . . .

'Joyce!' The shout was panic, but he now knew she was not there to hear it. He snatched up his mobile phone, but couldn't remember her number. It was on the confirmation she'd sent when he'd booked the cottage ... bag ... no, behind the ornament on the mantelpiece. Shaking fingers hit a wrong button and he had to start again.

'Thank you for calling. I'm sorry we're not in, but . . .'

Her voice, cordial and polite. Was she there and hiding from him? What time had she been at the cottage? He'd left shortly before two o'clock. If she'd called the police, they could be almost here. If he ran, she could tell them his car number. But that was irrelevant; he'd used his personal letter-headed paper to book the holiday . . . He was sobbing and finding it difficult to breathe. He sat on the settee and stared at the laptop, the words blurred as he struggled to decide what he should do.

Perhaps if he went to the house . . . If she was there, they could talk. I never wanted anybody to be hurt. You have to believe that. Giles had some sort of control over me – no, that's an excuse and I mustn't make excuses – but I never realized what he was really like. I'm scared; I've been scared for years. You were making it better, giving me something to build on. There were times when I wanted to tell you – I've wanted to tell someone ever since it happened – but I couldn't. They were your friends. Don't hate me. Please . . . I love you.

Chapter Eighteen

Amplified by high walls and the parquet floor in the front hall, the drilling note of the bell echoed stridently as Jowett frantically held down the button, flattened fingertip straining against it; her Honda was in front of the double garage and the upstairs windows were open, so surely she was in. He crouched and pushed up the brass flap of the letterbox, pressing his mouth against the opening.

'Joyce! It's me!' He lowered his eyes and peered through, then shouted again. 'Joyce! It's all right! Just let me in!'

'Who's there?' The voice was distant, apprehensive but challenging, like a hesitant sentry. He looked through the slot again, but there was no one visible.

'It's me! Randall! Where are you?'

Slippered feet and legs descended cautiously on to the highest stair he could see, then Grace Carstairs leant down to peer at the door, suspicious and offended.

'What do you want?'

'Is Joyce here?'

'She's gone out.'

'Where to?'

'Just a minute.'

He straightened up as he saw her continue down, smoothing his hair as though his appearance were important. Then the door opened and she looked at him with distaste.

'Are you drunk?'

'What? No, but I have to see Joyce. Where's she gone?'

'Don't cross-examine me, young man.' She was a very small

woman, but blazing with anger. 'I know exactly what's been going on between you and my daughter. Now you turn up shouting like a hooligan. As far as I'm concerned, you are not welcome at this house, Mr Jowett.'

'It's important.'

'Is it indeed? Has she put an end to this nonsense with you? Perhaps I talked some sense into her. Now, please go away.' She began to close the door. 'Take your foot out of there at once!'

'Just tell me where she is!'

'I don't know! And if I did, I would certainly not tell you. Now, if you don't leave immediately, I'm going to call the police.'

'No! It's OK, I'm going . . . Will you tell her I have to see her?'

'She may not want to see you. I very much hope she doesn't.'

He had stepped back at the threat of the police; the door slammed shut and he heard her lock it from the inside. At least he'd established that Joyce was not in the house, so was she . . . What was the woman's name? Faith? No, Fay. Her husband had said they lived next door but one. There was only one house beyond the Hetheringtons', so it must be back towards the village . . . As he ran, he registered what Grace Carstairs had said. Why would Joyce have told her about them? Bewilderment was added to his pounding fright.

'Randall?' Fay immediately looked behind him. 'Is Joyce with you?'

'No . . . I wondered if she was here.' His face was glossy with sweat.

'She left after lunch. She was coming to see you. Didn't she turn up?'

'Yes, but . . .' Having established she was not there, he wanted to leave immediately. 'It's all right. I just thought she might . . . If you see her, can you tell her to call me?'

'What's happened?' Alarmed by his agitation, Fay reached for his arm. 'You look dreadful . . .'

He backed away, a fearful animal cornered. 'I'm OK! I don't want to . . . Tell her I'll be at the cottage.'

'Randall!' Fay called urgently as he turned, desperate to get away. 'She's told me about you. What did you say to her? Come back!'

For a moment she thought of chasing him, but he was already at the gate. She snatched up the phone and hit the first memory button.

Jowett realized that if Joyce's mother saw him sitting outside the house in the car, she might call the police, so he parked near the crossroads from where the house was out of sight but he could still watch the front gates . . . or would she go back to the cottage? After twenty minutes, the waiting became intolerable and he drove back to Windhover, now terrified that her mother might report her missing. Everything was out of his control.

Her foot bandaged with a strip of material ripped from the hem of her skirt, Joyce had limped along the hedge, then gasped with relief as she saw the tower of St Matthews less than half a mile away; she must have wandered in mindless circles. The stile on the far side of the meadow led on to a bridleway where she often walked, and from there trees would protect her until she was nearly home. Unless she'd dropped her bag after running out, it must still be . . . but there was a back-door key hidden under a stone by the swimming pool, left in case one of the children needed it. Wincing as pain needled at her foot, she slowly moved on.

The worst memories of all had now returned. Initial confusion at the way it was written, clumsily, as though he had difficulty expressing what he wanted to say; it was as if he were speaking to himself. Then the name of Tannerslade Farm making her cry out, and the sick, heart-splitting chill of disbelief. She could half remember running out of the cottage, but nothing after that until she had fallen. Now she was incapable of thinking of anything except that she needed to be in the safety of her home. If she had met someone and they had spoken to her she would have screamed.

When she reached the road and saw her house, she checked the time; her mother would be watching television. As she neared the gate, she jumped as a car passed and flipped its horn, the driver waving to her through the rear window; she didn't recognize him, but waved back, then reached the sanctuary of the front garden. Irritated at not being fed, Macavity miaowed and scratched the back door as she opened it, then scampered into the kitchen expectantly. If she didn't deal with him he'd howl, but the effort was agonizing. Slowly she went upstairs and began to run a bath. Her foot had stopped bleeding, but was inflamed round the wound and she deliberately forced it open again to wash out the dirt. Hot water blanketing her body was a welcome pain that gradually comforted her as she lay with her neck against the padded headrest, feeling sweat gather and dampen her face. She lay very still, conscious only of being secure and warm, wanting nothing but some miracle that would make it last for ever.

The first reality was the water growing cold and she pulled herself up, then concentrated on cleaning herself, stretching to reach the shampoo bottle and washing her hair before standing and turning on the shower to rinse it. She partly dried herself, put on a white towelling robe and went to her bedroom, sitting on the cane stool in front of the dressing-table mirror as she brushed her hair through the blast of the drier. Bathing had become a deliberate process to hide behind, and she extended it to filing her nails and plucking her eyebrows . . . Face close to the mirror, she saw strains of grief and fright gathered in her eyes. In her apartment on the top floor of the house Grace thought she heard a wail, like someone in pain, above the sound of the television, but decided it was either her imagination or a dog somewhere outside.

Joyce felt faint with hunger as she sat and contemplated desolation, but knew her stomach would disgorge anything but the plainest food. Cream crackers, perhaps, and soft cheese; no alcohol, but the balm of camomile tea. As she went downstairs the house felt totally empty, abandoned by life. Ralph was in town – playing with his personal sex toy – Rupert and Annabel away, her mother isolated from her; she had never felt so completely alone. There was no one she wanted to talk to, because she could not even articulate anything for herself. She knew she ought to call the police but the thought was overridden by desperation to keep him – but on what terms? Had Fay asked her that morning what she would do for Randall, she had been so obsessed with the thought of him she would have offered anything ... If you weren't prepared even to die for someone, did you really love them? So would she lie for him? If what he had written was the truth, this Giles was the murderer, not him. Why should Randall be punished for that? But until a few hours ago the thought of the subhumans who had killed Ben and Annie, Cheryl, Thomas and Mandy finally being caught and punished would have brought immense comfort. After Tannerslade it had been a long time before she had been able to rebuild her belief that hanging was wrong. Now there were no certainties.

The answerphone showed there were two messages, and she switched it on as she prepared her meal.

'Hi. It's Fay at ... ten to six. What the hell's happened? Randall's just been here asking for you. He looked paranoid. We're going out for dinner in an hour, but if you can't call before then, for God's sake leave a message. If it's a real crisis, we'll be at the Cross Keys in Bury. I'll come back if you want me to and ...' She sighed. 'Call me as soon as you can, darling.'

The tape clicked and whirred, then her body froze as the second message began. His voice was strained and clipped.

'Are you there? Pick up the phone if you are.' There was a silence. 'OK, if you are there, I understand. Just ... don't do anything. OK? Let me talk to you. I'm still at the cottage. I'm not running away. We can sort this. I wanted to find a way to tell you. Call me back, yeah? Your bag's here, incidentally ... in case you were worried. I'll be in all the time, and ... No, I can't say anything on this machine. I'm sorry.'

She thought about what she should do as she finished spreading the cheese and making the tea. If she left no reply, Fay would start pressing panic buttons.

'It's me. I'm all right, but I can't talk about it at the moment. I'll call you in the morning. Don't worry.'

The silence of the house was oppressive. She put on a CD, chosen without interest, conscious only that it was sound, and began to eat, soaking away sudden, uncontrollable outbursts of tears with the sleeve of her robe. She went to her leather-topped writing table by the window and took out her letter pad, gazing at the garden for several minutes before starting to write. She heard the phone ring, but had left the answerphone on.

Weariness of mind and body greater than she had ever known overcame her as she sealed the envelope, and she had to use the arms of the dining chair to stand up. Sleep, which she would have thought impossible, was beginning to drug her, as though her brain were turning off. Climbing the stairs was a physical struggle against surrender, and she almost sank on to the thick, soft carpet rather than make the effort of reaching the bed. She was only half conscious as she sat down, the fading remnants of strength pulling her legs off the floor. As she lay curled on her side, the last thing she was aware of seeing was the rose on the bedside table.

Jowett flinched back from the window as the car pulled up outside the cottage. It was not Joyce's, and who else would come to the cottage at nine thirty in the morning unless . . . It was not a marked police car, but didn't the CID use . . . ? Then he recognized Fay and was at the door before she reached it.

'Is Joyce all right? I've been trying to call her, but there's no reply. I was about to go round and—'

'Don't do that. She won't tell me why, but she doesn't want to see you at the moment.' This was not the woman who had made him welcome at the pageant, introduced him to her husband and other people, been interested and warm. 'She asked me to collect her bag.'

'What? Oh, yeah. It's in here.'

She followed him inside, a hostile, suspicious presence. He held out the bag like a peace offering.

'Thank you.' She reached into the pocket of her skirt. 'Joyce asked me to give you this.'

He took the envelope. 'Did she get my message? On the answerphone.'

'She didn't mention it.'

'What's she told you?'

'Nothing. That's what's worrying me. She told me yesterday that she was hopelessly in love and was ready to give up everything for you. Did you realize that?'

He shook his head. 'No.'

'Well, that's how deeply you reached her, Randall. Now she just refuses to say what happened yesterday afternoon ... So will you explain?'

Fay had never meant to keep her promise not to question him. When she had gone to see Joyce first thing that morning she had looked desperate, face blotched with weeping, bloated with clinging sleep, but urgent, as if she had been given only days to live. She wanted Fay to go to the cottage, collect her bag and give Randall the letter. She couldn't talk about what he'd said or done ... She'd deal with it ... Fay mustn't worry ... It was all right. Demands for explanations had brought impatient anger. It was impossible for Fay to understand. However Jowett might have rejected her, Joyce's reaction was too extreme. And now he looked haggard as well; unshaven, feverish with tension, anxious about Joyce.

'I can't explain.'

'Well, I can't help unless one of you agrees to talk.' She gave a sharp sigh of frustration. 'Let me make one thing very clear, Randall. You must know enough to realize that Joyce is vulnerable. I don't know what's going on here, but I can get very nasty towards people who hurt my friends. Remember that.'

'I'd never want to hurt her.'

'Well, you seem to be doing a very good job of it.'

'Did she say I'd hurt her?'

'She didn't need to. But she wouldn't tell me how – and apparently neither will you. But I've known Joyce a long time, and eventually it'll come out.' The instant dread in his eyes excited the worst of her fears. 'For Christ's sake, what is it? Have you got Aids? I'll kill you if you have!'

'No!' He was starting to cry. 'Please . . . I must talk to her. Just tell her that for me!'

'All right.' Fay believed his denial; he was in too much of a state to lie. 'But I'm not guaranteeing she'll want to see you at the moment. You mustn't go anywhere near the house. I'll act as go-between if necessary . . . Is that it? I just tell her you want to talk?'

'Yes. She'll understand.'

'Well, that's more than I do.' She gave a bitter smile. 'Why the hell didn't you choose somewhere else to write your damned book?'

'Has she told you about it?'

'What?' Fay was startled by the edge of fear in his voice. 'No. I've said she won't tell me anything. Why?'

'It . . . it doesn't matter.'

'It obviously does . . . Have you been writing all this up as a hard porn novel? Is that how you got rid of her? You're seriously sick if you did.'

'It's nothing like that . . . I said I wouldn't hurt her. The book's just . . . I've told you before. It's something private.'

Fay glared with impatience. 'I can't be doing with this. If one of you comes to your senses, you know where I am.'

Jowett remained where he was as she left, then returned to the window and watched her drive away. The terrors were multiplying. At least Joyce had not gone straight to the police, but how long would it be before Fay coaxed the truth from her? He had no hold on Fay's heart. He realized he was still holding the letter and tore it open; six sentences, with what looked like a tearstain smudging one line, signed just with her initials.

I feel sick, but I can't bring myself to hate you. I need time on my own, so please don't come to the house again. You've deceived me terribly, and at the moment I can't think straight. Don't make it worse by running away again.

I'm going away for a few days and we'll talk when I get back. But I can't promise I'll still love you then.

He groaned, feeling as though hammers were smashing down six years of lies. He was unable to cope with this. He opened his wallet and took out the business card, then called the number.

'Lambert.' It was not the voice last heard on the Moorgate pavement, surprised and insanely friendly. This was the crackling City executive, efficient, impatient, his name snapped out like a challenge.

'Giles? It's Randall . . . Randall Jowett.'

'Randy?' The name he'd never liked being called, the tone instantly relaxed, no apprehension because Giles never expected danger. 'Good to hear from you. Look, I've got someone with me at the moment. Where can I get back to you?'

'No . . . There's a problem.'

'What sort of problem?' The relaxation vanished as quickly as it had appeared.

'A heavy one.'

'Hang on.' The phone went dead for a few moments, then he was back, tight with aggressive urgency. 'What the fuck's happened?'

The call lasted less than ten minutes, by which time Lambert's ability to bully had made Jowett helplessly admit where he was, why he had gone there, meeting Joyce, what he had realized when he had seen the laptop—

'*You fucking stupid dickhead!*' Jowett winced and jerked the phone away from his ear. 'Jesus Christ! Are you out of your fucking mind?'

'I'm sorry!'

'Sorry!' His voice was shaking with fury. 'What fucking use is sorry? Christ, let me think . . . Where are you?'

'I'm still in Finch. In the cottage.'

'You've not even had the bloody sense to get out? You've got a death wish . . . No, hang on. Stay there. Don't do anything. I'll be there in . . . How far is it?'

201

'About a couple of hours from London.'

'Right, I'll be there ... say twelve thirty. How do I find you?'

'Go to the church and turn down the hill ... It's called Windhover, the name's on the gate ... What are you going to do?'

'Christ knows, but I'll think of something. Got a pen? This is my mobile; call me if anything happens before I arrive ... You're certain she's not gone to the police?'

'She can't have done. It was yesterday afternoon when she ... No. This friend of hers who came just now would have gone for me if she knew. And if she's not told her, she won't have told anyone.'

'So we're OK at the moment ... I hope she was a bloody good fuck, because it could cost you for screwing her. Right. Don't go out, and don't call anyone except me.'

Jowett was shuddering as the line went dead. It was exactly like it had been in nineteen ninety, Lambert totally able to control him. But he'd been right; they hadn't been caught. Perhaps he'd have an answer this time as well.

Chapter Nineteen

Arms folded, Fay leant against the frame of the bedroom door, anxious, demanding, silently questioning, never taking her eyes off Joyce as she selected clothes from her wardrobe.

'There's no need to stare at me like that. I'm not a freak.' Joyce snatched a linen trouser suit off its hanger.

'You look like one from where I'm standing. And I'm not leaving this house until you tell me where you're going.'

'Just away.' Hastily folded, the jacket and trousers were laid in the suitcase and Joyce looked round as if checking she hadn't forgotten anything. Her voice was artificial, detached. 'I'll send you a postcard.'

'If you don't tell me, I'll call Ralph and tell him you're ill.'

'Don't do that. It isn't true, and anyway he'd only start getting concerned if you told him I was dying.'

'What about Rupert and Annabel?'

'They won't be back until next week, and . . .' A lock failed to operate and she became irritated. 'Back off, will you? Please. I need to be on my own for a while. That's all.'

'Let me help you with that.'

'I can manage!' The lock snapped shut as she hit it with the heel of her hand and lifted the case off the bed. 'Where's my sketchpad? I think it's downstairs. Can you look? Probably on the sofa in the sitting room.'

'I'm not going to help you unless you tell me.'

'Then I'll do it myself . . . Excuse me.'

Fay rubbed her forehead wearily as Joyce pushed past her,

then she followed her downstairs, collecting the sketchpad and a pack of pencils before joining her on the drive.

'Here you are.'

'Thank you.'

'What have you told Grace?'

'That I'm going away. I'm allowed.'

'Doesn't she want to know why?'

'Not really . . .' She put the pad on top of the case. 'The only thing she wanted to know was that I was going on my own, and I've assured her I am.'

She slammed the boot shut and walked towards the driver's side, activating her key control. Fay took hold of her before she could open the door.

'You're worrying me sick! What the hell did he say to you? It can't be that bad. You can sort it.'

'I hope so.' She looked down from Fay's pained and searching eyes. 'I told you. That's why I have to get away from here. I need time to think.'

Her neck stiffened and she tried to turn her head as Fay put her hand beneath her chin.

'No! Look at me . . . Christ, I'm terrified you're going to kill yourself!'

'I won't do that . . . promise . . . I'll ring you this evening. All right? And I'll be back soon. I only need a couple of days.'

'OK.' Defeated, Fay kissed her, then dropped her arms in despair. 'What do I tell him if he turns up on my doorstep again?'

'That I'm not here . . . No, call him to make sure.' Joyce sighed and opened her bag, taking out a ballpoint pen. 'I don't want Mummy having another row with him. Will you do that?' Unable to find a piece of paper, she wrote the number on Fay's palm. 'Say I'll talk to him when I get back . . . He'll understand.'

'I wish I did. Is there anything else?'

'I don't think so . . . Oh, yes. Can you feed Macavity? I've forgotten. You'll find everything in the cupboard under the sink . . . and tell Tom just to leave one pint for Mummy . . . and, no, it's all right. Anything else can sort itself. I'll talk to you tonight.'

Fay rested her hand on the car roof, pulling it away and waving as Joyce drove off, then blotted tears with her fingertips. Every question she'd asked had been deflected or ignored, every effort to make contact thrust aside. Whether Randall had been unspeakably cruel or killed it with gentleness made no difference. Joyce would have wanted to talk to her of all people. Cry on her shoulder, lament her stupidity, become maudlin over too much drink; not this void of unspoken pain. And Randall had looked dreadful that morning as well, as if Joyce had rejected him and he was desperate for a chance to persuade her to return. There was no sense to it.

Lambert pulled into a lay-by just outside Ipswich and punched Jowett's number into his mobile.

'It's me. Has anything happened?'

'No . . . Where are you?'

'On my way . . . no sign of the police, then?'

'No.'

'That's good. When do you reckon she read that laptop?'

'Sometime yesterday afternoon.'

'So she's still not reported it, has she?' He poured reassurance into his voice. 'They'd have picked you up by now if she had. Where is she?'

'I don't know. She's gone away. A friend of hers called to tell me.'

'Where's she gone?'

'I don't know, but Fay – she rang me – says she wants to talk to me when she gets back.'

'Then we're OK for the time being. Just hang loose. I'll be there in about half an hour.'

He switched off. If the police had answered, he'd have raced back to London and got out of the country any way he could, but this woman obviously hadn't gone screaming to them yet. There could be time to do something. Curiously, a traffic jam had calmed him down; furious at the hold-up he'd found some

Valium in the glove compartment, left over from a bad time in his life, and taken them. As his mind calmed, he began to feel unexpectedly good. This was Randy Jowett, the puppet he could make jump any way he wanted; as long as the woman held off – and for some reason she was still doing that – he could get up there and grab this situation before it went critical.

He pulled out and drove on, calmly running over the possibilities, the way he had in nineteen ninety. More risks than he'd have liked, but sometimes you had to take them. What was the alternative? Waiting like a sacrificial goat for them to get him? Making a panic dash with little more than fifteen grand and rotting in South America or wherever until they traced and extradited him? He'd killed five people and got away with it for six years; you don't just give up after that. He stopped just outside Finch and rang Jowett again, pretending he was lost. Still no police.

Driving down The Street he remembered the baker's shop, the old-fashioned metal sign in the shape of a cottage-loaf above the window – and he noticed the house with the crooked chimney. He'd been in control while Jowett was shitting himself; he wasn't going to be brought down by a wimp like that. He slowed as he dropped down the hill from the church, watching for flashing blue lights or other signs, ready to drive past if necessary. But there was just a scarlet MGF on the Tarmac hard-standing – was that Randy's? He was the type who ought to own a Sierra, which he washed every Sunday morning. As he parked on the opposite side of the road and stepped out of the car, Jowett opened the cottage door.

'Got anything to eat?' Lambert asked as he opened the gate.

'What?'

'Food. I haven't had lunch.' See, no panic. The Valium had got his head together.

'Yes. I . . . I haven't eaten either. I wasn't hungry.'

'Well, I am.' Lambert followed him inside and closed the door. 'Come here.'

'Why?'

'Just come here.' Jowett stepped forward, then staggered

back, stumbling over a chair as Lambert slapped him viciously. 'I needed to do that. Now make a sandwich or something.'

Jowett got up nervously and walked out of the room. Lambert walked into the front room and found the laptop.

'Have you wiped this?' he called.

'Wiped what?'

'Your fucking life story.'

'No.'

'Christ Almighty,' Lambert muttered. He took out the machine, leant it against the angle of the tiled hearth and the floor, then savagely stamped his heel on it until it shattered.

'What are you doing?' Jowett appeared in the doorway, holding a butter knife.

'What you hadn't got the sodding sense to do. If she goes to the police now, there's only her word that she read anything.' Jowett watched in dismay as he collected the pieces and put them in the bag.

'I needed to write that.'

'It's no great loss to literature. We'll have to dump this somewhere.'

'Giles, that was important to me.'

'Important?' Lambert laughed. 'The only thing that's important is that we don't go to gaol. And I'm going to have to sort that out again, aren't I? Isn't that why you called me?'

'I expect so.'

'Then leave it to me and do as you're told. Now, are you just going to stand there waving that knife about or do we eat?'

Jowett stared at him for a moment then looked away, defeated. Lambert followed him through to the kitchen. 'When did you get this call about her going away?'

'Just before you rang.' Jowett was twisting the key on a tin of corned beef. 'She says she'll talk to me when she gets back.'

'When's that going to be?'

'Only a day or so apparently . . . Do you like chutney? It's home-made.'

Lambert laughed again. 'Christ, you're the perfect host. No, I can't stand it. Got any booze?'

'There's beer in the fridge.'

'Scotch?'

'There's some gin in the other room.'

'I'll find it.' Lambert went back, knowing he'd have to be careful after the Valium, but needing a drink. He couldn't understand this woman. Instead of turning Jowett in, she'd simply vanished . . . and wanted to talk to him when she came back. Did not compute, unless . . . He returned to the kitchen.

'So why hasn't she gone to the police?'

Jowett cut two slices of bread in half. 'I'm not sure.'

'How about she's working out how much you'll pay her to make sure you don't end up inside?'

'No. She wouldn't do that.'

'Why not? Unless she's totally thick, she must have realized you've got money. How much did those wheels outside cost, for a start?'

'You don't understand.' Jowett pushed the plate towards him and lit a cigarette. 'I think she's in love with me.'

Lambert sneered. 'Please. Do me a favour . . . How long have you been here?'

'Just over three weeks.'

'Well, you've had plenty of time to screw her, but what the hell makes you think it's more than that?'

'What she's said. The way she's been with me.' Jowett sounded slightly defiant. 'I mean it, Giles. That's why I think she hasn't told anyone. She'd never blackmail me. She's got money. You should see her house.'

'How old is she?'

'She wouldn't tell me, but . . . over forty.'

'Married?'

'Yes, but her husband's a prat.'

'They don't usually fall in love with their toy boys . . . What's so special about you?'

'I don't know. It just happened.'

'She must have been desperate.' Lambert bit into a sandwich. 'I've got to make a couple of calls, then I want to know a lot more about all this.'

He took out his mobile and pressed a memory button. 'Hi, Kim. It's Giles. Can you put me through to Steve . . . Steve? Giles. She's not too bad, but they've admitted her. I'll need to stay a few days. OK, thanks. If you need me, try the mobile.'

'What was that about?' Jowett asked.

'The office thinks my mother's ill.' He pressed a second button. 'It's me. I'm in Coventry. Mother's had a heart attack. I'm calling from the hospital. What? I tried, but you were out . . . I don't know. Two or three days probably . . . I can't help that . . . No, but I'll get some stuff here . . . It depends on how she is . . . I'll ring you again.'

He ended the call and pushed back the aerial. 'My ever-sympathetic wife, otherwise known as the bitch from hell . . . Where are the nearest decent shops round here?'

'Bury St Edmunds. Why?'

'I need some clothes, I didn't have time to go home and pack.' He chewed the last of the sandwich. 'I'll follow you and leave my car there somewhere.'

'What for?'

'Think, shit for brains. Two cars outside means two of us here and people might notice. Why do you think I parked on the other side of the road when I arrived?'

Frightened and confused, Jowett nodded agreement. Seeing Lambert brutally destroy the laptop had horrified him – but it meant he had the strength to try to find a way out for both of them.

Perhaps it was because she had grown up near the sea that Joyce had gone back to it, even though Fay would have regarded Great Yarmouth as final proof that she'd gone mad. She found a hotel on the north side of the town, its original middle-class Edwardian comfort decaying, stair carpets wearing thin, the proportions of its spacious bedrooms dissected and ruined by dividing walls to increase accommodation. Most of the guests resembled fading remnants of Empire, carrying with them an air of bamboo chairs on hot colonial terraces.

She had not wanted dinner, but had ordered tea and sandwiches in her room before going out and across the road to the beach. From her right came the distant clamour of a fairground, and the garish lights of the resort were starting to glow faintly against slow mother-of-pearl twilight; to her left, a man digging for lugworms was a lone figure on a barren strand that stretched away to dunes. The tide was turning, barely breathing water bubbling into a thin string of silver froth as it sleepily stroked the beach. She walked away from the town, avoiding the fisherman, and on to slopes of soft sand and harsh marram grass, her feet slithering down into a silent hollow from where she could sit and stare at shimmering sea.

She lifted back the pages of her sketchpad to the portrait and now recognized what she had been unable to identify and capture. The secret guilt of an evil she would never have dreamt possible. But that was unthinkable in this gentle, pleading face that she had seen glow with gratitude or fired by the hunger of love. He must be terrified now – but Fay had said he was still at the cottage, still wanting to see her. She lay back and closed her eyes. There had been no alternative to running away from it, but that offered only false escape, not answers – if there were any that did not break her heart and all her hopes. Surely she was allowed to be alone for a while with such a thing, but staying away would solve nothing. So . . . She would spend tomorrow trying to think, remember a friend and her children – and ask forgiveness – then return to Finch in the evening. It was impossible for her to see beyond that, but they had to be together and discover if anything could be saved.

The last time Jowett and Lambert had been together in a pub had been the night of the murders; now they were back in one, although this time it was a Beefeater steakhouse chosen by Lambert because it was on a main road where passing trade meant strangers would not be noticed. Jowett chewed at a thumbnail as Lambert bought more drinks at the bar, trying to interpret his feelings. At some point Joyce and he had confusingly become like people without guilt, playing with visions of happiness. Such dreams were mad, but more powerful than reason . . . Lambert's chair scraped on the flagged floor as he sat down again, scratching his jaw as he thought.

'OK,' he said finally. 'She might well have a thing for you, which could mean there isn't a problem. How serious do you think it is with her?'

'She's talked about . . . you know. What it would be like if there were just the two of us.' Jowett saw Lambert's cynical sneer. 'I'm sure she meant it.'

'Yeah, well, they have different brains from us – but if she didn't feel something, you'd be in a cell by now. So . . . bollocks.' He reached into his inside jacket pocket as a shrill cheeping sounded; other customers looked slightly contemptuous. 'It's not mine . . . Have you got one?'

'Oh . . . yeah.' Alarmed that anyone should ring him, Jowett pulled out the phone and connected the call. 'Hello?'

'Randall?' Even on a bad line, he recognized her. 'Where are you? I can hear voices.'

'In a restaurant. I . . . came out for a meal.'

'But you're still at Finch?'

'Not far away.'

'I'm glad of that. I didn't want you to run back to London.'

'Where are you?' Lambert had seen the reaction on his face and was leaning forward, straining his ears to hear.

'That doesn't matter, but I wanted to let you know I'm coming back tomorrow evening. We have to talk.'

'I know. I want to explain about . . . I can't like this.'

'Of course not.'

'I can come to the house.'

'No. You mustn't do that. Promise me. And I don't want to come to the cottage. It would be better on neutral ground. There's a hotel in Stowmarket called the Crown. It's on the market square. I'll be there by seven o'clock. All right?'

'Yes. I . . . I'm sorry.'

'So am I.' He heard her voice catch. 'Please be there. I deserve that.' The line went dead.

'Was that her?' Lambert asked.

'Yes. She's coming back tomorrow night. She wants me to meet her . . . I think it might be OK.'

'Tell me in a minute. I need a slash.'

Lambert had not wanted to risk Jowett seeing his agitation over what he had suddenly realized. The lavatory was unoccupied and he stared at the tiled wall as he thought. With the laptop destroyed there was no proof – real proof – that Jowett had been at the farm. But he could be traced back to it. His father had sold both shotguns to a friend, so the police could find them – and he'd once read that they were as identifiable as rifles or revolvers to forensic experts. All that woman needed to do was to leave her husband, move in with Jowett – who was in no state to refuse her – then send the police an anonymous tip. They'd find the lock-up and start tracking down what he'd sold; it only needed one dealer to recognize him. He could drag Jowett in, but suppose she simply told him to deny it, even lied to give Jowett an alibi? She could probably manipulate him better than anyone. There would be hard evidence against Giles Lambert, but, however suspicious the police were, a lawyer could knock down an accusation against Jowett based on nothing more than his word. So she would end up with everything; Jowett in her bed and him in gaol for the murders. Women were like that . . .

Get a grip, it's not a problem. Randy will never work this out and she won't do anything until she's got him on the hook . . . so, turn it round. Who knows I'm here? Only Randy. I've told the office and Victoria I'm in Coventry, and they're not going to question it. Which means . . . Holding his hands beneath the drier, he began to think urgently. It could be dangerous, but what else is there? Why do I feel sick?

'Go on,' he said as he returned. 'She said she wants to meet you.'

'Yes . . . in a hotel in Stowmarket.'

'Why there?' He'd have preferred the cottage.

'I think she wants it to be somewhere without any . . . you know. Somewhere we've not done it. No vibes.'

Lambert shrugged. 'I can't see what difference it makes . . . but I'll come with you.'

'You can't! She read your name on that disk.'

'I'm not going to ask you to introduce me, you prat! We'll get there early and I'll just sit in the bar. I don't want to listen.'

'Then why come at all?'

'I'd like to see her for myself. OK? Come on, you owe me here.'

Jowett wanted to argue, but knew there was no point; Lambert simply wouldn't allow him to go alone. But why did he want to? The worst fear, the one he'd refused to recognize, stunned him.

'Giles, for fuck's sake, you can't be thinking of killing her!'

I was beginning to think you'd never make it to the real world; you've been living in a fantasy one for long enough. I'll get you back there. Lambert shook his head, forging a smile of regret.

'You never understood me, did you? How long did we know each other? Did you really believe I was the type to kill anyone?' He paused, letting the suggestion take root. 'Remember what it was like. We were planning nothing more than a robbery, but we were hyped up. Yeah? It wasn't the sort of thing we made a habit of. I never meant to fire that gun, but when that mask snapped, it just went off. I was on my nerve ends.'

'You told me it wasn't loaded.'

'I know . . . How would you have felt if I'd told you it was? But it wasn't for them. I'd thought out every detail of what we were doing . . . and farmers usually have dogs. As it turned out they didn't, but one bloody great alsatian and we were in trouble. That's the only reason it was loaded.'

'But you killed them all – and you weren't bothered afterwards.'

'Wasn't I? Grant me something, Randy. I felt like shit. Do you know who the worst one was? The boy. He had more bottle than I had.' He blinked and turned away. 'You've told me how bad it's been for you, but you don't know how often I've thought about that kid.'

'Why didn't you tell me this then?'

'The state you were in? I was trying to hold you together. We'd still be looking at a lot of years in gaol if I'd cracked as well. And what would that have achieved? I couldn't bring any of them back, but the least I could do was try to protect our families. If they'd got us, it would have crucified them. The only difference between you and me was that you showed it and I kept it in. But it hurts just as much.'

He kept his voice low and guileless and, apart from the moment he deliberately looked away, his eyes didn't leave Jowett's.

'I never realized all this.'

'There was no point in telling you . . . The fact is I killed five people – me, not you – and it's easy now to say I should have stopped after the first and we'd have got out of there. I've never understood why I didn't, but . . . well, there aren't any ways to turn clocks back. Pity.'

'So . . . so you've never thought of . . . harming Joyce?'

Lambert looked down again, rubbing his fingers against the sides of his forehead as if he were suddenly very weary. 'Can't you hear what I'm telling you? I know I bollocked you when you called me and bloody hit you when I arrived, but imagine how I was feeling. I'm sorry about that. But have I said anything – anything at all – to suggest I want to kill her? I don't know how we'll get out of this, but believe me, I don't want another life on my conscience. I've got more than enough.'

If you could see your face . . . why did I ever hang out with you? I could talk you into topping yourself if I wanted.

Chapter Twenty

Sleep had betrayed Joyce the second night; longed for but refusing to come. Passing traffic, voices and activities in the hotel were loud and intrusive to someone accustomed to the dark silence of a village, uneasy in a strange bed, tormented by the unthinkable. It was the wrong time to think, of course – the smaller the hour, the greater the problem – but it was almost impossible to move her mind to anything else. She tried reciting poetry, including a sonnet she had once written herself.

> The dialogue between my mind and heart,
> Considering my love's accomplishment,
> Was crossed in disagreement from the start
> Of all such unavailing argument.
> His sugar'd words of love the mind condemns
> As but the mask to hide unfaithfulness,
> But from the heart all absolution stems
> And lovers' eyes are blind to wantonness.
> Each accusation brings a counter-claim,
> Fresh evidence is met with alibis.
> The summer of his smile refutes the blame
> Of all that logic's art can realize.
> Concerning love, the heart may reason ill,
> Yet triumphs over penetration's skill.

That had been when she was nineteen – the first time she'd fallen seriously in love. He'd been reading English and she'd wanted to impress him . . . Now his name wouldn't come back.

'But from the heart all absolution stems, and lovers' eyes are blind to wantonness.' How much absolution could she grant? More than she knew, otherwise she wouldn't be hiding and he wouldn't be free. It was unbelievable. She was an unremarkable woman with two teenage children, a bad marriage, an ageing mother and what she feared were the first creepings of arthritis in her fingers; living a life of quiet desperation perhaps, but not the doomed heroine of tragedy. All she'd wanted was an affair, for the fun and daring of it, until love had ambushed her. And even that had been all right, because he'd been kind – until a truth that belonged in Gothic horror had emerged, as though a mask had been torn from his face and she had screamed at the decay beneath . . .

Stop it. There's always a way out, however dreadful. Sing to yourself, pray for sleep. That's not much to ask God for at the moment . . . What sounded like a juggernaut rumbled past, fading until she could hear the whisper of waves again.

When she opened the curtains it was a glittering morning, the rising sun molten on rippling water dyed pale blue by shining sky. Across the road a family were early on the sand; a father and two sons kicking a red plastic ball, while the mother held the hand of a tiny girl who was jumping with delight in the sea's shallow edge. Joyce watched them for a long time, before ordering a continental breakfast in her room; polite conversation downstairs would be unbearable. Then she showered, packed, settled her bill and left; it was eight hours before she was due to meet him. She felt better in daylight, her emotions more governable, leaving space for clearer thought. She bought cheese, apple and a fruit drink in Bungay, then drove south again, half aimlessly, the car radio on to occupy her mind, before stopping within sight of a windmill and walking across the fields to it. The sun was now blazing and she sheltered in its shadow. Still another five hours. Come on, look at this head-on.

Find the nearest police station and . . . No, she'd promised to talk to him first. So allow him that, then explain she had no choice but to . . . but not until he had time to get away – if that was what he wanted. Which meant she didn't want him to be punished? But he'd killed them ... No, he hadn't. He'd been there, but she'd read how dreadful he felt, why he'd come to Finch, how desperate he was to find forgiveness. Couldn't she, of all people, forgive? How would she feel when everyone turned on him – and it came out that she had given herself to him? Fay would be sympathetic, but who would understand? What would cruel children say to Rupert and Annabel? Are you the ones whose mother fucks killers? She remembered what the tabloids had been like in nineteen ninety and her revulsion at them; if anything, they were worse now and would tear her to pieces. So what would telling achieve? Randall in gaol, so beautiful they'd be queuing up to rape him; her life and the children's destroyed; Ralph and her mother disowning her; all the condemnation. And five bodies would still lie in the churchyard, no better for it.

She unwrapped the cheese and bit off a corner. Of all the men she could probably have slept with, even found herself in love with, what malign fate had made it him? Emotion was no use, and thought made it worse. The alternative was to keep loving him, protect him, help him to become a complete person, not the sixth victim of Tannerslade. Of course, it would mean this Giles, the one who'd been truly wicked, would still walk free, but there was always a price, however bitter. Her mind went back to Sunday night at the house, the closeness of his body, watching from the window as he found the rose, the unutterable warmth of feeling she was slowly bringing him into her private harbour, the pure joy when he had lifted her to the morning sky. If that had been real, it should be unalterable. 'Beareth all things, believeth all things, hopeth all things, endureth all things' ... How many times had she said that, convinced it had to be true, because if love failed what was left? Greed? Jealousy? Vengeance?

She gave a small, bitter laugh at how simplicities could be subtly distorted. Facts. I can identify the murderers of five innocent people, including two children; and, I knew them; the law, which I always observe, insists I must tell the police. That's what real life is about. This isn't grand opera, I'm not a portrayal of a soul in torment. So why am I sitting here agonizing? Because I'm scared – and have no more idea about what to do than I had before. Unless I could run away.

Jowett felt trapped in the cottage, but Lambert refused to leave and would not let him go out alone.

'We'll have to chance it this evening, but we mustn't be seen together if we can help it. I'm not meant to be here, remember. How long to get to this Stowmarket place?'

'I've not been there, but . . . half an hour?'

'And she said seven o'clock, so we leave here at five thirty. You drop me off somewhere and we don't know each other until you pick me up again.'

'I still can't understand why you want to be there. I'll tell you what she says to me.'

'We've been through that. I want to see what sort of woman you managed to pull.' There had only been one Valium left in the car, and Lambert was having to control his nervousness. 'I'm assuming she looks like a dog.'

'No, she doesn't.' Jowett felt protective, partly insulted on Joyce's behalf. 'You wouldn't think she's as old as she is, for a start. I'm not going to . . . Just don't slag her off, OK?'

'All right, I'm . . .' Lambert forced himself back into the mood he needed to maintain. 'I didn't mean it. I'm just on the edge here, you know? She might have changed her mind and be talking to the police right now.'

Jowett shook his head. 'She wouldn't lie to me. I know that.'

'OK, it's all right . . . How many cigarettes have you got?'

'One more pack after this.'

'Jesus. I need more than twenty to get me through today.'

'I'll go out for some.'

'No way. I'll manage. Let's watch some crap on TV.'

By mid-afternoon, they had lapsed into silence. Jowett wished Lambert would talk, explain what he was planning in more detail since they had discussed it the previous evening after Joyce's call. If their best hope – that she would somehow not want to hand him over – failed, Jowett was to play on her sympathy, asking for time to go to France to confess to his sister, preparing her for when he gave himself up. He'd told Lambert she would probably agree. That would buy them a few days, during which Jowett was to raise as much money as possible and Lambert would transfer it to his overseas account. Then it would be Eurostar across the Channel, hidden among crowds of day-trippers, a plane out of Paris to anywhere on one of the less efficient airlines, then on to the Cayman Islands.

'It's not perfect,' Lambert had admitted. 'But it won't make it easy for them to find us. Anyway, we may not need to do it. If she hasn't gone straight to the police, she might not go at all. Turn your charm on.'

Relieved that Lambert was so capable, Jowett also knew that once he'd handed over the money, there was nothing to stop Lambert disappearing. He'd felt bad suggesting it, as though it showed a lack of trust.

'Think about it,' Lambert had told him. 'If I'm not at Waterloo when you expect me, you'll go to the police and they'll turn Interpol loose. I know they'll get you as well – she'll make sure of that, anyway – but we've got to trust each other on this, Randy.'

And Jowett had accepted it. Why not? It sounded plausible enough. Not as refined as planning Tannerslade had been, but there wasn't time to perfect it. Lambert found a pack of cards among the assorted games supplied in the cottage and insisted they played three-card brag, German whist, cribbage – anything to keep Jowett's crazy mind occupied.

Lambert bought a copy of *The Times* in Stowmarket and folded it so it looked as if he was doing the crossword as he sat on a barstool in the Crown; he surprised himself by solving half a dozen clues. The quiet, soft-carpeted lounge was immediately inside the entrance: two grey imitation leather settees and a handful of low tables with armchairs, muted crimson lighting. Three men and a woman were the only other customers until Jowett walked in at twenty to seven, not looking at Lambert as he bought a gin and tonic and sat near the door. He lit a cigarette, then took a handful of peanuts from the bowl on the table and ate them one at a time. Lambert concentrated on the paper; the answer to six across was Coppelia. Behind him low voices, bland violins playing Andrew Lloyd Webber and the barman joshing with a waitress who came through from the dining room with a drinks order. One of the men told a dirty joke and the woman laughed politely; perhaps he was her boss. Lambert checked his watch against the lounge clock; it was three minutes slow. Where was she? The barman glanced at his glass to see if he wanted a refill, then continued playing with a pocket computer game.

It was ten past seven when Lambert saw the revolving door move; Jowett had described her, but not well enough. Statuesque, the sort of woman to make him wonder what she had looked like twenty years earlier when her beauty had been fired by carnal greed. High heels, olive green cotton shirt taut across good breasts, then sloping in to a wide leather belt and full skirt. She hesitated, then saw Jowett, and seemed both relieved and apprehensive. He stood up and they spoke before he went back to the bar and bought a St Clements with ice. Lambert stared at twenty-three down, ears strained but they were speaking very softly, leaning towards each other.

'I'm so relieved you're here.'

'Why shouldn't I have been?'

'Because you could have run away from me . . . May I?' She indicated his cigarettes, holding one between inexperienced fingers as he lit it, then coughed. 'Sorry. It's years since I've had one. I never thought anything would drive me back.'

He could think of nothing to say as she drew in and instantly expelled smoke several times, examining him curiously, as though he were someone she knew intimately who had become a total stranger.

'Where've you been?' he asked.

'Not far . . . But it was a hell of a long way back. I just had to be somewhere on my own after . . .' She stubbed out the barely smoked Dorchester in the cut-glass ashtray impatiently, as though asking for it had been a weakness. 'And before I say anything, I want you to swear to tell me the truth. You've lied by default, if nothing else. If you don't promise to be honest from now on – and for God's sake I deserve that – I may as well walk straight out of here.'

'Don't do that. Please.' She had her back to Lambert and Jowett could see him glancing across occasionally. 'I promise.'

She held his eyes as if trying to see deception. 'All right. Thank you. The first thing I have to know is . . . When I read what you'd written you said it had never been planned as murder . . . Don't interrupt. You said this Giles had told you the gun wasn't loaded and you were horrified when it happened. Was that true?'

'Yes.' He held his palms open for emphasis. 'What would have been the point in lying when I was writing about it? No one else was meant to see it, but I've been hiding from this for six years, and . . . there's a lot I can't explain. Writing it down, making myself read it again . . . I thought it might help me.'

'And did it?'

'In some ways . . . at least that's what I told myself. I was beginning to think that coming back here was helping as well.'

'Even though what happened between us took your mind off it?' She sounded slightly caustic.

'It didn't,' he said simply. 'Can't you understand? Nothing I do is separate from that day. It . . . possesses me.' At the bar Lambert was ordering another drink.

'So when you said it had been crucifying you, you meant that? Really meant it.'

'Did you read the part about when I tried to kill myself?' She nodded. 'I don't know how well I explained how I felt when I couldn't go through with it, but not having the courage to do it made me hate myself even more. Finch was the last place to go. If I fail here, with you, I might find the courage to try again. At least that would end it.'

She wondered how much the sudden twist of pain showed in her face. 'And *you* didn't kill them?'

'No, I didn't! You've got to believe that.'

She rested her elbows on the table and raised her hands to her lips, looking away, eyes troubled. He wanted to reach across and touch her, but feared rejection.

'All right, I do,' she said finally. 'But what happened afterwards? After you told him you wanted nothing more to do with it.'

'I just got out. Started trying to run away from it. As far as I was concerned, Giles could keep what we'd stolen and I never wanted to see him again. I didn't care what he did.'

'But you did see him again. On Moorgate. I read that.'

Randall fumbled with the cigarette packet. 'Yes, but it was just a chance meeting. I didn't even know he was living in London.'

'Tell me about him.'

'Why?'

'Because he turned you into somebody I know you're not.' She shook her head in dismayed disbelief. 'How could you let him do that to you?'

He looked directly at her, despite the urge to look beyond. 'He just did it ... He's very clever and I ... I'll never understand myself, but he could argue so well and I let him persuade me. What I need forgiving for is not what I did, but what I didn't do. I should have told him to forget it right from the start, then at least tried to stop him when it happened. And I should have given myself up.'

'Do you think he's evil? You didn't make him sound it.'

'If I said he was, wouldn't that be as if I were making an excuse for myself? He's ... hard, determined, you know the type. They succeed because they don't give a damn about people they hurt. Perhaps he's more extreme.'

'Wasn't he worried you'd betray him?'

'How could I? If the police ever picked him up, he'd drag me in even if I hadn't been the one who told them. I've dreaded hearing that they'd got him and knowing it was me next.'

She sipped her drink, before opening her bag and taking out a handkerchief, holding it briefly against each eye in turn as she sniffed. 'I know exactly what I ought to do, of course, but ...'

Her voice caught on a small hiccup. 'Well, if you didn't believe me before when I said how much I love you, I hope you've grasped it now. I can't bear the thought of you ... Just swear you're telling me the truth!'

'You've read the truth.' Lambert saw him take hold of her hand across the table. 'I came here to see if I could sort myself out, but meeting you confused me even more ... I've never been loved, I don't know what it's about.' He tightened his grip. 'I can't stop you going to the police, but if you do, that's it for me. I've read a lot about prison and I know I'd kill myself in there.'

She sighed. 'I know that as well ... So what do we do?'

'That's up to you ... but I didn't run away.'

'No you didn't.' She smiled. 'Thank you for that ... I need more time, all right? My conscience is tearing me apart at the moment. I'll have to see if I can make peace with it. I promise I won't do anything – but you must promise to stay at the cottage and I'll come to see you tomorrow evening. We'll talk again then. Please, please don't come to the house ... Oh, of course, you don't know about my mother seeing us, do you?'

'No.' He looked puzzled. 'When I went there to find you, she obviously knew something. I was trying to work out why you'd told her.'

'I hadn't, but when we were saying goodbye on Monday morning ... It doesn't matter.' She raised his hand and kissed it. 'I want to meet you on this, darling. I just pray I can. For both of us.'

Lambert watched her leave, then waited a few moments before folding his paper and following. Jowett found him waiting by the MGF in the market square; he'd seen Joyce drive away and noted the number of her car.

'Well?' he demanded.

'She wants more time.'

'What for?'

'To think ... But she doesn't want to hand me in.'

'Did she say that?'

'Yes ... Well, not in those words, but I'm certain she doesn't.'

'So what does she want time for?'

'She said she wants to think some more. She's coming to the cottage tomorrow evening to talk about it again.'

Lambert turned and dropped *The Times* in a litter bin by the car. 'How sure are you that she won't shoot her mouth off?'

'Positive at the moment . . . although she could change her mind. But I'm certain she'll agree if I ask for time to tell Ruth, so we'll still be OK.' He unlocked the car and they got in.

'I'll give you one thing,' Lambert said. 'She may be pushing it, but she's still a looker. What was she like in the sack?'

'I don't want to talk about that.'

Lambert laughed. 'The guys I work with have a rule that you're a winner if you've screwed more birds than you've driven different cars. I'm three ahead. What's your score, Randy?'

He smirked crudely when Jowett didn't reply, then stared out of the window as they drove away.

Chapter Twenty-one

The graves stood bare now, but next week there would be
flowers on them for the anniversary, not only from Trevor and
Janet Godwin but others in the village; Joyce and Fay always
bought them together and stood under the yews for a few
minutes, recalling and remembering, aware that the pain was
fading, before going back to their lives. Now Joyce sat alone on
a bench, her attention caught by a pewter tabby cat stalking
delicately as it slithered through long grass towards an unaware
thrush; she clapped her hands sharply and the bird flew off. The
cat's head flickered to follow the fluttering movement, then it
paused to wash before seeing her and trotting over for affection.

'Villain,' she murmured, stroking the purring body and rigid
tail trembling with pleasure. 'They feed you well enough at
home.'

The nearer headstone was that of Cheryl and the children,
pale marble mottled by six winters a visible sign of the decaying
bodies beneath the earth. As a child Joyce would have imagined
them white and winged in some vaguely defined pastel-coloured
heaven; now she thought of them as intangible spirits in an
unknown dimension. Were they aware of what had happened,
and waiting for her to inflict punishment? Or didn't it matter to
them now? Whatever, there were no signs, no inner or outer
voices, telling her what she must do. All the churchyard offered
was solitary peace to contemplate what in Jowett's case was
crime and in hers what used to be called sin. But the graves
made no demands. The decision, when it came, was neither
right nor wrong, but instinctive, and there were no tears as she

gazed at Cheryl's chiselled name, no need for forgiveness. Cheryl would understand that to love someone so deeply was a valuable thing.

The clock struck eleven, and she was aware that she'd been sitting there for nearly two hours. She thought about going straight to the cottage, but wanted more time alone to think about the consequences that lay beyond her decision. Explaining to him, facing painful practical and emotional problems . . . What was that line from Chesterton? 'Ruin is a builder of windows.' Emerging from dark confusion, she sensed the possibility of light.

Lambert had allowed Jowett to go out for food, whisky, more cigarettes. He rang the office again, telling them his mother had passed the crisis but remained seriously ill; it might be Monday before he could return. There was no need to call Victoria; she would be grateful that he was out of the house. Was there a lover? Lack of proof didn't undermine his conviction, and she was devious enough to hide it; they were probably at it like knives once Becky had been taken to nursery . . . he physically shook images away. The claustrophobia he felt in the cottage was deepened by being in an alien world. In London you were anonymous; still, insular Finch was filled with eyes that watched. He stayed away from the windows at the front in case he was seen and somebody later remembered.

He had lain awake deep into the night. There were weapons – the meat knife in the kitchen was new, the blade leaving a hairline of blood when he had stroked it experimentally across his finger – and neither of them would be prepared. Jowett had accepted his spurious guilt and denials of ever wanting to kill, and the woman was unaware of his presence. Attacking them together would be dangerous, but if one of them came upstairs to use the bathroom . . . He had read somewhere about how it should be done. Strike hard – the body was remarkably resistant – and upwards, just below the ribcage. Then deal with the other one . . . sorted.

He thought about possible problems, trying to drive off the

returning sense of fear that he might not be able to go through with it. There was evidence of him all over the house; things he had been in contact with, the bed he had slept in. So he would have to wipe every surface he might have touched ... Then torch the place. Wait until night, siphon petrol out of the MGF's tank and soak the bed linen in it, add those old deckchairs and anything else that would burn quickly, pile it all on top of the bodies. The building was old, the timbers dry ... and there was a gas oven. The chapel next door was disused and Jowett had told him the couple in the attached cottage were invalids, wife bedridden, husband half deaf. With no other houses around until you reached the church, nobody would know anything until the actual explosion, and the nearest fire station must be miles away. There would be virtually nothing left by the time the police arrived.

Escape. He would start the fire, say around two in the morning, then leave taking Jowett's Ordnance Survey map and head towards Bury St Edmunds. It would be tricky walking in the dark and he'd have to avoid roads wherever possible, but it would be light by the time he reached the town and nobody would take any notice of a man going to catch an early train. His Saab was parked in an unrestricted zone just outside the town centre. Someone might have seen it there, but why should they connect it with two deaths in Finch nearly fifteen miles away? He could do nothing about that now, anyway. He'd spend one more day away – he had bought clothes and would take one of Jowett's cases to become just another businessman booking into a bed and breakfast where they'd accept cash and not ask for identification – then back to London. Not as seamless as Tannerslade had been, but then there had been weeks to plan and perfect it; this was being created in emergency.

The weaknesses were tolerable. Nobody knew he had come to Finch; even after the fire, forensic experts might still find traces of another person in the cottage, but he was unknown to them. The only connection between Giles Lambert and Randall Jowett was Cambridge ... unless there was something in

227

Jowett's flat. The police would go straight there; had the prat written down anything else? He'd have to ask him, making it part of the scheme to escape together. The great thing with Randy was that he couldn't lie. And if there *was* something . . . he'd worry about that if it happened.

And afterwards he would just carry on shifting the stuff until he'd had enough. His only regret later would be that it had been impossible to come up with a method of murdering his wife that offered any hope of getting away with it. Unless one day his life brought him into contact with a contract killer; that would be a good way to close the chapter. But that was daydreaming; he must concentrate on the dangers of the next few hours.

He heard a car pull up outside and withdrew into the kitchen, in case it was some unexpected visitor, but then heard Jowett calling, as if anxious to confirm he was still there.

'You took your time.'

'There was a queue. It's a small shop.'

Lambert took the whisky bottle from the carrier bag and twisted the top loose, then half filled a tumbler and topped it up with tap water. Alcohol could be used as a fire accelerant as well.

'What time do you think she'll be here?'

'I told you. She just said this evening.' Bizarrely, Jowett was putting things in cupboards. 'Seven o'clock.'

Lambert checked his watch; eight hours of keeping Jowett under control, dealing with his weird conscience. He momentarily thought of simply killing him, getting that over with, then waiting for her to walk through the door, but there was a possibility she might ring and change the arrangements, perhaps not even come. He needed to ensure they were both where he could deal with them.

'Did you get a paper?'

'In the other bag. *Times* and *Telegraph*.'

'You should have bought all of them. Anything to pass the bloody time.'

*

Joyce felt comfort in having chosen her road, having made her decision after so much agony. She could even persuade herself that so terrible a secret might bind them together. But the most immediate problem, one she would have avoided if somehow possible, was explaining to Fay. Truth was out of the question but her lies were transparently inadequate.

'All right, I admit the whole thing's mad.' Seeing Fay's bewilderment moving from impatience to temper, she retreated to defiant acknowledgement. 'But it's a damn sight better than what I've got. OK?'

'The hell it is!' Fay snapped. 'Where do you want me to start? Your mother's going to hate you. Ralph is twisted enough to demand the kids, even though he doesn't want them, so God help those two. You've told me before that Ralph controls the money, and he'll find some high-octane bastard lawyer who'll make you fight for every penny. I can think of a dozen people off the top of my head who'll turn on you. And for what? A man years younger than you whom you jumped into bed with but still know damn all about . . . and how do you know he'll agree?'

'He just will. I know that.'

'Why? Christ Almighty, they'll all say they love you if that's what it takes to get you on your back again. Haven't you learnt that yet?'

Joyce looked down to where she was twisting her wedding ring on her finger. 'I obviously can't explain it, can I? Will I lose you as well?'

'No. Never that. But don't expect me to cheer . . . and you've still not told me what happened to make you go away. What the hell did he say to you? That was Tuesday, and you looked as if you wanted to kill yourself. Now it's Thursday, and suddenly he's the only thing you want in your life.'

Joyce flinched as Fay took hold of her, fingers digging deep and urgently into her shoulders as she cried in frustration, 'Why are you lying to me? Tell me!'

She replied like a tearful and captured child, head lowered.

'There's nothing to tell. What happened on Monday was just a misunderstanding. We've sorted it now. It's all right.'

Fay peered at her, as though trying to see the hidden truth through the tears, then shook her head. 'No, it's not. And you know that . . . but I can't help if you won't trust me.'

'I don't need help.'

'Oh yes you do. And when you realize that, just call Auntie Fay.' She hugged her. 'OK, no more quarrelling. This is dreadfully wrong, but . . . Well, I said you might have to crash and burn. Do you want to talk about practicalities? You're not planning to pack up and walk out today, are you?'

'Of course not. I must talk to Rupert and Annabel for a start, and Christ knows how many complications there are in this. It'll take for ever to sort them out . . . and I've got a weekend from hell coming up.'

'You're going to tell Ralph you're leaving him?'

'Yes. I think he'll stop short of locking me in the attic, but he and Mummy will get the thumbscrews out.'

'You know you can always come and stay with us.'

'Thank you.'

'And what about Randall? He'll still be here, won't he?'

'No. I'm seeing him this evening and I'll ask him to go back to London while I . . . get the worst of it over. He'll understand.'

'You mean he'll back off while you deal with all the shit on your own.'

'It's not like that. I've got to handle this. He'll . . . be there.'

Fay shook her head sorrowfully. 'I hope you're right, darling, but all I can see for you in this is grief.'

Sultry and slow, the afternoon crawled as shimmering thermals seeped in to shade and Finch took on a greater stillness, stunned by cauldron heat. Only flying insects moved through the fevered air as cats sprawled death-still, and the wet tongues of dogs hung loose; bricks were warm to the touch, as if fresh from baking ovens; blinding with light, the sun appeared stationary and horizons were blurred.

Stripped to a pair of Jowett's shorts, Lambert sweated as he stood just by the back door of the cottage, unable to venture into the open in case someone saw him. But there would be little point; outside was no mercy of breeze. He rolled a cold beer can across his chest, then swallowed the last mouthful. He should commit the killings virtually naked so there would be no danger of blood on his clothes; another detail in place. Then a bath – the cottage had no shower – before preparing for the fire. A twinge of fear came back, more difficult to wrestle away. Of course there were risks, but not as great as the alternatives; nothing in life was foolproof, but you either made things happen or they happened to you. What was the use of going down without a struggle? He'd become a murderer six years ago and had remained free, so why not again? And if he succeeded this time, there would be no more enemies. He couldn't lose it now.

He went back inside, then stopped himself as he opened the fridge and reached for another beer. He could handle it, but the heat and three whiskies were beginning to make him feel sluggish – and he must stay calm and prepared for this evening. Apprehension flickered back as he walked through to the sitting room.

'What the fuck are you watching?'

Jowett lay on the sofa, staring at the television. 'It's a game show.'

'For the brain dead?' Lambert sat in a captain's chair, oak briefly cool against his skin, but almost immediately becoming adhesive. Also wearing only shorts, Jowett was in good condition, lean but with a stomach hard and flat, forearms crafted with slender muscle. It would be best if he was first, taken by surprise, not alerted if he heard her scream. And once he was out of the way, she would be weakened by terror when a man burst in unexpectedly, almost naked, carrying a knife blazoned with blood. She would probably freeze, voice choked to silence, unable to move. The soft flesh below the breasts, diagonally upwards, all his strength behind it . . . No more than a minute from first to second strike. He could do that.

'What else is on?'

'What? Kid's stuff, I think. Might be something on BBC2. Shall I switch over?'

'No, just turn this crap off.' Jowett obediently pressed the control and the cottage became silent. He picked *The Times* off the floor.

'Do you want something to eat?'

'No . . . Yeah.' It would help to soak up the alcohol. 'Some of that cheese and one of those rolls. Thanks.'

Look at you waiting on me. No wonder she can twist you any way she wants.

It was a brief calm between storms – and there would be many of those. French doors wide open but curtains closed, the pale sitting room faced west, so the sun was only just touching it and the parquet floor was cool. How much would Ralph fight over what she would want to take? From this room the portrait of herself as a child, her porcelain thimble collection, the silver salver her father had left her, the carriage clock that had been a fortieth birthday present from Fay and Oliver. Mentally she ran over the rest of the house; apart from her clothes and books there were remarkably few things she treasured. Too many of them were associated with Ralph. So little baggage – apart from anguish over the children, which would surely pass as they grew older; there was no reason why she could not continue to be a good mother, if in a different way . . . And, of course, her share of his guilt.

'Oh, hell,' she whispered to herself. 'Forgive me for that.'

Loneliness was so absolute surely it could grow no worse. Her mother remained frigid with disapproval, impatient for Ralph's return so that this unpleasantness could be dealt with. Worried and confused, knowing she had been lied to, Fay waited for her to find her way back to sanity, unable to reach her until she did. There was only Randall, scared and pleading, alone like herself, offering desperate – and, to be honest, mad – hope she was able to weave into dreams that she couldn't allow to be false.

The carriage clock chimed six and she went upstairs to

shower and change. Something lightweight and simple – but nothing that made her look desirable. This was not the time for sex, however much she might long for it. They had to talk, to find ground where only they could meet, agree that the past could not be buried but must be accommodated in the heart. She could help by forgiving, and surely once such darkness had been lifted, they could build. But she knew it must not be through compulsion or a sense of terrified gratitude. If Randall did not come to her willingly, she would have to let him go and live with herself . . . which meant there was a more absolute loneliness.

Chapter Twenty-two

'You weren't planning to get her into bed again, were you?' Lambert mocked his captive, a diversion to take his mind off his own increasing nervousness. 'I don't think screwing's on tonight's menu – so there's no problem about me being upstairs.'

'You could go out. No one's likely to see you and they don't know you anyway.'

'Read my lips – I'm staying here. Got it? I'm not wandering round the sodding countryside while you two talk. She could be here until midnight. I'll take a book up with me.'

'You won't try to listen?'

'What for? You're going to tell me afterwards. We haven't got time for secrets here.'

Jowett turned away, convinced Lambert would listen from the stairs, limiting how he dare answer if Joyce wanted to talk about him again.

'Suppose I can't persuade her? You know – worst case scenario.'

'We worry about that if it happens. But it's been four days and she's still not gone to the police. Even if she says she's decided to do it now, she'll give you time to see your sister. I'd put money on that.' Lambert smiled. 'Sweet talk her.'

'She's not a fool.'

'Tell me about it . . . OK.' He held up his hand against the instant resentment in Jowett's face. 'Let's just hope she's panting for you as much as you think.' He picked up the whisky bottle. 'I'll take this for company. I'll get a glass. You stay here and watch for her. She might arrive early.'

Lambert took the knife from the kitchen drawer, hiding it inside a newspaper as he went up to the spare bedroom. Twenty to seven; say two hours before one of them might need to come upstairs. He poured a drink and sat against the headboard of the bed, staring through the window opposite, waiting to hear a car. Why did he need to hold the glass in both hands to prevent it from trembling? More Valium would have helped, but . . . shit! What are you taking on here? A dickhead and a woman. They're all that's between you and . . . It was easier to think beyond it to the safety of knowing that he had succeeded again, of ceasing to be Giles Lambert, of finding some obscure, corrupt country where a white man with money had power and there would be compensations for what he'd had to give up. Perhaps he'd open a bar with girls to attract the sex tourists, entertain the police, a little discreet gambling in the back, become a character. Not the sort of life he'd planned at Cambridge, but things didn't always work out . . . He felt the first twinges of a headache.

From the path came the sound of footsteps, then the click of the catch on the gate; she must have walked. That was good; it meant she didn't plan to rush away. He heard Jowett open the front door, and muffled voices came from the room below before someone went into the kitchen; he must be getting her a drink. There was no need to listen; what they said to each other would never matter. He just had to wait.

Joyce spoke the moment Jowett returned from the kitchen. 'I want to tell you this straight away . . . I'm not going to the police.' She shared the reaction in his eyes. 'I've nearly gone out of my mind thinking about it, but I can't.'

'Thank you.' He handed her the wine. 'I didn't kill them.'

'I know you didn't. It's not in you.'

'But you must still blame me.'

'For some things . . . but I don't want to discuss that at the moment.'

She sat in the centre of the narrow padded windowseat, positioning herself to discourage him from joining her. It was curious that the worst thing could have been resolved so easily.

He looked exhausted and she felt regret for what he had suffered.

'So what do we do?' he asked. It would have been so much better had he cried with relief, with gratitude that she felt so much for him. It would have been so much better had he understood why she could not tell.

'What do you want to do?'

Jowett looked at his glass, held in both hands as though he were clasping a chalice. He told himself he had been forgiven, that his life might start again. He wanted desperately to be alone.

'You know why I came here. To try to . . . exorcize it.' He appeared unable to continue.

'And have you . . . or have I?' Her eyes forced him to look at her. 'Do you just pass the guilt on?'

'No. That wouldn't be right. I'd feel no better if I did that.'

She looked out of the window, watching a mother walking her daughter home from Brownies. Sandra Dean, sang in the church choir, soon old enough to take care of the little ones at Sunday School, dreaming of becoming a vet like her father when she grew up. A fragment of Joyce Hetherington's life.

'I want to say something and you mustn't interrupt.' She remained looking at mother and child, holding hands as they walked up the hill. 'I've decided to leave my husband – and my children, and everything I've spent half a lifetime making. I know it's insane, but it's not a matter of reason. If it was, I'd have gone to the police by now.' As she looked at him again, his face was blank. 'But you mustn't feel trapped. Either we do this on the right terms or we don't do it at all. And if you can't do it because you don't love me, then all I ask is that you go away – and I mean tonight – and never come back. What I said before will still stand, so you'll have nothing to be afraid of. That's it. End of speech.'

Jowett felt culpable; he had not trusted her, not recognized the intensity of her feelings – which was why he had called Giles. But this was the best they had hoped for; once Giles knew she would keep their secret, he would go away again. But he needed to know . . .

'What about Giles?'

She sighed. 'My conscience is giving me hell. If I could see a way to punish him and protect you at the same time, I'd take it this instant. He didn't just kill them, he destroyed you as well. I've just got to try to drive him from my mind . . . He mustn't matter to you and me.'

And you've still not responded to what I've said. I'd accept it with tears, with disbelief, with any promises . . . as long as you're honest with me. Or I'll accept rejection and live with it because I could never hate you so much that I'd . . . Both of them jumped at the sound of shattering glass above their heads. In the bedroom, Lambert swore at the broken bottle that had slipped from his grasp.

'There's someone upstairs!'

'It's OK. I left the window open. The wind must have blown the curtains.'

'There isn't even a breeze!' She leapt up, but he stood in front of her.

'I'll go and check! There's no one there.'

'Don't be stupid! That was something heavy. Someone's broken in!'

'They can't have done! We're here.'

'They can't see us from the back. Did you leave the door unlocked?'

'I think so . . . yeah.'

'Where's your mobile phone?'

'Why?'

'To call the police!'

'I've told you. I'll go and check.'

'Stay here!' She grabbed his arm. 'They could be dangerous. I don't want you thumped over the head. Just find your phone and we'll get out . . . listen!' The fourth stair had creaked for years. 'Christ, they're coming down! Put something against the door!'

When he didn't move, she snatched up a dining chair and jammed it under the knob. 'Bring the table over . . . There it is!' She leapt at the phone on the mantelpiece.

'We've called the police!' she shouted, punching the buttons as she saw the door strain against the chair. Jowett had still not moved. 'They're on their way!' The chair legs slid fractionally and the door opened a few inches. 'For Christ's sake, the table! Go on ... Hello? Police! Come *on*! Yes? Windhover Cottage, Finch. Near the church. Someone's broken in! They're trying to attack us ... quickly!'

She dropped the phone and grabbed the table herself, in the strength of her panic managing to push it across the floor until it slammed the door shut again. From the other side came a bellow of rage.

'For God's sake, what's the matter with you?' She was starting to sob with terror. 'Do something!'

She screamed at a violent bang behind her, and the knife blade burst through one of the door panels. 'Randall, please! Help me!'

Jowett snapped out of inertia. 'Get out! It's all right!'

In the hallway Lambert struggled to pull free the knife he'd plunged at the door in fury, but it remained fast. He'd heard her on the phone and knew the message had got through. Where were the keys for the MG? Jowett had them on him. Was there time to get his own? If he didn't ... He raced upstairs, snatching up clothes. How long before the police arrived? He daren't trust it would be long enough for him to get dressed. He grabbed jacket, trousers and shirt, then thrust bare feet into his shoes. Back or front? Front too dangerous; he'd have to risk finding his directions across the fields. He pounded downstairs again.

'I think he's gone!' Still pressing her weight against the edge of the table, Joyce was gasping with fright.

'I'll go and look.'

'No! Wait for the police ... Pass me my drink.' She was conscious it was the first time Jowett had moved. 'Who the hell was he?'

'He must have been a burglar.'

'With a knife? Trying to kill us? No way. He was a lunatic.' Through turmoil, she remembered something. 'Why did you shout at him to get out?'

'I was telling him to go away.'

'But you didn't say "Go away" . . . and what did you mean about it being all right?'

'I meant . . . he couldn't get in here. We were all right . . . and the police were coming.'

'But I'd yelled that at him.' She stepped away from the table. 'I don't understand you.'

Their heads jerked towards the window as car brakes screeched outside and they saw Christine Sheaffer leap out, talking into a hand radio as she ran to the gate, her jeans and shirt mottled with paint. Joyce pulled the table and chair away as they heard her dash into the cottage.

'Police! Where are you?'

Joyce opened the sitting-room door. 'What are you doing here?'

'I'm with CID. Someone remembered I lived in Finch and called me.' She raised her radio. 'I'm in the house. Two adult persons present, both unharmed. Hang on . . . Is there anybody else here?'

'No. He ran off.'

'How long ago?'

'Only a few minutes.'

'Did you see him?'

'No. He went out the back.'

The radio was raised again. 'Suspect apparently escaped. I'll check the premises.' She turned off the radio, then indicated the knife. 'Did he do that?'

'Yes. He was trying to kill us.'

'Don't touch it.' They heard her race upstairs and into the bedrooms, then she returned. 'There's no one else here. Are you all right if I leave you? Other officers should be arriving soon. OK. I'm going after him.'

'He's dangerous,' Joyce warned.

'So am I.' As she left, they heard the faint approaching howl of a siren.

*

Lambert felt shriekingly visible as he ran across empty fields, like a hunted animal in naked desert. The windows of a farmhouse a quarter of a mile away caught the sun, turning them into searchlights that pinned him down. He reached a stile and scrambled over it, the flapping leg of the trousers clutched under his arm tearing on an exposed rusty nail. A lane, barely the width of a car, but it must lead to a proper road. His desperate compulsion was to keep running, but he had to stop and put his clothes on. Gasping for breath he dropped the bundle, then snatched up the shirt, leaving it unfastened as he dragged on trousers and jacket. A wild scarecrow figure without socks, patched with dust, he started running again. Had he left anything behind that would identify him? He slapped his hand against his chest and felt his wallet in the inside pocket. There was nothing else . . . apart from his fingerprints all over the place and Jowett exposed to questioning. He began to sob, angry tears mixing with sweat, then yelped in terror as he passed a gate in the hedge and the dark bulk of a cow lumbered away, booming in alarm.

Then there was a road, and he stopped at the T-junction, ignorant of which way to go; there was no signpost. Which direction was the cottage? It was impossible to know. He'd run blindly and wasn't familiar with this open, menacing country-side. The police could have arrived by now, calling for dogs and helicopters . . . Through smeared eyes, he saw a car appear, heading towards him, and he stepped into the centre of the road, windmilling his arms frantically. He could only see the shape of a driver . . . and it was a woman. She stopped a few yards in front of him and he ran to the driver's door; secure in her country life, she was too innocent to have locked it.

She screamed as Lambert wrenched open the door, grabbed hold of her hair and dragged her out, then savagely slammed her head against the edge of the roof until she went slack. Leave her in the ditch? No, she might come round. He dropped her and reached inside for the keys, then opened the boot and bundled her into it. Road blocks? They hadn't had time – and who knew he had a car? It was a Volvo, capable of speed as soon as he reached a main highway. When he started it the radio came on playing Sibelius, and he switched it off. There was still the question of which way. If Finch was the nearest village, she could have been heading there . . . Tyres squealed as he turned round. Within half a mile he reached a crossroads. He'd guessed right – Finch was behind him – but none of the four wooden arms on the gibbet-like post said Bury St Edmunds. He scrabbled in the glove compartment, flinching as a stitch of pain stabbed across his stomach, but there was no map. At least the road ahead was straight, taking him farther away. The woman's bag lay on the passenger seat and he fumbled it open. No cigarettes, but a wallet which he snapped open and looked into as he drove. Photograph of a teenage girl in a frame pocket protected by a plastic film, credit cards in a column of thin slots . . . and money. He pulled out the notes and counted them on the dashboard with one hand. Five twenties and four tens . . . his head jerked up as the car rocked violently. He had drifted across the road, wheels ricocheting against the step of the opposite kerb. He swerved back. Concentrate; an accident now would be sick.

The road rose and curved across an abandoned railway line, then ran to meet a dual carriageway; Bury St Edmunds was to the right and he seethed with impatience as he waited for a gap to appear in the traffic. As the roar of a car transporter faded, he heard a hollow banging and muffled yells; he whirled round, but the road behind was empty . . . The bitch had come round. An approaching van was signalling to turn into the side road, and there was just enough space if he . . . Violent acceleration forced him back in the seat. The banging had grown louder, shouts amplified in the metal box. If he had to stop and another driver heard it . . . there was a left turn marked just ahead. Tyres screamed as he braked and hurled the wheel over to screech round the sharp corner into another back road; within a few hundred yards he was in isolation again.

She looked terrified as he opened the boot again, but instinctively tried to sit up towards light and air. Lambert's fist smashed against her jaw, then he lifted her out and dragged her

241

into a patch of trees by the road, hysterical with frustration. One unlaced shoe slipped off and he swore as his unprotected foot trod on a sharp fallen branch. Then it felt cold as the ground became soggy and he stumbled; he lay panting for a moment until she moaned and started to move. Just beside them was a shallow, slime-covered pond and he forced her face into it, knee on her back as she struggled. It seemed a very long time before she went limp, and he fell back, staring at her.

'I'm sorry.' Almost gently, he pulled her out. Brutalized, her face still showed her beauty, and he wiped away the blemish of wet green threads of water plants, as though such consideration might bring forgiveness. Then he began to cry uncontrollably, not now tears of panic, but of fear and a sense of desolation he had never known. He remained beside the body as darkness gathered.

Chapter Twenty-three

Shocked and inquisitive, Finch's attention centred on the cottage and the police vehicles outside, roof lights flickering blooms of blue glare, radio messages crackling in the quiet. Gathered at a discreet distance, a knot of villagers exchanged rumours as alert alsatians were led into the fields behind. It could only be murder; Joyce Hetherington's holiday guest, the reserved, courteous young man from London. She was probably being questioned about him, telling what little she knew. But did murder mean there was some blight of violent death in this place? How long ago was it now? Six years – the anniversary was next week – and they had never caught them. What evil had come back? In God's name, why here?

Joyce's hands trembled as she held the cup of tea, disliking its sweetness, but accepting it would help.

'I must let my mother know.' The realization burst into her whirling brain.

'We've already taken care of that.' The Inspector was sympathetic, but not prepared to let her leave. 'I've sent an officer round to your house. What about your husband?'

'He's in London. He stays there during the week.'

'We can contact him if you wish.'

'That doesn't matter. He'll be back tomorrow. How long do I have to stay here?'

'We'll be as quick as we can . . . Excuse me.'

Haggard left as a man looked round the door and said he was wanted in the kitchen. The cottage was full of noise, people apparently in every room. She and Jowett had been separated. Sheaffer had returned and was sitting with Joyce.

'You didn't even see him then?'

'No,' Sheaffer replied. 'He could have run anywhere. The dogs are very good, though, and the helicopter should be up there any time now.'

'I didn't know you had anything to do with the police.'

'I hadn't advertised it, but it meant I was nearby.'

'Yes. Thank you.' She forced down more tea as Haggard returned.

'We'll need to take a statement from you, Mrs Hetherington, but there are some points I want to sort out immediately.'

'I've told you what happened. I don't know anything else.'

'How long has Mr Jowett been staying here?'

'He arrived on the eighth of June.'

'And he was on his own?'

'Yes.'

'Was that unusual?'

'It's happened before. There was a man last year. He came to fish.'

'And why were you here this evening?'

She replaced the cup on a side table. 'I'd just called in to see Mr Jowett.'

'What about?'

'Nothing important . . . Just for a chat.'

'Do you make a habit of that with your guests, Mrs Hetherington?'

'Not a habit, but . . . I like to make sure everything's all right.'

'But he's been here for nearly a month, any problems would surely have been sorted out by now, wouldn't they?'

'Yes . . . but I'd got to know him.'

'How?'

'We'd met in the village, talked to each other. He came to the pageant last Saturday. I knew he was on his own and . . . I like to be friendly with people who stay here.'

What was stopping her telling the truth? Did she fear Haggard and Sheaffer would be shocked – or vulgarly amused? Earlier that evening she had been prepared to face her husband and mother with it and damn what anybody thought. Now she was prevaricating, making what could become traps with evasive lies.

'I see . . . And you're certain nobody else was staying at this cottage?'

'Absolutely. Why?'

'Obviously we're in the very early stages of this investigation, but there are signs of another person having been here.'

'That's impossible.'

'Do you know which bedroom Mr Jowett used?'

How loaded was that question? 'The back, I think.'

'The one in the front has also been slept in and there was a glass of water beside it.'

'But we heard whoever it was in there. It's right above this room.'

'Was he having a sleep, Mrs Hetherington? Had he found a glass and poured himself some water?' Haggard waited, but, confused, Joyce said nothing. 'You also say that the first thing you heard was the sound of glass breaking, then he came downstairs and immediately tried to force his way in through this door . . . yes?'

'That's right.'

'But you've also told us that the knife belongs to the cottage and was kept in the kitchen. If he ran straight down to this room, how did he get hold of it?'

'He could have gone into the kitchen first – before going upstairs – but we didn't hear him.'

'That's possible,' Haggard agreed. 'But it makes no sense. This wasn't an opportunist thief who saw an open door and decided to try his luck. People like that don't arm themselves – and they get out as fast as possible when they realize they've made a mistake and someone is in the house. And why go upstairs when anything worth stealing would be down here? And what about the whisky? Unless Mr Jowett kept a bottle in the spare bedroom for some reason.'

'He doesn't drink whisky.' That came out spontaneously.

'Indeed? We'll check that with him.' Haggard nodded at Sheaffer, who left them. 'So if it wasn't a chance burglar, Mrs Hetherington, who might want to harm you or Mr Jowett?'

'Nobody. It's impossible.'

'No, it's not . . . It happened.' Haggard hesitated. 'Is there anything you're not telling me?'

She shook her head. 'I've told you exactly what happened.'

'And there's nothing you want to add?'

'No.'

Haggard had seen too many people lie. 'Would you like to call your solicitor, Mrs Hetherington?'

'What! Why should I need to do that? I've not done anything.'

'Possibly not, but what you and Mr Jowett have told us so far raises a great many questions. A serious offence has been committed, and I have to be absolutely certain that neither of you is holding anything back.'

'For God's sake, are you going to charge us? What with?'

'At this moment I have no reason to charge anyone with anything.' Haggard was growing impatient. 'But I'm not leaving anything to chance. You've lived in Finch long enough to remember Tannerslade Farm.'

'Tannerslade?' The name terrified her. 'What on earth's that got to do with it?'

'Possibly nothing. But we never caught those men, and now there's an extremely dangerous individual out there somewhere. If you and Mr Jowett hadn't managed to keep him out of this room, I could be investigating two more murders. I want him caught, Mrs Hetherington, and until I'm satisfied you're telling me everything you know, I have the power to keep you here.'

'I don't know anything apart from what I've told you.' Apart from the fact that . . . No, she had to protect him. 'Why should I keep anything from you?'

'One of my officers will take your statement. We can do it here. Please wait a moment.'

As he stepped into the hall, Harry Pugh and Sheaffer appeared from the room opposite.

'How's it going?' Haggard asked.

'He says he bought the whisky for a nightcap,' Sheaffer said. 'To help him sleep.'

'How stupid does he think we are?'

'He's lying through his teeth about everything,' Pugh growled. 'But he won't budge. Swears he was the only one staying here.'

'Lean on him, Harry. Drop the idea that she's told us something.'

'Has she?'

'Nothing that's any use. Get back in there and take her statement, Chris. I want to find out if there's any sign of our villain yet . . . What is it?' Turning away, he was stopped by a woman constable.

'I've just been to see Mrs Hetherington's mother, sir—'

'Good. No need for her to be worried.'

'—and she says they were having an affair.'

Haggard looked at Pugh. 'That's both of them lying, Harry.' He turned back to the constable. 'Why the hell did she tell you?'

'She was in a state about it. Said she was disgusted with her.'

'So much for mother love . . . Is she all right on her own?'

'She had a visitor, some woman she knows. I said Mrs Hetherington would probably be home soon.'

'Don't hold your breath.' He turned to Sheaffer. 'Ask her where we can contact the husband. I want to know where he's been tonight.'

As Haggard stepped out of the cottage, a helicopter clattered overhead and began to sweep across the fields.

Lambert stared as a longhorn beetle crept over the back of his hand, its legs probing the hairs, as if blind, before it slipped off and crawled away. His eyes went to his watch; he must have been sitting there for more than two hours, almost as still as the woman. Why had she been so different from the others? Because he had killed her with his hands, battled to defeat her desperate fight for life? The gun had been an impersonal tool that involved no connection. And he'd been younger, perhaps crueller, more fiercely determined that his life had not yet begun and must not be destroyed. Now he had failed because his weakness had been to pretend he had strength. There was nowhere left to hide. Jowett would crack, and all the love of all the women in the world could not prevent it. The most bitter thought was of Victoria's satisfaction that would feed off her hatred . . . Could he drive back to London to kill her? He didn't have the courage – neither did he have the courage to face the threat of gaol with which he had terrified Jowett. But there's one thing, Randy; I've got the guts to get out.

Standing up took an enormous effort and he walked back to the car like an old man. Summer stars were appearing in the dusky mauve sky; he had known their names once.

Harry Pugh broke Jowett mercilessly, pouncing on every moment of fear, slamming back contradictions, accusing him of lying even when he was telling the truth. This wasn't an official interview that would have to be recorded, but the first round of a serious inquiry, and if Pugh had ever worn gloves he would have taken them off now.

'Bollocks, Mr Jowett!' His accent was deepening with emotion. 'We've found fingerprints to match the ones on that knife all over this place, including the room you and Mrs Hetherington were in.' In fact, the police had only just started in there, but Pugh would make ammunition where he lacked it. 'So he didn't just walk in here tonight! Did he?'

'He must have done!'

'With a bottle of whisky from the village shop? Who'd been sleeping in that other bed?'

'I don't know!'

'Don't know? What *do* you know, Mr Jowett? I'll tell you what I know. You've been having it off with Mrs Hetherington. Randy little bugger, aren't you? Can't keep your hands off another man's wife. Was that it? Did you use different beds? Bit of novelty?'

'Leave her out of this.' Jowett began to cry, red meat for his tormentor.

'But we can't leave her out, can we? She was here with you tonight. Planning some more nookie, were you?'

'Shut up!'

'Was it her husband? The man upstairs?'

'No!'

Pugh pounced again. 'But if you don't know who he was, how do you know it wasn't him?'

'He spends the week in London.'

'There's handy. All the time you want to get your end away.'

'It wasn't like that.' Jowett could feel himself cracking.

'But you're lying to us. You're both lying. Why?' Tearstained and quivering, Jowett's face pleaded for relief. Pugh's voice dropped to persuasion. 'You know who he was, don't you? Come on, lad. It'll be better if you tell us. It's important. We have to catch him.'

'May I have some water, please?' The question was croaked out.

'Of course you can.' Pugh nodded an instruction to the constable in the room with them, then sat down next to Jowett, a menacing presence now reduced to an overweight man on a chair. 'How about a cigarette?' He held out a packet, invitingly. 'There you are ... Better? Now take your time. We know somebody else was staying here, all right? And you must have known him, mustn't you? Was that a yes? Good, we're getting somewhere. What was his name? Pardon? Giles. Friend of yours, was he? Not really a friend ... Hang on, here's your water.'

He watched while Jowett drank. 'Not too fast, you'll give yourself hiccups ... All right, so he wasn't really a friend. So why was he here? When did he arrive?'

There was a silence as Jowett smoked. 'May I speak to Joyce, please? It's very important.'

'Just a few more questions first. Where does Giles live?'

'I don't know ... honestly. In London somewhere.' Jowett turned his face to Pugh again and there was nothing but defeat in it. 'I want to make a statement.'

'Of course you can, but tell me more about Giles. Do you know where he's gone?'

249

'No. He just ran away.'

'Has he got a car?'

'Yes . . . but he left it in Bury St Edmunds.'

'Whereabouts?'

'I can't remember . . . Parked in a road.' He frowned as if trying to see it. 'There was a pub nearby . . . Marquis of something.'

'Granby?' Pugh coaxed.

'Yes. I think so. It's a grey Saab.'

Pugh snapped his head at the constable. 'Corner of Lattimore Street. Get someone on to it . . . Thank you, Mr Jowett. So how do you know him?'

The dam had burst and Jowett was helpless in the flood. 'Joyce had nothing to do with it. Promise me you believe that.'

'All right,' Pugh coaxed. 'Take your time.'

Jowett's head sank in despair, and when he spoke again the Welshman strained to hear his voice, little more than a croaking whisper.

'We were the ones at Tannerslade Farm.' Staring at the floor, he did not see Pugh's eyes harden. 'It was only meant to be a robbery, but Giles had a gun. I never wanted them to be killed.'

He looked up pleadingly, then it felt as if his head had exploded as a massive hand, swung like a club, smashed against his face. He was hurled backwards, then rolled out of the chair, blood pouring from his mouth.

'You fucking shit! Christ, I've been waiting for this, boyo!'

Jowett scrambled away, hand held up for protection, as the sergeant moved towards him.

'Leave it out, Harry!' Alerted by Pugh's shout, Haggard had burst in.

'He killed them.' A thick finger shook with fury as it pointed at Jowett cowering against the wall. 'At Tannerslade. Two minutes, Peter. Then you can come back in.'

Haggard leapt between the two men. 'I said out!'

'They were kids!'

'We all know that, Harry. I was there as well. Now, I haven't seen anything, but either you get out right now or I break you. I mean it. Don't push your luck.'

Jowett whimpered as Pugh remained glaring at Haggard before walking out of the room. The Inspector helped Jowett to his feet. 'Is what my sergeant just said true?'

'Yes.'

'And the man who was here tonight was also involved? Very well, Mr Jowett. I must advise you that I am placing you under arrest. One of my officers will caution you, then you will be taken to Suffolk police headquarters for questioning. You can call your solicitor from there.'

'I have to speak to Joyce first.'

'I'm afraid that's impossible at the moment.'

'She knew nothing about it.'

'You can include that in your statement.'

Joyce was numb as she was driven back from Ipswich at two in the morning. Beside her in the back, Sheaffer watched her carefully.

'I could stay with you tonight, if you like,' she said. 'I don't want to intrude, but if it will help . . .' Joyce's head gave the tiniest shake of refusal. 'What about calling your doctor? He could give you something.'

'I don't need anything.'

'Look, I'm not happy about your being alone. I know your mother's there, but . . . You're positive you don't want us to call your husband?'

'Will you stop it, please?' she begged. 'I don't want to talk.'

The car slid through the night, Joyce staring out of the window, Sheaffer rarely taking her eyes off her. Lambert's car had been found and his address traced, but there was no sign of him. In the morning the media would be printing and screening his picture, warning people not to approach him; airports and seaports were on full alert. Wanted for questioning in connection with the murders of Ben and Annie Godwin, Cheryl, Thomas and Amanda Hood at Tannerslade Farm, Finch, Suffolk in July 1990. A second man was in custody and would appear before magistrates. Lambert's mother, with a strange irony, had suffered a heart attack when she had been told and was in the hospital where he'd pretended she was. His wife was hiding from the anticipated press pack at her parents' home.

There was a light showing downstairs as the car reached Joyce's house.

'This is my number,' Sheaffer gave her a slip of paper. 'Call me if you want. It won't matter what time.'

Joyce put it in her pocket as if she had instantly forgotten it was there and slowly climbed the steps to the front door. Grace was asleep on a chair in the front room.

'Oh, you're home, dear.' She smiled with relief as Joyce gently touched her arm. 'The police wouldn't tell me what time you'd be back, but Lillian stayed. I made her go to bed. What's happened?'

'I'll explain in the morning, Mummy. It's very late.'

'But they said someone had attacked you. At the cottage.'

'I'm all right . . . Did they tell you that?'

'Oh, yes. They were very good. They came to see me . . . Was it him?'

'Who?'

'You know. The one I saw you with.'

'No. Not him. He'd never hurt me, Mummy.'

Grace grimaced as she tried to move. 'Oh, I'm so stiff . . . I tried to ring Ralph, by the way.'

'Why?' However inevitable, Joyce was still dismayed she had done it. 'I'd have let him know.'

'You'll still have to. There wasn't any reply. He must be out somewhere. He'll be so worried when you tell him.'

'Come on. Let's get you to bed.'

Holding her mother's arm she helped her slowly up the stairs; at the door of her room, Grace stopped.

'You will stop this . . . this business with him, won't you? He can't be worth it, and I'd be so terribly hurt.'

Joyce swallowed painfully. 'I don't think . . . you needn't worry about that now.'

Grace smiled and stroked her cheek. 'That's good. All I want is for us all to be happy.'

Joyce kissed her goodnight, then walked across the landing and lay fully dressed on her bed; within moments, a dreadful form of sleep closed off reality.

There had been no point in going to collect his own car; the Volvo was fast enough on night roads. Lambert drove south, skirting London, across the Thames at the Dartford bridge, through Kent and into Sussex, an image of chalk cliffs in his mind, of childhood holidays and many things long lost. Dawn was lighting the Channel as he passed through silent Eastbourne and up the hill on to Beachy Head. There'd been a pub near here – the Tiger at East Dean – where he had played on the green when the family had stopped for lunch forever ago. The unfenced road climbed until all he could see was the slope of the Downs, then he pulled off on to short smooth grass and the sea appeared ahead of him. He stopped the car and switched off the engine, listening to morning gulls and the distant crash of waves. Jowett must have told them everything by now, and they would be hunting him. A cigarette would have been good, but he had not wanted to stop and buy any. OK. Do it . . . The woman's face came back, the stranger who had chosen the wrong road at the wrong time. It was curious that he felt worst about her. Would he see her again soon, one of the newly dead, or was that just superstition? And if he met her, would he meet them as well? He would soon know . . . unless this was the threshold of oblivion.

He unbuckled his seat belt and released the handbrake. For a moment, the car remained stationary, then began to roll forwards, hollow rumble of tyres the only sound. He crossed his arms to resist the urge to grab the wheel and forced his legs back from the brake. See, Randy, I always had the guts. Faster and faster. The car was rocking as it raced to the cliff's edge, blurred by the vibration. There was a desperate, terrifying second of wanting it to stop, then complete silence and the sea flashing across his vision as the car dipped like a saffron diving fish.

Lambert's own weight hurled his head against the roof, then he fell back and whiplash snapped his neck. The car turned over once again, then smashed on to the rocks, the windscreen splintering in fragments caught by a breaking wave that scattered in a seething silver cascade of glass and violent spray.

'Suffolk Constabulary.'

'Good morning, I don't know who I should speak to, but my wife hasn't come home and—'

'One moment, please.'

'Control Room.'

'Good morning, I'm concerned about my wife. She didn't come home last night.'

'Where had she been, sir?'

'She was visiting friends of ours in Gedding. I've spoken to them and they say she left there about seven o'clock.'

'And she mentioned nothing to them about going on somewhere?'

'No . . . She wanted to leave in time to watch a television programme.'

'Why haven't you reported this sooner?'

'I've been on a business trip. I only returned half an hour ago. Our daughter's away on an art course at the moment, otherwise she'd have let me know what had happened.'

'And you're absolutely sure your wife was going straight home?'

'Yes. There's nowhere else she might have gone. She was expecting an interior designer here this morning. We're having our . . . It doesn't matter . . . She'd have kept the appointment.'

'Was she all right when you last saw her?'

'Perfectly . . . I tried calling about ten o'clock last night, but got the answerphone.'

'And you weren't concerned?'

'There was no reason to be . . . She could have been in the shower. I just left a message confirming what time I'd be back.'

'Have you tried contacting any other friends?'

'Some of them, but they can't help. This is completely unlike her. If she'd been held up, she'd have let me know. I'm worried something's happened to her.'

'That's obviously a possibility, sir, but in most cases like this people turn up safe and sound . . . Where do you live, sir?'

'Finch.'

'Finch? One moment please.' In the pause there were muffled voices, then a faint sense of urgency. 'May I just confirm these details, sir? Your wife left Gedding about seven o'clock and was going straight to Finch . . . Would she have used the road through Ash Sounder?'

'Probably. It's the quickest way . . . Why?'

'I just needed to check it, sir . . . Are you at the house at the moment?'

'Yes.'

'Will you remain there, please? We'll send officers round.'

'Thank you, but . . . what's happened?'

'Have you seen the papers this morning, sir?'

'No. I set off before breakfast.'

'Did you listen to any news on the radio?'

'No. I don't . . . What are you talking about?'

'The officers will explain when they arrive. I don't want you to worry unnecessarily, but there has been a serious incident in your area. We're hunting a man who may have stolen a car.'

'Oh my God.'

'I'm sorry to have had to tell you this, but it is an urgent inquiry.'

'Is he dangerous?'

'Yes . . . but it may have nothing to do with your wife. Can you ring anyone else you can think of and let us know immediately if she turns up?'

'Of course, but . . . You think something's happened to her?'

'We're just taking every precaution, sir. It's very important that we trace this man . . . Are you still there, sir?'

'Yes . . . all right. But she'd have let me know if . . . How dangerous is he?'

'Please, sir. I'm sure your wife's perfectly safe, but we have to . . . What make of car does she drive?'

'A Volvo 850 saloon . . . yellow.'

'Do you know the registration number? Thank you. We'll put out an immediate alert. In the meantime, the officers are on their way . . . I'll need your name and address, sir.'

'Graveney. Oliver Graveney . . .'